———————————— ★ ————————————

I reached out to nudge her, gently pulling back the blanket. Staring down in astonishment, I saw that I was wrong on both counts. It was not Megan and she wasn't asleep. It was Roni, and unless I was very much mistaken, she was dead.

She was lying on her side, her beautiful eyes wide and staring. The silent grimace of her lips reminded me of Edvard Munch's painting *The Scream*. Except Roni's hands weren't clutching her head; they were frozen, clawlike, at the place in her chest where a large kitchen knife protruded.

I must have started screaming, but I don't really remember. I found myself at the other end of the terrace surrounded by the catering staff and soaked from the rain.

I dragged my eyes away from the the horrific sight of Roni sprawled on the chaise, fighting the waves of nausea rolling through my stomach, and forced myself to concentrate on the rose-covered trellis. But there was no relief to be found there. All my eyes could see were the roses that were now wilted and dying, their delicate petals edged in brown. Death, it seemed, was all around me.

———————————— ★ ————————————

Previously published Worldwide Mystery titles by
TRACY KIELY

MURDER AT LONGBOURN

MURDER
ON THE BRIDE'S SIDE

TRACY KIELY

W💿RLDWIDE®

TORONTO • NEW YORK • LONDON
AMSTERDAM • PARIS • SYDNEY • HAMBURG
STOCKHOLM • ATHENS • TOKYO • MILAN
MADRID • WARSAW • BUDAPEST • AUCKLAND

For my husband, Matt

Recycling programs
for this product may
not exist in your area.

MURDER ON THE BRIDE'S SIDE

A Worldwide Mystery/November 2012

First published by St. Martin's Press

ISBN-13: 978-0-373-26823-8

Printed in U.S.A.

Acknowledgments

I need to thank several people for their support and help while I wrote this. Barbara Kiely, Mary Melanson, Ann Mahoney, Mary Doyle, Judith O'Neill and Terry Mullen Sweeney were all kind enough to read early versions of this and listen to me yammer on about everything and nothing (it's a particular skill set I have). The Bunco Ladies helped me stay positive and kept my mind sharp ("Hey, are we on threes?"). I still haven't figured out what I did to deserve my agent, Barbara Poelle, who is a Force of Nature, but when I do, I will light the appropriate candles. My editor, Toni Plummer, was wonderful and her edits always make my writing stronger. I owe a great big thanks to Cynthia Merman and her excellent copyediting; she misses nothing! Bridget Kiely was, as always, simply amazing. Her wit (which I continually steal) and her willingness to reread slightly altered scenes over and over again ("Is this better? Are you sure? How about this?") never cease to amaze me. As a fellow Janite, her input was invaluable. My husband, Matt, patiently suffered through numerous conversations involving murder and mayhem and was invaluable in spotting certain (ahem) plot holes. My children, Jack, Elizabeth and Pat, were just lovely and helped me keep it all in perspective. Thank you all!

Death in particular seems to provide the minds of the Anglo-Saxon race with a greater fund of innocent amusement than any other single subject...the tale must be about dead bodies or very wicked people, preferably both, before the Tired Business Man can feel really happy.

—*Dorothy L. Sayers*

ONE

It is bad luck to be superstitious.
                                    —Andrew W. Mathis

"A DEATH IS COMING," Elsie remarked blandly, glancing upward.

I followed her gaze and saw three seagulls gliding on crisp September air. My left temple throbbed slightly at this news. Not, ironically, out of any fear that her prediction would come true, but rather at the explosive effect it might have on the people with me. Elsie is a sophisticated, educated woman, but she has a propensity for fortune-telling that would try the most patient of souls. The year I turned twelve, she told me that I would grow up to "marry a rocker and live a life of international travel." I had a mad crush on Peter Gabriel at the time and immediately began practicing what I anticipated to be my married name, Elizabeth Gabriel. I even envisioned myself managing his world tours. Obviously, I wasn't the most perceptive child. I'm now twenty-seven, have never been married, and work as a fact-checker for a local paper in Virginia. As for the international travel, I did once accidentally wander into the duty-free shop at the airport, if that counts.

Elsie's declaration hung in the air, much like the seagulls. Next to me, I was relieved to see that Blythe's only response was a simple roll of the eyes. Twenty-eight years as Elsie's daughter-in-law has inured Blythe to Elsie's fondness for predictions. It still irks her, but she has learned to hold her tongue. Bridget, however, Blythe's daughter and Elsie's granddaughter, has not yet learned such restraint.

"Elsie!" she burst out. (No one in the grandchild generation ever calls Elsie anything other than Elsie—the mere idea of calling her "Grandma" or "Nanny" is laughable). "For Christ's sake! Don't start this crap now. The wedding is tomorrow and my nerves are shot as it is!"

Elsie and Blythe, polar opposites in most everything, were united in their response. "Don't swear, Bridget," they said automatically. It was a refrain I had heard directed at Bridget many times over the years. It had never had any effect, of course, but that didn't stop her family from trying.

Elsie tilted her black Jackie O. sunglasses down an inch and gazed at Bridget with tranquil blue eyes. "I am only stating what I see. And what I see are three seagulls flying overhead—in a *city*. Which is," she continued calmly, "a well-known sign that a death is coming."

"You know what's another well-known sign?" retorted Bridget with feigned politeness.

I grabbed Bridget's hand before she could illustrate the gesture, hoping to prevent what would have been the twenty-sixth argument of the day, but Elsie only laughed.

I've known Bridget since the fourth grade, and I've known Elsie almost as long. In many ways, they are a lot alike. Both are ruled entirely by their emotions, emotions for which moderation has no place. Sadness was desolation, happiness was ecstasy, and irritation was fury. It made for some high drama at times, regardless of whether those times warranted even the *slightest* bit of drama.

"Oh, look," I said, hoping to distract them both. "We're here."

"Here" was Grey's Bridal Shop, a white, two-story brick structure in the heart of downtown Richmond, Virginia, and a veritable tradition among Richmond's older families. Happily, our arrival had the hoped-for effect and no more was said about signs and death.

Elsie entered the shop first, the small silver bell atop the door cheerfully announcing our arrival. René, the owner, beamed enthusiastically. He was a fussy little man with a thick mane of white hair that never moved. It was widely rumored that his real name was Jim and that he wore a wig, but no one cared because he had exquisite taste and stocked the most beautiful dresses in town.

"Ah, Mrs. Matthews," he cooed, hurrying over to kiss Elsie's hand. "It is always a pleasure to see you."

"And you as well, René," replied Elsie, taking advantage of René's bent posture to covertly study the man's hairline. "Are our dresses ready?"

"But of course," said René with a flamboyant swoop of his pudgy hands. "If you ladies will please follow me."

We dutifully followed René's mincing footsteps, crossing the store's thick cream carpeting to the large dressing rooms in the back where our gowns awaited us.

Bridget, as the bride-to-be, slipped into hers first. Unlike the others, it was not from the store but was Elsie's mother's gown from the 1930s. A sleek creation of creamy silk with an empire waist, it was perfectly suited to Bridget's eclectic sense of style and her petite frame. Bridget had uniformly dismissed the more modern designs as making her look like an overdone meringue.

She somberly gazed at herself in the large three-way mirror before turning to us. "Well?" she whispered nervously.

A gentle sigh escaped from Blythe as she surveyed her daughter from head to toe. "You look lovely, Bridgie," she said, with a slight catch in her voice. Thankfully, she made no mention of Bridget's short spiky hair—a constant source of irritation for the conservative Mrs. Matthews. Bridget herself had made some concessions in deference to the occasion, by toning down the color from near magenta to a more sedate red.

"You look beautiful, Bridge," I agreed. "Colin is going to flip when he sees you."

"He most certainly will," agreed Elsie, with a firm nod that sent the elaborate upsweep of her silver hair teetering precariously to one side and then the other before coming to a halt only millimeters from where it had started. "As my father would say, you look monstrously pretty. Colin is a lucky man. And speaking of Colin, has your mother told you everything you need to know?"

"About what?" Bridget answered absently, still twirling happily in front of the mirror.

"About your wedding night, dear. About sex."

Bridget's eyes blinked in surprise and a color not unlike her hair seeped over her cheeks. "Um, yeah, Elsie," she mumbled. "I think I know everything."

"Oh, I'm sure you know the *basics,* like what goes where. I'm talking about satisfaction."

"Elsie!" Blythe yelped, her eyes growing wide over the rims of her half-moon glasses. Although Blythe had served for twenty-odd years as the headmistress of a local boarding school, and had no doubt been exposed to her fair share of explicit girl talk, Elsie nevertheless always took her by surprise. Elsie had that effect on a lot of people.

"What?" Elsie replied blandly. "You know perfectly well that men can be a bit, well, *selfish* in that department. You have to show them. That's why I brought you this, dear. I always found it most helpful." She reached into her ever-present hounds-tooth handbag and pulled out a well-worn book. The graphic sketch of the couple on the cover gave no doubt as to its contents. Elsie fingered the frayed binding almost reverently. "This book was a blessing for Walter and me," she said with a wistful sigh. "God, I miss that man."

"I'm going to try on my dress now," I said, diving into one of the empty dressing rooms. Bridget caught my eye in the mirror and mouthed the word *coward*. I nodded in full agreement before shutting the dressing room door tightly behind me.

I closed my eyes and rested my forehead against the cool wood of the heavy door. When Colin proposed to Bridget last New Year's Eve, no one was happier than I. But now, eight months later, I felt on the verge of a nervous breakdown. From the moment they announced their engagement, there had been a nonstop whirlwind of activity. As maid of honor, I wasn't at the center of the storm, mind you. That spot was reserved for Bridget and Colin. No, I was off to the side, where, as any meteorologist will tell you, the real brunt of the tempest lies. I'd attended engagement parties, engagement teas, and engagement brunches. I'd participated in endless earnest discussions about china place settings versus the everyday kind. I'd tried (stupidly) to referee numerous conflicts between Blythe and Bridget. The wedding was tomorrow and rather than experiencing the proverbial calm before the storm, we'd increased our frantic pace.

To make matters worse, if that was even possible, as maid of honor I was expected to give the toast at the rehearsal dinner. An actual toast, made in public and in front of actual people. That fact alone loomed over me like an executioner's ax. I love Bridget and Colin dearly, but my skills at public speaking are second only to my skills as a sumo wrestler. Glancing at my watch, I saw that I had six hours to go. My insides promptly transformed to hot goo and I fancied I heard that weirdly German/mechanical voice from the James Bond movies intone, "Six hours and *counting*."

As a result of all this stress, my once-vanquished vices were sniffing around me like long-forgotten friends. I was overeating and seriously considering taking up smoking. Not start smoking *again*—just start, period. It had been that kind of a month. Don't get me wrong. I've known Bridget and the Matthews family for most of my life and I consider them an extension of my own family. Which is why, I suppose, they have the ability to drive me so absolutely batty. Only family can worm its way under your skin like that.

I glanced longingly at my canvas tote bag, where I had stashed my copy of *Sense and Sensibility*. Some people turn to spas for stress relief, others to holistic herbal remedies. Not me. Let me curl up with a Jane Austen novel and I'm good to go. Bridget had once accused me of using the novels as a kind of security blanket. She was absolutely right. Among other reasons, Austen's books are populated with eccentric, trying individuals. When your favorite heroine has to deal with such characters, it can make your own daily encounters a little easier to bear.

Normally, *Pride and Prejudice* was my go-to book in times of distress, but lately I'd been rereading *Sense and*

Sensibility (and watching the DVD). There was something reassuring about Elinor Dashwood's almost transcendental calm in the face of chaos; in an odd way it gave me hope. Especially in light of the new tactic I'd adopted for myself over the last few months—one of restraint and control. Too often in the past I'd let my emotions get the better of me. The results were never pretty. But no more; I was determined finally to acquire an inner strength. And if that meant I had to squelch every last one of my natural reactions, then so be it.

With more than a little apprehension, I shrugged out of my red polo dress and into the pale yellow gown. Cautiously, I glanced at my reflection in the mirror.

I've been told that I resemble a young Audrey Hepburn. Granted, it was only the *one* time and was said by my great-aunt Mitzie—who was not only tremendously fond of her Baileys Irish Cream but also in dire need of cataract surgery. Still, it *was* said and so I count it.

What the rest of the world sees is far less glamorous. I'm five foot seven, 125 pounds (usually), with shoulder-length brown hair, and have been told that I have the map of Ireland stamped on my face. This is a polite way of saying that I'm pale and freckled. As a kid I used to wish that my freckles would merge together—then at least I'd have a semblance of a tan. Now I just hoped they didn't look like premature age spots.

I shifted my attention from my complexion to the actual fit of the dress. I've never had much luck with wedding attendant dresses. Their main goal seems to be to make the bride look good by comparison. The worst one was for my friend Violet Mitchell's wedding. She had insisted that all the bridesmaids wear—you guessed it—violet dresses. I looked like an ailing grape. The guy I'd been seeing at the time broke up with me shortly after that. I still think it had something to do with the dress. But, as I studied my reflection with a critical eye, I allowed that this one was different. Its basic design was similar to Bridget's, and with its high waist and sleek lines it disguised not only those areas of my body that were underdeveloped but those that were overdeveloped as well. Better still, as her only attendant (Bridget having adamantly stated that she did not want to be preceded down the aisle by a Stepfordesque chorus line), I did not have to compete with other figures in an identical dress.

As I tentatively craned my neck to check the dreaded rear view, I decided that not only was the dress a far cry from my last wedding, but so was my date. The thought of Peter McGowan brought a warm flush to my checks. It still took me by surprise that we were dating. I'd known him as a kid, but it hadn't been a pleasant experience. In fact, for years I put him in the same category as clowns, intimidating grade school teachers, and other nightmares of youth. A series of bizarre events last New Year's (which included two murders and an insufferable cat) had thrown us together again. Since then, Peter had been atoning for his obnoxious past, and I spent a lot of time keeping my fingers crossed that nothing would happen to ruin everything. My dating track record would make the most hardened of bookies seek out Gamblers Anonymous. Things had been bumpy lately due to my immersion in wedding duties and Peter's immersion in his work, but I told myself that once this wedding was over things would get back to normal.

My reverie was interrupted by an impatient call from Bridget to come out and show everyone the dress. I pushed open the door to my dressing room and stepped out.

"You look very pretty, Elizabeth," said Elsie matter-of-factly.

"You do look lovely," Blythe agreed, adding, "You're more of an Irish rose than ever. That dress is the perfect color for you. It looks wonderful with your dark hair and it really livens up your complexion."

I had smiled, a polite thank-you hovering on my lips, when Bridget shot me a knowing grin. "Oh, I don't think the dress is responsible for her coloring."

Almost before I knew what I was doing, I found myself parroting, "Well, whatever your conjectures may be, you have no right to repeat them."

Bridget immediately retorted with, "I never had any conjectures about it, it was you who told me of it yourself." Maybe I *had* been watching the DVD a tad too much back at the apartment Bridget and I shared.

Our brief exchange, however, was enough to excite Elsie's interest. "Oh? Then what *is* the reason?" she asked, instantly on the alert. "Now don't shake your head at me, Elizabeth. There's no point trying to hide anything from me," she teased, wagging her finger at me. "I'll get it out of you one way or another!"

In addition to considering herself entitled to know the intimate secrets of everyone around her—related or not—Elsie fancies herself a skilled matchmaker. What others think of her efforts in this area is far less complimentary. While "infernal, meddling bull in a china shop" is not the most frequently used expression to describe her, it is the least profane.

I gave a shudder at the thought of what Elsie would do should she realize the extent of my feelings for Peter. It would not be enough for her to know that we were dating. She would not be satisfied until Peter had proposed, preferably while she stood behind him, beaming proudly. I turned agonized eyes toward Bridget. She seemed to belatedly realize the inherent danger in exciting Elsie's matchmaking inclinations and now tried to defuse the situation. "Don't get yourself all worked up, Elsie. There's no secret," she said quickly. "I was only teasing Elizabeth about her boyfriend, Peter. And he's already crazy about her, so there's no need for your interference!"

"Interference! Of all the silly ideas!" Elsie protested. Tapping her chin thoughtfully, she then ruined this sentiment by adding, "Still, it would be romantic for your best friend to get engaged at your wedding, don't you think?"

"No, I don't," said Bridget. "As a matter of fact, if you *really* want to know what I think—"

"Oh, Peter's such a nice young man," Blythe interrupted, trying to steer the conversation away from Bridget's thoughts, which no doubt contained various obscenities. "He's coming tonight for the rehearsal dinner, isn't he?"

"Yes," I said. "His flight gets in at six." Peter had recently joined his parents' hotel business. He'd just helped them open a hotel in Los Angeles and was due back tonight. I hadn't seen him for three endless weeks. Up until a few moments ago, I'd been anxiously counting the minutes until he arrived. Now, seeing the calculating look on Elsie's face, I began to rethink that excitement.

"Bridget," said Elsie with a knowing smile, "pass the book on to Elizabeth when you're done with it. Leave everything to me and I guarantee that she'll be need-

ing that book for her own wedding night—and before
too long!"

Bridget rolled her eyes in defeat and tossed me the
book. It flew past my outstretched hand and landed—
open—on the carpeted floor. I won't say what the couple
in the book was doing, but the caption of their activity
was "Happy Death." Bridget and I dissolved into a loud
fit of giggles. After a moment of shocked silence, Blythe
gave up and began laughing, too. Only Elsie didn't join
in. Cocking her head, she stared down at the illustra-
tion, her thin lips pulled into a frown.

"Death again," she said slowly.

TWO

Nobody, who has not been in the interior of a family, can say what the difficulties of any individual of that family may be.

—Jane Austen, Emma

OUR DRESSES IN TOW, we returned to Elsie's house. Although *house* really isn't the word I'd use to describe the structure. It isn't quite a mansion, but only by a hair. It looks like a place where foreign dignitaries might sign treaties—or map out invasions. Located just outside Richmond, the Revival-style building sits on the remains of Elsie's great-grandfather's tobacco plantation. Over the years, much of the property has been sold off, but the main house, which affords a view of the James River and surrounding land, is still intact. An entry porch, with a gable above, dominates the two-story white brick façade. Four gleaming white columns with shallow square bases line an equally gleaming front porch. The only spot of color is the glossy black-paneled door topped by a semi circular fanlight. When I was a kid, it reminded me of something out of *Gone With the Wind*. Which is why, although the actual name of the place is Barton Landing, I have always privately referred to it as Tara.

We stepped into the ornate entrance foyer, roughly the size of my entire apartment. A large mahogany table stood center, topped by an enormous blue-and-white vase, yellow roses spilling out. Knowing Elsie, the vase could be from either Pier 1 or the Ming Dynasty. To the right and left stood arched doorways with intricately carved moldings. Directly in front, a wider doorway led to the living room. It was from here that Elsie's newly acquired black Russian terrier puppy, Anna (as in Anna Karenina), came charging. Her paws hit the waxed wood floor and she lost control, skidding sideways into the wall.

"Anna! No!" admonished Elsie. Anna paid no attention. Untangling her legs, she righted herself and charged again. Bridget and I instinctively stepped back, pressing against the wall and out of her path. Placing her hands on her hips, Elsie turned and yelled, "Vronsky!"

Anna's furry ears perked and her hind legs pulled up, slowing down her onslaught. She skidded to a halt inches from Elsie's feet.

Elsie looked down and smiled proudly. "Good girl."

Blythe couldn't believe her ears. "Vronsky? You trained her to stop on Vronsky?"

"What's Vronsky?" asked Bridget.

"Who, not what," replied Blythe absently. "Count Vronsky was Anna Karenina's lover. The one she gave everything up for."

Elsie nodded. "Exactly. When Anna is about to do something really naughty, I simply yell, 'Vronsky.' It's much more effective than 'no.'" Anna sat complacently at Elsie's feet, happily thumping her tail against the floor.

Blythe stared suspiciously at Elsie. "You *are* kidding me, right?"

Elsie's answer was lost in the arrival of her daughter, Claire. At forty-two, Claire looked exactly as she had at eighteen. She wore an ankle-length floral print

dress that minimized but did not obscure her plump-
ness, and her straight auburn hair was cut in a pageboy
style. Over the years, I had seen only two variations
to Claire's hair. Her bangs were either pulled back off
of her round face with a tortoiseshell headband or left
hanging in an even line above her brown eyes. Today
she had opted for the latter. While some women find
a flattering hairstyle and stick with it for life, Claire's
homage to an entire look had more to do with her husband, David Cook, than with a becoming fashion.

David and Claire had gone to high school together,
but that's not to say that they had been high school
sweethearts. Far from it, in fact. Claire, a plain, shy, and
not particularly athletic girl had adored David with his
thick ash blond hair, ruddy complexion, and toothy grin.
He had been the revered captain of the football team. He
was also, as he would tell anybody in earshot, destined
for big things. Unfortunately, in his senior year a knee
injury had ended that career path. Instead of continuing with his plans to go pro, he had married Claire and
accepted a position in the Matthewses' family business,
the Secret Garden. The marriage was a puzzlement to
most until six months later when Claire gave birth to
their eight-pound baby daughter, Georgia.

These days David's athlete's build was giving way to
a middle-aged paunch and his ruddy complexion was
more of a bourbon blush. That said, there were many
women who still considered David very handsome; a
fact of which David openly took considerable advantage. For the most part Claire turned a blind eye to
David's womanizing. Claire had never been the head
cheerleader (or even on the squad, for that matter), but
she had nevertheless married the captain of the football
team and it was her crowning glory. So, in a manner of

speaking, she froze time. She wore her hair the same, dressed the same, and convinced herself that she had a happy marriage.

As for Georgia, she had just started her freshman year at Cambridge in the UK. It was a long way away and her first time living abroad. Bridget's family thought that the impetus for Georgia's escape was the same as Claire's lack of transformation: David.

Seeing us now, Claire smiled at our garment bags. "Oh! You got your dresses!" she said. "How is René?"

"Effusive as ever," said Elsie. "Have I missed anything here?"

"No, I was just looking for David. You haven't seen him, have you?"

Elsie's upper lip curled slightly at the mention of her son-in-law's name. "Have you checked in the study? That's where the liquor cabinet is, after all."

Claire sighed. "Please don't start, Mother. David's going through a very difficult time right now."

"David is *always* going through a difficult time," countered Elsie.

"Please," Claire repeated wearily. "Work has been very stressful for him. He's taken over some different client accounts and has been working very hard to win them over."

I hid a smile as Elsie murmured, "Yes, I imagine *that* would be very hard work for David."

Claire did not seem to hear the remark and continued. "And then those stock options didn't pan out the way David imagined. You know he's never been very good at handling stress."

"I see," said Elsie. "May I ask what exactly he *is* good at?"

Claire picked up one of the fallen rose petals on the

table, crushing it between her thumb and forefinger. "Look," she said, her voice low, "I know David has his faults, and I know that you don't like him, but he is my husband and I expect you to treat him with a modicum of respect. You don't realize how your behavior affects *me*."

Elsie sighed. "Claire, I wouldn't hurt you for the world. But you could do so much *better*—"

"Please, Mother, not again," Claire interrupted. "We've had this conversation too many times already. David is my husband and that's that. I can't believe you can be so cavalier about a marriage. I said until death do we part, and I meant it." Flinging the crushed petal on the table, she swung around and stormed out of the foyer.

"From her mouth to God's ears," Elsie muttered, watching her go.

Claire had just disappeared through the arched doorway when another face appeared in her place. It was Bridget's father, Graham. The second of Elsie's three children, Graham Matthews favored his mother. A successful trial lawyer, he was tall and lean with angular features. His faded blue eyes peered out from underneath bushy black eyebrows with a mix of irreverence and intelligence that had helped sway many a juror to his side of an argument. Like his mother, he was driven and opinionated. But whereas Elsie had become increasingly dogmatic in her views over the years, Graham had not. Much of this softening seemed due to Blythe. She was the perfect foil for her husband, both physically and mentally. Round and plump, she possessed a keen understanding of human nature thanks to her years as a schoolmistress. She was also thoughtful and slow to judge—traits not commonly associated with the Matthews family.

"What's the matter with Claire?" Graham asked, seeing Elsie's dark expression.

Elsie gave a casual shrug, but her pursed lips and furrowed brow gave away her annoyance. "David is the matter with Claire."

Graham shot Elsie an appraising look. "Have you been after her again about him? I realize you don't like the man. Hell, I don't think *any* of us like him, but they've been married for almost twenty-two years now. I think it's time we face the fact that he's here to stay."

Elsie scoffed. "Here to stay, my foot. How can you speak such nonsense? You yourself once said that you would do anything in your power to get rid of David."

Graham gazed at his mother with studied indifference. "I never said any such thing and you know it. Don't foist your own absurd wishes onto me. David is here to stay. Bullying Claire about him isn't going to change anything."

Elsie lifted her chin and gave Graham a level look. "That's *your* opinion. A mother can always hope. Now if you'll excuse me, I have some things I need to attend to." Pausing in the doorway, she turned and said, "And for the record, I have never *bullied* anyone in my life." Sending Graham a curt nod, she swept out of the foyer, leaving the rest of us in open-mouthed shock. I fancied that even Anna looked startled. Elsie could write a primer on the fine art of bullying.

Graham shook his head in bemused disbelief before turning back to us. Focusing on me, he pulled me into a tight hug. "Elizabeth! It's wonderful to see you! When did you arrive?"

"Just this morning," I answered, happily returning his

hug. I smiled at the familiar feel of his tweed sport coat scratching my cheek. I'd always been fond of Bridget's father, having practically grown up in their rambling house, but I'd become even closer to him in the past few years after my own father's untimely death. Graham had unobtrusively stepped in and filled that void, becoming almost a surrogate father to me.

"Well, all I can say is thank God you're finally here. You always have a much-needed calming influence on Bridget."

Turning now to her, he kissed Bridget on the cheek, saying, "And speaking of which, how's my baby girl?"

Bridget scoffed. "Dad, I'm getting married tomorrow! I'm hardly a baby anymore."

Graham chucked her lightly under her chin. "My mistake. You are, as always, correct. How's my decrepit old maid?"

Laughing, Bridget said, "Oh, I'm fine. But Elsie thinks someone is going to die."

Graham cocked one of his bushy eyebrows. "Dare I ask why?"

"Because of the seagulls she saw."

Graham's eyebrows now pulled together and he turned to his wife. "Seagulls?" he repeated.

Blythe rolled her eyes and handed him her garment bag. "Yes, seagulls. Apparently, it's a *sign*."

"Sounds like I missed quite a time."

"You have no idea. Come on, I'll fill you in on all the details upstairs."

They left, leaving the foyer empty save for Bridget and me. Moving toward the table, she picked up one of the fallen petals and gazed at it thoughtfully. "Maybe I should just elope," she said.

"Don't you even think about it!" I snapped. "After

all I've been through this past year? You most certainly are not going to run out on me now!"

Bridget spread her hands out defensively. "Okay, it was only an idea. But the way everyone is carping at each other, this is turning into a nightmare rather than a dream wedding. And all this fuss really isn't my style, anyway. Martha Stewart centerpieces are more up your alley."

"Meaning?"

"Meaning that if Colin and I *did* elope, then you and Peter could take our place. You guys get married with all the trim and pomp, and Colin and I will run off to Vegas."

"You're forgetting two very important points," I said, ticking them off on my fingers. "One, if you run off to Vegas, your entire family will tan your hide. And I'll hold you down while they do it. And two…"

"Yes?"

"Peter hasn't asked me to marry him."

Bridget waved her hand. "A minor detail and one I'm sure he'll rectify soon."

I rolled my eyes. With Bridget to wish was to hope, and to hope was to expect. "Nice try," I said with a laugh, "but no dice. *You* are getting married. *Here. Tomorrow.* Not me."

Bridget placed her hands on her hips. "Don't you want to marry Peter?"

I felt my face flush. "I don't know…" I sputtered. "We've been dating less than a year…"

With an arch look, she said, "Seven years would be insufficient to make some people acquainted with each other, and seven days are more than enough for others."

That caught me by surprise. "Is that…?"

Bridget grinned smugly. "Jane Austen? It is indeed.

Now answer me this: you are in love with him, aren't you? I mean, he is the 'one,' isn't he?"

"Bridget, I don't know. And keep your voice down. I mean, I like him. A lot. But, well, we haven't really discussed it and—"

Bridget cut me off with a derisive snort. "You 'like him'!? Coldhearted Elizabeth! Oh! worse than coldhearted. Ashamed of being otherwise. Use those words again and I will leave the room this moment."

After a beat, I said, "Okay, now you're scaring the crap out of me."

"Well, what do you expect? You've played that damn *Sense and Sensibility* DVD so many times over the past month that now you've got *me* quoting it." She paused. "Actually, to be honest, I'm beginning to see the attraction."

Rallying my composure, I said, "Bridget, this weekend is about *you,* not me. Besides, after this past year, going through another wedding is the farthest thing from my mind."

Bridget didn't say anything, but from the sudden twist of her mouth, I don't think she believed me.

Which was only fair, considering that I didn't quite believe me, either.

THREE

He is a rogue of course, but a civil one.
—Jane Austen, letter to her sister, Cassandra

"What do you say, Elizabeth? Let's make it a double wedding."

We were standing in the back room of Richmond's most romantic restaurant. The private room boasted dark paneling on three of its walls with a polished bank of windows making up the fourth. The city below shimmered silver and white against the dusky, indigo sky. The low melody from a strings ensemble mingled with the occasional clink of crystal and murmured laughter. It was the perfect place and moment for a proposal. Unfortunately, these words were whispered to me not by Peter but by Bridget's cousin, Harry Matthews. Ten years ago I would have jumped at a proposal from Harry. Hell, who am I kidding? I would have jumped at a mere proposition from the man. Harry is three years older than me and for a long time had been my idea of perfection. Tall, with light blond hair, cobalt blue eyes, and a cleft that rivaled Cary Grant's, he was easy to fall for. But as I grew older, I realized he had a bad-boy streak a mile wide. Trouble didn't just follow Harry; it stalked him.

I gently unclasped my hand from his. "Harry, please. What makes you think I want to marry you? I asked you to put a fried scallop on my plate."

"Yes, but it was the way you asked that gave away your true feelings."

"I think I should tell you, fried food and I have a very special relationship."

"We could be good together," he persisted. "Don't you know I've been in love with you since I was thirteen? It's always been you."

"And all those other girls, they were…?"

"Mere distractions."

"Apparently you get distracted mighty easily," I scoffed, thinking of the endless parade of girls through Harry's door over the years.

"Not anymore," he said softly. He took a step closer to me and I could smell his spicy aftershave. Like most of the other men in the room, he was wearing the standard Southern uniform: a blue blazer with khaki pants. Unlike the other men, Harry's clothes were, as usual, slightly rumpled. Rather than making him look unkempt, it only gave him the look of an errant little boy. Over the years, Harry had cultivated this look to great advantage.

"Really?" I said, closing my eyes. "Then tell me, what color are my eyes?"

There was a pause. "Blue?"

I laughed. "Nice try. They're green." I thrust my plate forward. "May I have my scallops now?"

Harry sighed and took my plate, deftly spearing three large scallops from the hors d'oeuvre table next to us. After he handed it back to me, he said, "It's because of this Peter fellow, isn't it? Is it true you two are getting married?"

I paused in surprise, my fork halfway to my mouth. "Who told you that?"

"Elsie. She said it was a done deal."

"She actually *said* that Peter and I are getting married?"

Harry shrugged. "Well, not in so many words, but she inferred it."

"Implied it."

"Whatever. Is it true?"

"Not as far as I know. Elsie appears to know more about it than I do," I said with what I hoped was casual indifference.

"Well, are you going to marry him?" Harry pressed.

I made a noncommittal gesture. What was it about being in a wedding that made people feel they had the right to query you on your own matrimonial plans? Since Bridget had gotten engaged, everyone around me felt quite free to ask if Peter and I had any plans of our own. From my mother (who stated outright that I wasn't getting any younger) to my sister (who kept hinting that I'd better not "blow this relationship, too") to my boss (who flat out told me that she didn't want me to run off and get married and pregnant and leave her "high and dry"), the subject of Peter and me was a popular one. The only person who *hadn't* asked me about it was Peter.

"Well, if he's so wonderful," Harry persisted, "then why isn't he here?"

"I've told you, he should be here any minute. His flight only got in at six."

As if on cue, a tall man walked into the room, pausing uncertainly in the doorway. With his presence, the room suddenly seemed a brighter place. His dark brown hair curled slightly at the ends. His nose was patrician, his eyes were an unusual shade of amber, and he had a large mole on his right forearm. Not that this was visible underneath his tailored pin-striped suit; I just knew it was there. My heart gave a happy leap. Smoothing the folds of my navy blue sheath dress, I shoved my plate into Harry's hand, turned, and rushed over to him.

"Hey, stranger," I said as I approached. Peter smiled and pulled me into a tight hug. "I've missed you," he said into my ear. "Are people watching or can I ravish you right here?"

"People are indeed watching, but don't let that stop you."

Peter gave an appreciative growl but gave me only a chaste kiss. He talks big, but at heart he's an old-fashioned guy.

Before I could respond with a kiss of my own, I heard a shriek of excitement behind me and was abruptly pushed aside by Bridget. "Peter!" she cried, enveloping him in a bear hug. "I'm so glad you could make it. Thanks again for coming: I know you must be tired."

"A little," admitted Peter. "But I wouldn't miss this for anything."

"Did you get my fax?" Bridget asked.

A small smile played on Peter's lips. "I did. Thank you."

"What fax?" I asked. "Why did you send him a fax?"

"For the reading he's doing tomorrow," Bridget explained. "I sent him a copy and underlined the words that he needs to emphasize."

"You're kidding, right?" I asked. Ever since Bridget and Colin had asked Peter to give one of the readings at the mass, Bridget had constantly been on Peter's case to add more "dramatic flourish." She felt his usual style of delivery was too tame.

"They're only suggestions," Bridget said defensively.

"Bridget! Peter reads just fine!" I said. "It's a church reading, not a recital of Cowper!" Bridget rolled her eyes at the reference but did not look convinced.

Colin appeared next to Bridget, putting an end to the debate. With his curly brown hair and soft brown eyes,

Colin resembles an enormous teddy bear. He is six two, but he looks taller. This is probably due to Bridget more than anything else. Even in the spiked heels that she considers a mandatory element of every outfit, Bridget is only about five three. "Thanks for coming, Peter," Colin said, extending his hand. "It's good to see you. How was L.A.?"

"Great. The opening went really well, but I'm a bit jetlagged. I hope I'm not too late."

"Not at all," I said. "Are you hungry? They have scallops, if you're interested." Peter nodded, and with Colin and Bridget in tow, I led him back to the hors d'oeuvre table where Harry stood, still holding my plate.

"You must be Peter," Harry said, handing me back my plate so he could shake hands. "I'm Harry. I've just been trying to get Elizabeth to run away with me, but to no avail. I'm told you're the reason."

"Well, that and good common sense," I added.

"Oh, yes." Harry nodded affably. "That goes without saying."

Peter looked blankly at me and then at Harry before shaking his head. "I think I need a drink before I can do this conversation justice," he said.

Harry laughed. "A man after my own heart. Let me get you something from the bar. I'm in need of a refill myself. What would you like?"

"Heineken, if they have it, thanks."

Harry went off to the bar, while the three of us tried to talk to Peter at once.

"How was your flight?"

"How are your parents?"

"Colin hates my shoes, Peter. I say he's blind. What's your opinion?" This last question was posed by Bridget. She twisted her leg out for Peter's appraisal. We silently considered the item in question, a bright purple-and-blue-plaid pump, the heel of which was not only zig-zagged (and green) but a good three inches high. I may have mentioned that Bridget has eclectic taste.

"I saw something very similar when I was out in L.A.," Peter said wonderingly.

Bridget turned to Colin with a triumphant smile. "See? He saw these in L.A. and everyone knows that L.A. is fashion central."

"He probably saw them on a hooker," Colin dead-panned.

"Colin!" Bridget yelped. "What an awful thing to say!" Colin looked as if he were about to apologize, when Bridget amended with a rueful glance at the pumps, "Okay, maybe they are a teensy bit over the top. But I had to do something outrageous. Tomorrow I'm going to look...well, I'm not going to look like *me*."

Her shoulders slumped underneath her neon apple green dress (a fashion statement in and of itself) and she stared dejectedly at her feet. It took all of my self-control not to burst out laughing. Colin smiled at her and grabbed her hand. "Honey, I don't care if you wear a bathing suit tomorrow."

Bridget's green eyes glinted and I thought she was about to take him up on the offer when Harry returned. Thrusting a bottle into Peter's hand, he said hurriedly, "I'd drink this quickly if I were you. Elsie's spotted you. I don't know if Elizabeth warned you about her, but she considers it her duty to, well...to test those who date the ones she loves. And from the look in her eyes, you are about to be tested."

We all turned to see Elsie bearing down on us. Her silver hair was pulled back into an elaborate bun and her royal blue floor-length dress billowed out behind her

as she skillfully maneuvered her way across the floor
with the aid of a silver-tipped mahogany cane. There is
nothing wrong with Elsie's balance. The cane is just for
dramatic effect, a bit like Bridget's shoes. Nevertheless,
she looked haughty and intimidating, like one of Jane
Austen's characters who make life hell for everyone else.

"Elizabeth!" she said crisply. "I don't believe I've
been introduced to your young man."

I have known Elsie since I was nine years old and I
still found myself stifling an urge to curtsy. I could only
imagine what Peter must be thinking.

"Of course," I said quickly. "Elsie, may I present
Peter McGowan. Peter, this is Bridget's grandmother,
Elsie Matthews."

"I'm pleased to meet you, ma'am," Peter said, extending his hand. Elsie took it and held it in her own heavily bejeweled hand.

"Elsie," said Bridget, a warning note in her voice.

"Hush, Bridget," Elsie replied, not taking her eyes off
Peter. Firmly holding his hand, she said, "You remind
me of a man."

I groaned. Elsie not only loved old movies, she
considered them a mandatory element of any proper
education, like history or algebra. Bridget shot me a
sympathetic look and shrugged.

"What man?" Peter replied pleasantly.

Elsie's blue eyes snapped. "Man with the power,"
she continued conversationally. People started to gather
around; they, too, were used to Elsie's tests.

Peter did not miss a beat. "What power?" he said. I
breathed a sigh of relief.

Elsie's lips turned up appreciatively. "Power of hoo-
doo."

"Who do?"

"You do."

"Do what?"

"Remind me of a man," finished Elsie, letting go of Peter's hand with a snort of laughter. "I'm impressed, young man. Not many people know that one. For instance, I bet David here doesn't," she said, turning to her son-in-law. As usual, David had plastered his thick hair with products and was preparing to do the same to his liver from the looks of the very full glass of amber liquor in his right hand.

At Elsie's challenge, I tensed. So did most everyone else, for that matter. When he was younger, David had been nothing more than a good-looking blowhard. His dreams of one day being a football hero buoyed him through any hard times and kept him upbeat. But once he realized that those dreams were never going to happen, he changed. His drinking increased and his moods became mercurial. In the early part of the day he was still the jocular backslapping friend to all—annoying but not threatening. However, somewhere between his fifth and sixth scotch, he turned nasty. Rather than a slap on the back you were more likely to get a punch in the face. Not an enjoyable prospect from a man who was six three and weighed somewhere north of two hundred pounds.

Luckily, David was still shy of his fifth drink. He threw back his shoulders and laughed. It was a sound not unlike a donkey's bray. "Of course I do, Elsie," he said. "It's from that movie with…um, Gregory Peck."

Elsie brandished her cane at him, causing David to take an involuntary step back. *"Ha!"* she cried triumphantly. "No! It's from *The Bachelor and the Bobby-Soxer* with Cary Grant, Myrna Loy, and Shirley Temple."

"Yes, I know, Elsie," David said. "I was only teasing

you." Turning to Peter, he continued smoothly. "So you must be Peter. I'm David Cook. We've heard a lot about you. Elizabeth said you were out of town on business. What is it that you do?"

"My family runs a hotel chain," responded Peter.

"Hotels? You don't mean McGowan and Company?"

"That's me," replied Peter.

David pulled his drink away from his mouth long enough to let a low whistle escape from his thick lips. "Jesus," he said. "You must be loaded, huh?"

"Uh…not really," Peter said. "It's my parents' company." He shot me a quizzical look and I shrugged in response. Among David's many odious traits was an obsession with money, mainly other people's money, as he never seemed to have any of his own.

"Say, Pete," David continued, "why don't we talk later about you guys using us for your landscaping needs? Given Elizabeth is practically family, I'll give you a good deal. But then, maybe I'd better talk to Elizabeth first," he said with a broad wink, "and find out how serious you two are before I start handing out discounts."

My cheeks flushed. "I would never dream of asking for special favors for anyone, David," I said as diplomatically as I could.

David threw back his head again and made a noise somewhere between a laugh and a snort. "Oh! Watch out, Pete! Did you hear that?" he jeered. "You don't even rate the discount yet!"

Beside him, Claire saw my flush and quickly interjected, "David's only kidding."

David's eyes briefly glanced in Claire's direction, as if surprised to find her next to him. "Huh?" he asked.

Claire did not answer. Instead, Elsie spoke. "As

grandmother of the bride, I insist that there be no business talk to night. Let's just enjoy the festivities."

David took a large gulp from his glass and shrugged his large shoulders. "What ever you say, *boss*."

Elsie's eyes narrowed and her nose pinched as if suddenly assaulted by a foul odor. David missed the look, but Claire did not. Two red spots flamed brightly on her pallid cheeks. Glancing uneasily at Elsie, she gently tugged on David's sleeve and pulled him away under the pretext of making an introduction. Elsie's eyes followed Claire as she dragged her husband across the room.

Seeing her glower, Harry leaned over and said, "Let it go, Elsie. She's a grown woman. She can make her own choices."

"The man's a jackass," Elsie muttered.

"True, but as someone once said, 'There is probably nothing like living together for blinding people to each other.'"

Elsie turned to him with a reluctant grunt of amusement. "Since when did you get to be so smart?"

"I've been taking a correspondence course," he said, extending his arm. "Now, why don't you buy me a drink?"

As we watched them go, Bridget turned to Peter. "Nicely done, by the way. Not many people know that movie."

Peter laughed. "I don't think anyone could hang out with you two and *not* know that movie."

Bridget nodded. "Elizabeth has Jane Austen; I have Cary Grant."

"Not tonight, you don't," said Colin good-naturedly. "Now if you two will excuse us for a second, I need to introduce Bridget to my cousin."

Peter turned to me. "Okay, just so I'm clear. I've been

here only ten minutes and so far someone has informed me that he wants to run away with you, a drunk I just met wants me to hire him, then I had to pass a test on old movies. Is there anything else I need to be worried about for this weekend?"

"Nothing at all," I said laughing, hugging his arm and feeling warm just standing next to him. "The worst is over."

What a whopper that turned out to be.

FOUR

She was not a woman of many words; for, unlike people in general, she proportioned them to the number of her ideas.
—Jane Austen, *Sense and Sensibility*

AT THE PROMPTING of the waitstaff, we took our assigned seats. Bridget and Colin settled in at a table with their parents, while Peter and I were seated with the rest of Bridget's family. I quickly introduced Peter. The first to speak was Bridget's uncle Avery—Elsie's oldest son and Harry's father.

"Elizabeth," he said as we sat down, "it's nice to see you again. How have you been?"

"I'm fine, Avery," I answered. "How have *you* been?"

Avery has a long sad, horse like face, salt-and-pepper hair, and slate gray eyes. Until recently, he ran the Secret Garden, the Matthews family's business, with worka-holic zeal. However, a stroke a few months back had confined him to a wheelchair and left his role as company president in doubt. Seeing him now, I was taken aback by his frail appearance. The stroke had severely damaged his once-lean, athletic body. His left side had been primarily affected, but his right side seemed just as weak. His whole body seemed to have simply given up. He was only fifty-eight years old, but he looked at least a decade older.

He produced a determined smile. "Oh, I'm fine. Getting stronger every day. I'm quite sure I'll be out of this contraption soon." He lightly slapped the arm of his wheelchair. "I owe most of my recovery to Roni, really. She's been my angel."

Roni, Avery's much younger second wife, had been married to Avery for only a few years, but for most who knew Roni, that was deemed long enough. With delicately winged eyebrows framing sapphire blue eyes, a flawless complexion, sleek black hair, and a figure that simply has to be man-made, Roni is easy to hate. Happily, her monstrous personality removes any guilt one might feel about such superficial snap judgments. At Avery's praise, her coral lips curved into a coy smile and she patted his hand. "Oh, Avery, please," she purred with false modesty. "I haven't done anything special."

She was right, of course. Bridget had told me that Avery had been forced to hire a full-time nurse because of Roni's inability to be of any real use. In fact, she was so worthless that she was even staying in a different room from Avery. Avery claimed the reason for this was his recent difficulty sleeping, but no one believed him. While Roni's unintentionally honest assessment of her nursing abilities was lost on Avery, it wasn't on the rest of us. Claire quickly looked down at her lap, Elsie rolled her eyes, and Harry coughed uncontrollably into his napkin. Roni peered suspiciously at her stepson before continuing. "I just know that you'll be up on your feet by Christmas, honey," she said.

Only her brother-in-law David was impressed with her performance. He beamed at Roni with all the goofy admiration of a love-struck schoolboy. "That's right, Avery," he said. "I'm sure you'll be back at your desk in no time."

"Well," said Roni softly, fiddling with the tiny strap

of her lavender sheath. The small movement brought everyone's attention to one (or rather two) of Roni's most stunning features. For a moment, I thought that David would fall into his lobster bisque, but Roni's next words righted his posture in a jiffy. "That may never happen, if Avery decides to accept Landscape Garden's most generous offer."

Her words threw the table into stunned silence. The Secret Garden had been in the Matthews family for generations. The mere idea that it be sold—and to an impersonal corporate chain such as Landscape Gardens—was dumbfounding.

Elsie broke the silence. Slamming her spoon down, she bit out through clenched teeth, "I'm sorry, did I hear you correctly? Are you considering selling the Garden?"

Avery opened his mouth, but it was Roni who answered. "Well, yes, Elsie, we are." She leaned in close to Avery and slid her arm under his. Avery shifted uncomfortably. "After Avery's dreadful stroke, I thought it best that he concentrate on enjoying life rather than working so much. With this wonderful offer we could retire, travel, take it easy."

Elsie fixed her daughter-in-law with a glacial smile. "I wasn't aware that you *were* working, dear."

Roni fixed Elsie with a frosty smile of her own. "I just want what's best for Avery."

David for once was at a loss for words. Finally, he found his voice. "Selling to Landscape Gardens?" he exclaimed, his usually florid cheeks pale. "But you can't do that!"

Avery cleared his throat and spoke up. "This is all premature, I promise you. We haven't made *any* decisions yet." He shot Roni a quelling look. "And whatever we do decide, we'll do so as a family."

David was not mollified. He smashed his fist angrily on the table, causing both me and the silverware to jump. "You simply can't sell the Garden. It's preposterous!" he boomed. David's devotion to the Matthewses' business might have been more touching were it not for the fact that he was virtually unemployable anywhere else. David held his cushy job as vice president of marketing only because he was married to Claire. He might have been an idiot, but he wasn't so big an idiot that he didn't realize this simple fact. Claire said something to him under her breath, no doubt trying to calm his temper. For once, he seemed to listen to her. Taking a deep breath, he ran his large hand through his goopy hair. "Besides," he said in a more sedate tone, "you know what they say about getting back to work—sometimes it's the best thing for a recovery!"

Roni brushed aside these words with a lofty wave of her bright pink manicured fingers. The small movement sent a wave of Roni's trademark perfume across the table—a cloyingly floral scent Bridget referred to as Nauseating Narcissus. If Roni was aware of the mounting tension around her, she did a fine job hiding it. "Oh, *they*," she said, snorting dismissively. "I'm so sick of hearing people quote what *they* say. *They* say all sorts of things that we really have no way of proving. For instance, *they* say that dogs can only see in black and white. But really, how do they know?"

Roni's daughter, Megan, blinked and, turtlelike, raised her head from her salmon. "Dogs *can't* see in color, Mother," she said.

Megan was Roni's daughter from a previous marriage. At seventeen, she was everything her mother was not, which, to paraphrase Jane Austen, was enough to alone recommend her. She had blotchy skin and limp nut-brown hair and was what is politely termed a "full-figured girl." Megan also differed from Roni in that she was both smart and nice. But those traits are rarely consolation to an awkward teenager, especially to one with a mother like Roni.

Roni looked disdainfully at her daughter. "And how do you know that? Did you ever ask one?" Roni glanced coquettishly at the rest of us while she giggled appreciatively at her own cleverness.

"No," Megan said, unfazed by—or simply used to—her mother's condescension. "Their eyes don't have rods or cones. Rods and cones enable sight in color." She looked back at her salmon and took a bite.

Roni stared at her daughter for a moment, an ugly red blush staining her perfect olive skin. After a beat, she shrugged a tanned shoulder. Taking a sip of her wine, she said, "Well, whatever. Avery is *not* a dog." Pausing here as if just having made a meaningful point, she continued, "And I think he needs some rest. He's given his heart and soul to that business and it's about time he gave something to himself." Turning to me, she unexpectedly stretched out her hand in an inclusive gesture. "Elizabeth, I'm sure you agree with me."

I did not voice my dissent, so I gave no offense. Privately, of course, I did not think for one moment that Roni was concerned in the least about Avery giving something back to himself. Roni was concerned only about Avery giving something to Roni. The Garden had a thriving and loyal customer base. When Avery took it over it was a small local business. But under Avery's savvy business direction, it had been transformed into a huge and booming one. It had to be worth millions. Avery stood to become a very wealthy man if he sold. It was clear that selling the business was what Roni wanted. And Roni had an annoying way of usually getting what she wanted. I wondered what would happen if I actually voiced this opinion. For starters, Roni would probably stop seeking me out during family events. I didn't kid myself that she liked me; it was just that other than Avery, I was the only one who wasn't openly hostile to her.

Luckily, I was spared a response by the announcement that it was time for the speeches and toasts. Peter gave my hand an encouraging squeeze as I nervously got to my feet. With a shaky voice, I began the speech that I had been practicing obsessively over the last week. "Good evening, everyone. For those of you who don't know me, my name is Elizabeth Parker and I am Bridget's maid of honor." So far, so good, I thought, pleased that I had neither fainted, stuttered, nor burst into tears—all, unfortunately, actual events from past forays into the arena of public speaking. I took a deep breath and continued with my short speech. I explained that Bridget and I had been best friends since the fourth grade and that even though many things had changed since then—we no longer loved pink-bubble-gum ice cream or Corey Haim—our friendship had stayed the same. I touted her loyalty, her humor, and her sincerity. I also touted her horrific driving skills, specifically her cheerful disregard for speed limits. After all, it was only after she slammed her car into Colin's that they had met and begun to date. I closed by predicting that they would have a long and happy life together, especially if Colin handled the driving.

Finished, I collapsed heavily in my seat, my heart thudding in my chest. The table was strangely silent and I wondered if I had inadvertently said something stupid. I leaned over to Peter and whispered, "What's wrong

with everyone? Did I say something wrong? Are they
mad about the driving thing?"

He shot me a reassuring smile. "No! You did great!"
Glancing at the rest of the table, he added in a low voice,
"I think they're still upset about Avery talking about
selling the business."

A bespectacled waiter in a starched white coat hovered next to me. "Dessert, miss?" he inquired, offering me a plate bearing something decadently chocolate.

"Yes, please." He deftly placed the plate in front of
me. "It looks delicious," I said. "What is it?"

"Death by Chocolate," he responded before moving
away. Death again, I thought, sinking my fork into the
gooey concoction. By my count this made the third time
in fewer than twelve hours that death had been refer-
enced. I glanced at Elsie, wondering if she had heard.
The fierce expression on her face as she glared at Roni
made me bite my tongue. Elsie had an impressive temper. I didn't want to give her any ideas.

FIVE

*She's the sort of woman...one would almost feel
disposed to bury for nothing: and do it neatly, too!*
—Charles Dickens

TWO HOURS LATER, I was seated on Elsie's back terrace
with Bridget, Colin, Peter, and Harry, watching the fire-
flies dart and weave across the wide lawn and breathing in the lingering fragrance of nearby rosebushes. As
flashes of silvery water from the James River peeked
through the trees, lazy images of the Old South (or at least
David O. Selznick's sanitized version of it) featuring chiv-
alrous young men and demure ladies floated before me.

"Christ," said Bridget. "I need a drink. Anyone else?"

Harry rolled his eyes at Bridget before turning to
Colin. "She's like a delicate flower, my cousin is."

"Oh, shut up," Bridget said, kicking him. "I expect
you want one, too."

"Ow!" said Harry, shifting his long legs out of Bridget's reach. "Take those ridiculous shoes off before you
hurt someone. And yes, now that you mention it, I do
need a drink. You've no idea the intense craving for alcohol my lovely stepmother can inspire."

Colin stood up. "I'll play bartender if you can refrain
from swearing for ten minutes," he said to Bridget. "Remember, my mother is a retired schoolteacher from Il-
linois."

"Your mother is not here," Bridget retorted.

"Think of it as practice for tomorrow," said Colin.

"Your mother loves me!"

Colin paused behind her chair. "That she does," he said, placing a kiss on top of her head, then ambling toward the drink cart.

Bridget smiled up at him before turning back to Harry. "What did Roni do this time?"

Harry closed his eyes and rested his head against the cushioned patio chair. "She's trying her damnedest to convince Dad to sell the Garden. Apparently, he's received an offer."

Bridget's eyes opened wide. "Sell the Garden? Can he do that?"

"In a word, yes," Harry said, taking a beer from Colin. He took a long swig. "And it looks like he just might, too."

"Jesus!" whispered Bridget.

"Bridget!" admonished Colin, as he handed her a glass of white wine. "You're not even trying!"

Bridget took the glass from Colin without looking at him. Her eyes still trained on Harry, she took a quick sip. "Sorry, but this is huge! Does Elsie know?"

"Oh, yes. For a moment, I thought she was going to lunge across the table at Roni. Of course, if she had, I sure as hell wouldn't have stopped her."

"What happened next?"

"Nothing. Dad shut down the conversation and we were reduced to shooting evil looks at Roni's beautiful empty head."

"I still don't understand what he sees in her," Bridget continued, playing with the delicate stem of the wineglass.

"Well, he'd been alone for so long," said Harry slowly.

"I think he saw what he wanted to see." Harry was silent. Harry's mother, Ann, had died when he was just a boy. That would have been painful for anyone, but for Harry it was made all the worse because of his own illness. At age six, Harry had been diagnosed with leukemia. His mother, a devout Catholic, had prayed and prayed that he would get better. And he did. Two years later, when Ann was diagnosed with breast cancer, Harry had prayed just as his mother had. But in spite of his fervent prayers, she died. Harry was left feeling that he hadn't prayed hard enough to save her.

Harry took another long pull from his beer and stood up. "Right. Well, I'm off to bed." He leaned over and kissed me on the cheek. "See you tomorrow, sweetie. Peter," he said, extending his hand, "I guess I'll see you later, since we're bunking together. It was nice to meet you."

"You, too," Peter replied.

"Good night, Colin. Good luck tomorrow," Harry said, shaking his hand as well. Turning to Bridget, he pulled her into a tight hug. "All the best tomorrow, Bridgie. And you swear all you want," he said, releasing her and turning for the house. "After all, I've got a hundred bucks riding on it."

Bridget flopped back into her chair and looked at me. "He doesn't look good," she said. "He seems tired."

"Well, dinner was a tense affair," I said. "After Roni's little announcement, conversation came to a standstill."

"God, she is so vile," grumbled Bridget. "I really don't get what Uncle Avery sees in her. I mean, other than the fact that she has…" Bridget cupped her hands in front of her chest to indicate Roni's most notable characteristic.

Peter's dark brows pulled together in confusion. "Roni has arthritis?"

Colin burst out laughing as Bridget threw a cushion at Peter.

"You didn't think that I was going to walk into that one, did you?" He laughed as the green cushion sailed over his head. "Besides, I have eyes only for Elizabeth," he continued with mock adoration.

I picked up another cushion and threatened him with it. "You're full of malarkey is what you are," I said. "Hell, I'm a dedicated heterosexual and even I have a hard time not staring at them."

"Please don't ever tell me that again," Peter said, wincing.

Bridget interrupted. "Well, big boobs or no, she's a b…witch," she quickly amended, directing a syrupy smile at Colin. He raised his beer bottle in tacit acknowledgment. She continued. "If she succeeds in convincing Uncle Avery to sell the Garden, it will tear this family apart. My great-grandfather started that business!"

"I know, honey," said Colin. "But what can we do? It's really not our decision."

"Maybe we could poison her food," Bridget mused.

"Who are you planning on poisoning?" inquired a deep voice behind us.

Turning, we saw Graham, his black brows pulled together quizzically. Blythe stood beside him. She peered at Bridget over her half-moon glasses, her expression bland. Some mothers might be alarmed to hear their daughters casually contemplating a murder. Those mothers did not have Bridget for a daughter. Blythe had learned years ago not to let Bridget's flair for the dramatics affect her blood pressure.

"I was talking about Roni," said Bridget. "Is it really true that she's pressuring Uncle Avery to sell the Garden?"

Graham sighed and nodded his head. "It's true," he said quietly, with a backward look at the house. "Although everyone in there is trying their best not to talk about it, it's clearly on everyone's mind."

"She is such a bitch sometimes!" exclaimed Bridget.

"I give up," moaned Colin, throwing up his hands in mock frustration.

"Oh, please," she scoffed, "you know I'm right."

"Bridget." Blythe sighed with a shake of her head. "Do you have to be so contrary? It's very unattractive."

A sudden gleam lit Bridget's eyes. "Excuse me," she said formally, with a quick look in my direction, "but I did not know I contradicted anyone by calling Roni a bitch."

"Hey! Nice one!" I said appreciatively.

"Right?" She grinned at me in response. "I think I'm starting to get the hang of it!" Brushing her bangs off her forehead, she added, "But in all seriousness, can't we do anything about her?"

"Not tonight, dear," Blythe said firmly, pushing her glasses up a notch. "We've got more important things to worry about, such as tomorrow. And speaking of tomorrow, please be patient with Ashley. I know she's trying, but she *is* family."

Ashley is Bridget's five-year-old cousin. Born to Blythe's sister, Karen, and her husband, Lewis, later in their lives, she was hailed by them as a miracle. It was a sentiment that was becoming less and less shared, however, as Karen and Lewis pandered to Ashley's every whim, with the result that she was well on her way to becoming an obnoxiously spoiled little girl. In the name of family harmony, Blythe had pleaded, cajoled, and finally bullied Bridget into asking the little girl to serve as flower girl.

Bridget rolled her eyes now at the mention of the girl's name. "Mother! Please. Ashley is beyond trying. She demanded—demanded!—that her basket only contain pink roses because 'all other flowers make her sneeze.'"

"On every formal visit a child ought to be of the party, by way of provision for discourse," I said to no one in particular.

Bridget's head swiveled in my direction. "Movie?"

"Book."

"Good to know." Turning back to Blythe, Bridget folded her arms across her chest. "Simply put, Mother, Ashley is nothing short of a monster."

"She's not a monster. For heaven's sake, she's only five."

"Leona Helmsley was five once, too."

"Bridget! This is exactly what I'm talking about. Please, just try and be patient with her. After all, it's not exactly her fault. If anything, she's Karen and Lewis's creation."

"Well, obviously, but they're a little off themselves. I know she's your sister, Mom, but really, did you see what she sent for a wedding gift? A gold-plated *toothpick case*! What is that all about?"

Blythe shook her head in understanding while half-heartedly muttering something about it being an antique. Bridget continued, "In any case, I don't particularly care if Ashley's problem is nature or nurture. I just don't want her pitching a fit in the middle of everything tomorrow. What that child needs is a firm spanking. And if she tries any of her usual stunts tomorrow, I may just take the job upon myself."

"That would make for a nice addition to the wedding album," said Colin with a grin. "The glowing bride smacking around the little flower girl."

"You don't believe in spanking?" asked Bridget.

"Not until after the wedding," Colin replied primly.

"Kinky," Peter opined.

"Okay, enough, you two!" said Blythe. "Bridget, just be nice tomorrow. And as it is almost tomorrow, I think the two of you should say good night. Call me old-fashioned, but it's bad luck for the groom to see the bride before the wedding on their wedding day."

Colin stood up with a smile. "Point taken, Mrs. Matthews."

Forgetting the extreme height of her heels, Bridget hopped quickly to her feet. The sudden movement wreaked havoc with her balance and she teetered dangerously to one side before Colin grabbed her arm.

Once steady, Bridget grinned sheepishly at Colin. "Come on. I'll walk you out," she said.

"Yeah, good luck with that," Graham offered.

The laughter following this remark died in our throats upon entering the house. Normally, I love the living room at Barton Landing. With its bright yellow walls, blue-and-white-floral-patterned chairs, and charming watercolors by French artists whose names I can never pronounce, the room is cheerful and inviting. But tonight the palpable tension in the room, combined with utter silence, rendered its appeal more on par with a dentist's surgery chair.

Roni was curled up in one of the overstuffed armchairs. Her bare feet tucked up underneath her, she serenely sipped a glass of red wine. If she was aware of her in-laws' animosity, she was doing an excellent job of hiding her emotions. The same could not be said for the rest of the room's inhabitants. From her high-backed cane chair, Elsie glowered at her daughter-in-law without the slightest attempt at pretense. Anna lay flopped at her feet, her intelligent eyes watchful. Claire absently picked at her stunted fingernails, an overbright smile pasted on her face. She sat nestled in close to David, but I doubt he even registered her presence. He was, to put it bluntly, drunk. His bleary eyes shifted unseeingly around the room and his large frame was slumped so far back into the blue brocade cushions of the couch that he seemed to have been partially swallowed by them. Megan sat away from the group in a small leather armchair next to a large potted fern. She appeared to be reading a book, but she turned no pages. Between the sprawling branches of the fern and the generous folds of her green corduroy dress, she faded from view like the Cheshire Cat, except there was no smile on Megan's round face. I wondered if she came by her ability to disappear naturally or if it was a practiced trait. Next to Roni, Avery sat in his wheelchair, seemingly preoccupied with a mark on the chair's wheel. At our entrance, he looked up with an expression more normally associated with drowning men seeing life preservers.

"Ah," he said, forcing his long face into a smile. "There you all are! Come and join us for a drink."

"I'd love to, sir," said Colin, "but I'd better be getting back to the hotel."

"I'm going to walk him out. Be back in a minute," Bridget said, as the two practically ran from the room.

Avery's face fell at their departure, but, spying Peter and me, he rallied. "Elizabeth! I insist you join us, although it's strange to be offering you a drink. It seems only yesterday that you, Bridget, and Harry were young-sters bent on bedeviling Elsie." Avery turned to his mother with an inviting smile. "Remember the year that you hosted the local marksman tournament, and Harry threw a rubber chicken out his window and it landed at the feet of the club's president?" Elsie nod-ded her head slightly but did not answer. Avery pressed on, a note of desperation in his voice. "And what about the time the three of them snuck out of the house by crawling out onto the roof? Didn't one of them fall and sprain an ankle?"

Again Elsie's frozen expression gave no sign that she was going to answer, so I jumped in. "That was me," I said. "I had a fun time explaining that one to my mom. But since Harry's not here to defend himself, I have no qualms about blaming the entire incident on him." The whole thing *had* been Harry's fault, too. He convinced Bridget and me not only to sneak out, but to go out by way of the roof. Harry could climb like a cat, but my skills were far less nimble. I skidded off the roof, man-aged to grab hold of the gutter, and hung for a moment suspended in space before falling into an ungainly heap in the laurel bushes below. In a flash, Harry jumped down to my side—unhurt, of course. He carried me in-side and was so overcome with guilt at my injury that he waited on me hand and foot for the rest of my visit and carried me wherever we went. It was quite a heady experience for an impressionable twelve-year-old girl and effectively cemented my crush on him.

Avery smiled. "I've no doubt of that. My son has a talent for finding trouble. But still, you three always had fun together."

Bridget returned to the room in time to hear these last words. "Who had fun?" she asked.

"You, Elizabeth, and Harry," Avery answered, "when you were kids."

"I had a terrible childhood," Roni suddenly announced, pausing for effect. We all dutifully turned her way. Bridget caught my eye and quickly placed her right pinkie on the corner of her mouth in a dead-on imitation of Mike Meyers's Dr. Evil. I knew exactly what she was thinking—Dr. Evil's hysterical recital of his personal history during the therapy session: "My father was a relentlessly self-improving boulangerie owner from Belgium with low-grade narcolepsy and a penchant for buggery. My mother was a fifteen-year-old French prostitute named Chloe, with webbed feet." It took all of my self-control not to burst out laughing. Idly tracing the rim of her wineglass with her finger, Roni continued, "My father left when I was only six and my mother had to work two jobs to support us. We had no money and had to wear secondhand clothes. When I grew up, I swore I'd never let that happen to me. But, of course, it did anyway. Megan's father walked out on me just like my dad did."

From the folds of the couch, David mumbled something. I couldn't hear him, but Claire blushed and shushed him.

Roni stared at him a moment before shrugging her shoulders and continuing. "I never even had a proper vacation until I was twenty-three."

"How positively Dickensian," Elsie muttered.

"What's that supposed to mean?" Roni asked, her eyes narrow with suspicion. No doubt Roni fancied Elsie to be satirical, perhaps, I amended, without knowing what it was to *be* satirical.

"Bridget, would you be a dear," said Elsie, changing

the subject, "and play something for us?" She nodded toward the piano. "Nobody plays unless you're here."

Bridget smiled. "Sure, Elsie. I'd be happy to." Bridget was a very accomplished pianist, having studied the instrument for more than ten years. In college, she even made some extra money working in nightclubs. She settled herself on the padded bench and commenced with a jazzy rendition of Mendelssohn's "Wedding March." Elsie sat back with a smile.

As soon as Bridget began playing, Roni announced to no one in particular how much she enjoyed listening to the piano. "Of course, I never had the opportunity to learn. My mother could not afford such luxuries. It was the bare minimum in my house."

Purely for my own amusement, I mentally added, "But if I had ever learnt, I should have been a great proficient."

Leaning over, Avery patted Roni's hand. "Those days are gone, sweetie."

"Gone. Just like the business," David muttered. "Just like my job." This time Claire did not attempt to shush her husband. She stared at her lap, her face flushed.

"Now, look," snapped Avery angrily, slapping the arm of his wheelchair. "I did not say I was selling. I only said I was considering an offer."

"A very *generous* offer," Roni interjected.

The muscles in Avery's long face pinched. He briefly closed his eyes before continuing. "The point is, no decision has been made. And I don't want this to ruin the weekend. We can all talk later. In the meantime, can we please just drop it?"

"I agree," said Roni. Turning to Bridget, who had just finished the piece, she said, "Bridget, why don't you play something, you know, 'weddingy.'"

Bridget stared at her half a beat but made no answer. Bridget never had much toleration for those she found insufferable—even if she was related to them. Without another word, she launched into "Lydia the Tattooed Lady," complete with lyrics. She'd just gotten to, "On her back is the Battle of Waterloo. Beside it, the Wreck of the Hesperus, too," when Avery's nurse, Millicent "Millie" McDaniel, strode briskly into the room. An imposing woman in her mid- to late fifties, she wore her straw-colored hair scraped off her face in a severe bun, and her heavily starched white uniform practically cracked as she walked. A slash of red across her thin lips was her only concession to feminine vanity. Her overall shape was that of an inverted triangle, with impossibly tiny ankles and calves supporting an enormous torso. She looked as if she'd put on a girdle and, starting at her ankles, pulled every ounce of fat upward toward her neck.

"Excuse me, Mr. Matthews," she said in a low masculine voice, "it's time for your medication." Although maintaining her professional demeanor, Millie was clearly displeased that her patient was still up at this late hour. Her lips were pressed so tightly together that they were reduced to the barest sliver of red.

"Thank you, Millie. I'll be right there." Avery turned back to the rest of us. "Well, if you'll excuse me, I think I'd better call it a night."

Roni jumped to her feet and positioned herself behind Avery's chair. "Here, honey, let me get this. Good night, everyone," she called over her shoulder as she pushed the chair around. "Lead the way, Millie."

As Roni sashayed past Millie, the nurse's professional mask slipped briefly. A quick twist of Millie's mouth made it clear she held the same low opinion of Roni as the rest of us.

With their exit, some of the tension subsided. Elsie sniffed loudly. "Oh, what I would love to say to that little trollop. The way she eyes everything in this house like she's appraising it, wondering how much she can sell it for after I'm dead. But for Avery's sake I am biting my tongue. So much so that I'm going to need stitches."

"Yes, Mother," said Graham dryly. "You've been a model of restraint. Remind me to play poker with you sometime." Beside him, Blythe smothered a smile.

"Oh, shut up," Elsie retorted calmly. "Rather than fight with each other, we need to work out a way to convince Avery not to sell the Garden."

Blythe glanced uneasily at her mother-in-law. "I understand how important the Garden is to the family, Elsie," she began tentatively, "but really, isn't this Avery's decision? After all, he's been running the place and he is the majority stockholder. He's a workaholic and he's had a stroke, for goodness' sake."

"It's not just the fact that he's thinking of selling the business that my father built that upsets me," said Elsie, "although I admit that this is part of it. Mainly, it's the fact that *she's* pushing him to do it. When it comes to *her,* he shows absolutely no common sense. That's what makes me so furious. He can't think straight with her around. I know my son. Avery loves that business. It's a part of him and he will be lost without it." She paused and traced the blue-and-cream swirls of the carpet with the gold tip of her cane. "If I believed for one minute that he'd be happier or healthier living a life of ease and not running the Garden, then I'd sell the place in a New York minute. But he won't be either. Within two months he'll be bored out of his mind. And, if I'm not mistaken, within a year he'll not only be without a business, but he'll be without his money and his wife, too."

David's face bunched in an angry scowl. "You can coun' on me, Elsie," he said, turning bleary eyes in her direction. "Lil' bitch." His brief effort at speech proved too taxing for what was left of his mind. The cushions grabbed him back into themselves.

Elsie stared at her son-in-law with undisguised scorn. "Claire, please put your husband to bed."

At her mother's words, Claire scrambled to her feet, her hair falling over her face. A crimson blush peeked through the auburn veil. "David," she pleaded in a low voice, "let's go. Come on, it's time for bed."

"Leave me alone," he mumbled. Claire reached out and grabbed her husband's hand and pulled. "Leave me alone, you cow!" he barked. Elsie's face darkened and she gripped her cane until her knuckles showed white. Anna, sensing her mistress's emotion, leaped to her feet and growled at David, the black hairs on her back standing up in an angry salute.

Graham stood up and roughly yanked David to his feet. "How dare you speak to Claire like that!" he hissed, his black brows bristling. "Get out of my sight before I lose my temper!"

"Who the hell are you to talk to me like that?" David retorted, his face dark with anger. "She's my wife and I'll talk to her any damn way I please. You think you can stop me?" David pushed himself off the couch and onto unsteady feet. I held my breath. David was clearly well past his fifth glass of scotch of the night; anything was possible when he was this drunk. However, once he was upright, his body gave way and he fell into Graham.

"Graham, please," Claire pleaded. "It's okay. He doesn't mean it. You know how he gets when he's…"

She started to say drunk but finished with "tired." "Please," she whispered, "don't make a scene."

"I didn't," Graham shot back, as he attempted to prop David up. "He did!"

Blythe was now on her feet as well. "Graham, honey, calm down. Let's just get him to bed."

"Fine with me," Graham muttered, as he spun David around and roughly shoved him toward the stairs. Blythe put her arm around Claire's slumped shoulders and led her away as well. Elsie watched them go with a shake of her head. "It's a real toss-up which one of them I detest more. You know, sometimes I think the animal kingdom has it right. They have no problem thinning the herd when necessary—and both Roni and David certainly present valid arguments for us adopting the practice."

Turning back to Peter, Bridget, and me, she said, "I'm going to bed, my loves. And I suggest that you all do the same. Peter, I've put you upstairs with Harry in the green room. Bridget will show you. Now remember, the electrician hasn't finished rewiring the bedroom wall switches, so you'll have to use the lamps instead. Try not to trip over yourself in the dark, Bridget," she said, surveying Bridget's shoes with a critical eye. Waving her cane at us, she left, followed closely by Anna.

Bridget frowned at Elsie's retreating form. "Are you okay?" I asked.

Giving herself a shake, she looked at me, her lips pulled up into a sad smile. "I'm fine. It's just that after scenes like that, I realize how lucky I am. My parents might drive me crazy nagging me about my hair and clothes, but I know they love me. I can't imagine what a nightmare it would be to have either Roni or David as a parent."

From behind us a chair scraped across the floor. Horrified, I turned around. Megan! I had completely forgotten she was in the room. She stood up and walked out from behind the plant.

Bridget's face flushed bright red as she stuttered her apologies. "Megan, I'm so sorry. I didn't know you were still here. I didn't mean—"

Megan interrupted her. "Yes, you did mean it. But don't worry about it. Being Roni's daughter *is* a nightmare."

Bridget stared at Megan and then nodded her head sympathetically. "It must be. I'm really sorry."

Megan ducked her head, trying to hide her tears, and slowly made her way toward the staircase. "Me, too" was all she said.

SIX

Avoid running at all times.

— Leroy "Satchel" Paige

"WAKE UP!" This command was accompanied by a kick, a forceful kick.

"Unless it is a respectable hour, say anytime *after* nine o'clock, then get away from me," I muttered, rolling away and ducking my head farther under the pillow.

Bridget was undeterred. She was also an absurdly early riser. "Let's go for a run," she persisted.

I cautiously opened one eye and peered at the clock on my nightstand. "Bridget! It's not even six thirty!" I pulled the down comforter up over my head.

She poked me in the back. "Come on. I can't sleep. I'm a nervous wreck about today. I need to go for a run."

"Then by all means do so," I said, curling into my pillow. As friends go, I consider myself loyal and true, but I do have my limitations. Running through chilly early morning mist is one of them. Actually, doing anything through early morning mist qualifies.

"We could run along the path by the trees," she coaxed. "You know how pretty it is this time of year, with the all leaves starting to turn."

"It is not everyone who has your passion for dead leaves," I quipped.

She did not rebuke me for the line. Instead, she urgently whispered, "Elizabeth! Please?"

I eased the comforter down an inch and peeked over its snowy top to look at her. She was dressed in a purple tracksuit emblazoned with tiny orange roadrunners. I winced.

"Where on earth did you get that outfit?"

She looked down. "On eBay," she said proudly. "It was a steal!"

"I would hope so. Now, what's the matter?"

"I don't know. I couldn't sleep last night. I kept having nightmares."

"About what? Not about you and Colin?"

"No. Not exactly. I just have a feeling that something bad is going to happen today. Something really bad." She twisted her engagement ring around her finger, a habit of hers when agitated.

In addition to being an early riser, Bridget is convinced that she has a sixth sense about danger. A trait, I might add, that fails her utterly when it comes to her driving. It was on the tip of my tongue to point this out when it finally penetrated my sleepy brain that Bridget would never force (read: kick) me awake before eight a.m. unless it was really important.

"All right," I said with a sigh, flinging back the heavy comforter and swinging my feet out onto the cool wood floor. "You win. Let's go for a run. But don't be surprised if the 'really bad thing' you're foreseeing is me having to be carted away by ambulance."

THIRTY MINUTES LATER, we were off and running. Music from my headphones blared, but not loudly enough to drown out my pounding heart as I pushed my leg muscles to carry me forward. I need this, though, I thought as my lungs burned as I strained to match Bridget's stride. As I mentioned, I'd been mastering my stress in the same manner a baker masters a pie crust: with a lot of sugar and butter. From the corner of my eye, I saw that she was trying to talk to me. "What?" I huffed, pulling the headphones away from my ears.

"I said, how far do you want to go?"

"I'm ready to stop whenever you are."

She laughed. "Stop? We're not even out of the driveway yet!"

I turned in disbelief. Sure enough, there was the house, a scant one hundred yards behind us. I sighed and clicked off my music. "Bridget," I said, coming to a stop and resting my hands on my knees. "*Please* don't make me do this. I'm still half asleep. I haven't even had coffee."

Bridget placed her hands on her hips and considered me. "Are you telling me that you agreed to this run only because you didn't think I deserved the compliment of rational opposition?"

"Have I really been watching the DVD that much?"

"You have indeed."

"Well, you drove me to it." I sighed. "Bridget, I love you dearly, but can't we just take a walk while you tell me what's bugging you?"

"All right," she conceded.

I fell into step next to her as we continued down the gravel driveway. "It's not about marrying Colin, is it?"

"God, no!" she said. "It's just a feeling that something bad is going to happen and on my wedding day."

"When did it start?"

She twisted her ring as she thought. "It might have started last night when Mom told me that Julia is coming."

"Julia!" I said, stopping and staring at her. "Julia's coming? Jesus! Does Avery know?"

"I don't know."

We fell silent as we contemplated this potentially awkward reunion. Julia Fitzpatrick had been the best friend of Avery's late wife, Ann. After Ann died, Julia and Avery became particularly close. Julia's own marriage was miserable and Avery was terribly lonely. When Julia's husband, Tom, died, everyone in Bridget's family had assumed that Avery and Julia would marry. And they might have done so had it not been for the arrival of Roni in Avery's life. One look at Roni and Avery lost all reason. Julia had said nothing, but the consensus was that she had been deeply hurt by Avery's desertion.

I gave myself a shake. "Well, so what if Julia is coming?" I said firmly. "She isn't a vengeful woman. Even if she considers Avery a complete cad for throwing her over, she wouldn't come to your wedding simply to make trouble."

Bridget stopped. "You're right," she said with a relieved smile, "she wouldn't. I'm just being melodramatic."

"Gosh. You? That's so unusual."

"You're not nearly as funny as you think you are."

"True. But I was dragged out of bed at an ungodly hour, so I have an excuse."

"Whatever. Come on, I'll race you to the house."

"You're on," I said. "Ready, set...go!" She took off and was soon a blur of purple sprinting in front of me. I made no move to chase her and instead walked slowly up the driveway, listening to gravel crunch noisily underneath my feet. I was glad that I had been able to extinguish Bridget's fears. Now I just wished someone would do the same for this very uneasy feeling of mine.

I DRAGGED MYSELF UP the stairs, heading for my room. Rounding the corner, I was startled by the sound of David's voice, raised in anger. "I need that money!" he yelled. "You promised me that you'd get it!" His voice was coming from one of the bedrooms, but I couldn't tell which one. A second voice answered him; it was Roni. "That well is dry," she said, her voice laced with disdainful amusement. My question as to which bedroom they were in was answered a second later when David furiously burst out of Roni's room. I had a brief glimpse of Roni's laughing face before the door slammed shut. David looked terrible. He was wearing a faded green shirt that only served to make his pale and spotty complexion look even worse. I noticed, too, that his hair hadn't been properly shellacked yet. It was standing out in at least six different directions. Seeing me, he stopped. His face was bunched in a ferocious scowl and his eyes were black with rage. I knew his ire wasn't directed at me, but I nevertheless took an involuntary step back. David scared the crap out of me when he was like this. The long hallway seemed to shrink with his menacing presence, and I became acutely aware that I was several feet from the top of the stairs. I couldn't fathom how Claire could live with such a ticking bomb.

Thankfully, David wanted as little to do with me as I did with him. Quickly rearranging his face into a less antagonistic expression, he grunted at me and disappeared into his own room. I let out a sigh of relief. No sooner did his door shut than the door to the hall bathroom opened. Claire emerged. She was wearing an ankle-length cream-colored dress, the kind an ex-boyfriend of mine used to refer to as a "decoy dress." Pithy comments like that were just one of the many reasons

I broke up with him. Claire's hair was neatly pulled back from her face with a black beaded headband. Unfortunately, this only highlighted her blotchy skin and bloodshot eyes. Apparently, Claire had not had an easy night after dragging David to bed. All the same, she smiled brightly when she saw me. "Have you been out running? Wow. That's dedication. I don't know where you get the energy. I'm beat this morning. I could barely pull myself out of bed."

"Well, that's where I'd rather be, but Bridget made me go. I think she needed to work off some nervous energy. Not that I was much help," I added. "I made it as far as the end of the driveway."

"Well, it is a long driveway," Claire said sympathetically, returning to her room.

Back in my own room, I debated changing, but the smell of freshly brewed coffee proved too strong. I headed to the dining room, where breakfast was set up on the sideboard. On the way downstairs, I bumped into Megan, who was headed in the same direction. Most everyone else was already there, Peter among them. I poured myself a large cup of coffee, grabbed a poppy seed bagel, and sank down into a chair next to Peter. Looking askance at my outfit, he said, "Dare I ask?"

"Bridget and I went for a run."

Peter, who knew about my penchant for sleeping in, made an odd noise and asked, "You're kidding, right?"

I took a grateful swallow of coffee. "Sadly, I am not. She dragged me out of bed so she could work off her nerves."

His dark brows pulled together in concern. "Is she all right?"

"I think so. She had one of her premonitions."

"Ah," said Peter dispassionately. He was used to Bridget's superstitious tendencies. "Not about her and Colin?"

"No. She's worried about something bad happening during the wedding. She wasn't too specific." I spread a thick layer of cream cheese on my bagel, remembered I still had to fit into my maid of honor dress, and scraped some off.

"Well, I suppose it's not strange to be jittery on your wedding day," Peter said, taking a sip of his coffee.

"True, but even so, I can't imagine anything going wrong on Chloe the Tyrant's watch." I took a bite of bagel, decided I'd scraped off too much cream cheese, and added more.

Peter looked blankly at me. "Who?"

"Oh, sorry. I forgot you haven't met her yet. Bridget's mom hired this top-notch coordinator. Her name is Chloe Jenkins, but she marches around barking orders and generally inspiring fear, so Bridget dubbed her Chloe the Tyrant."

Peter choked on his coffee.

"Are you all right?" I asked.

Grabbing a napkin, he held it to his mouth and nodded weakly. He seemed on the verge of speech when Claire entered the room. She had added a black beaded cardigan sweater to her ensemble, making her look exactly like an ad for Laura Ashley, circa 1982. "Good morning, everyone," she said.

Elsie looked up from her newspaper. "Good morning, dear. Where's David?"

Claire ducked her head and headed toward the sideboard. "He's not feeling too well this morning. I think he's coming down with a cold."

"It's called a hangover, dear."

Claire bent her head low as she poured herself a cup of coffee. "Mother, please don't start."

Elsie spread out her hands in a defensive gesture. "Fine. Have it your way. I won't say another word. Except…"

Whatever Elsie was going to not say was lost in the arrival of Roni. Wearing a tight turquoise silk dress that left very little to the imagination, she was, to quote Jane Austen, at once expensively and nakedly dressed. She sauntered into the room and issued a cheery hello. Not counting Avery's response, her greeting was largely ignored. Her smile still firmly fixed, she turned to Elsie, who sat absorbed in reading the paper. "Any interesting news today, Elsie?" she asked.

Elsie did not look up. "None at all," she replied, continuing to read.

Taking a plate from the sideboard, Roni placed a few pieces of fruit on it and sat down next to Avery. Eyeing her daughter's full plate of eggs, bacon, and toast, she said with a sigh, "Really, Megan. You're never going to lose weight if you insist on eating like a truck driver."

Crimson crept up Megan's neck and across her cheeks. Without a word, she pushed her plate away, stood up, and left the room. I caught a glimpse of her pinched, angry face as she hurried out the door. Harry, who had been sitting next to Megan, glared across the table at his stepmother. "You're unbelievable," he said disgustedly.

Roni raised a delicate eyebrow in surprise. "What are you talking about? I'm trying to help her."

"Help her? How is embarrassing her helping her? She ran out of here completely miserable, thanks to you."

"Thanks to me? You have no idea what you're talking about. Her *weight* is making her miserable. She's constantly complaining to me about it. I'm only trying to help her."

"By being cruel and making her cry?"

"Of all the nerve! How dare you speak to me like that! Avery, say something!" Roni demanded.

Avery, who had been listening to the exchange with an expression of growing dread, now grimaced. He looked as if he might agree with Harry, but he nevertheless said, "Harry, I'm sure Roni has Megan's best interests at heart. Let her handle it."

Roni was not mollified. Scraping her chair back, she rose to her feet in one majestic movement. "That's not the point, Avery, and you know it. I'm talking about the insulting way he speaks to me while you just *sit* there and let him get away with it!" Flinging her napkin on the table, she stared piercingly at her husband.

"Roni, please," said Avery in a low voice. He glanced uneasily in Elsie's direction.

"I'm going outside to have a cigarette," Roni bit out before turning on her not insubstantial heel and striding away.

Avery turned to Harry. "Why do you always have to start something with her?"

Harry's mouth twisted in irritation. "I didn't start anything, Dad. She treats Megan like crap and you know it. Since nobody *else* thinks to stand up for the girl," he said pointedly, "I thought maybe I should. But apparently it's more important to you that Roni not be upset." Harry, too, threw his napkin down and left.

An awkward silence followed his departure. We all stared at our plates, studiously pretending not to have heard the exchange. All except Elsie. With her eyes still on the newspaper spread out in front of her, she said matter-of-factly, "The boy's got a point, Avery."

"I don't recall asking your opinion, Mother," Avery snapped, backing his chair out from the table and wheeling it toward the door.

Elsie sighed heavily, her eyes trained on Avery's retreating form. Graham watched his mother warily. He must have seen something alarming in her expression for he suddenly tensed and said sharply, "Let it go, Mother."

"Let what go?" she responded, her eyes wide with a practiced look of innocence. No one was fooled.

"Whatever it is that you're planning," said Graham. "Let them sort out their own troubles."

Elsie sniffed and got to her feet. "I can't imagine what would give you the absurd notion that I could ever involve myself in other people's affairs," she said loftily. "And now, to announce my departure, I will also throw down my napkin in a fit of pique."

After matching her words to action, Elsie marched out. Anna, who had been happily receiving scraps from almost everyone in the room, reluctantly followed. At Elsie's exit, Bridget laid her head down on the table and put her hands on top of her head. "Great. This is just great," she moaned. "I'm getting married in eight hours and most of the members of my family aren't speaking to each other."

Blythe walked over to her daughter and put a comforting hand on her shoulder. "Never mind, dear. I'm sure they'll all have sorted everything out by then. In the meantime, I need to go over a few last-minute details with you." Noticing Bridget's hands, Blythe leaned in and suspiciously peered at her fingernails. "Bridget! You've painted your nails purple! No! Absolutely not! What happened to the pink shade I bought you?"

Bridget popped her head back up. "You were serious about that? It looked like overdone cotton candy. I thought you were kidding."

Blythe took a deep breath, while Bridget gazed appraisingly at her nails. "I think they look nice," she said stubbornly.

"We'll talk about it later," said Blythe firmly. As she propelled Bridget out of the room, she launched into a rapid recitation of the two dozen or more things that needed immediate attention.

Graham watched his wife and daughter leave, his black eyes sparkling with laughter. "In about five minutes, I expect Bridget will wish her mother was one of the nonspeaking family members," he predicted. "But speaking of last-minute details. Peter, could I borrow you for a few seconds? Since you are in the hotel business, I want to ask your opinion on the setup for the reception tonight."

Peter stood up. "Sure. I'll be glad to help."

"Thanks. This way," said Graham, as he exited through the French doors at the back of the room.

Peter squeezed my shoulder lightly. "See you later," he said, following Graham.

I waved good-bye, took another sip of coffee, and finished my bagel. Claire sat with me for a few more minutes before excusing herself as well. The dining room was now empty save for me, and I settled into my chair and enjoyed the quiet. Resting my head against the top rung of the high-backed chair, I idly studied the long room. Icy lime green walls were topped with intricately carved crown molding. To me, it had always looked like thick icing on a wedding cake. A long mahogany sideboard ran along the left wall. Along the right stood two enormous hutches, each displaying several patterns of china and crystal. At the far end of the room was a set of tall French doors. There were three sets of these double French doors in all: one in the dining room, one in the living room, and one in the study. Each led to the stone terrace that ran along the back of the house.

After finishing my coffee, I stepped out onto the terrace. It was still early but the sun was already blazing. The weather-men had predicted that we were going to have an Indian summer today and apparently they hadn't been kidding. It was going to be a scorcher, I thought, cupping my hand over my eyes to block out the sun's glare. Below me the lawn swarmed with the staff from the catering agency. Clad in bright blue T-shirts emblazoned with the logo Elegant Events, they appeared to be everywhere at once. One group was transforming the normally lush green lawn into a sea of circular tables to seat tonight's three hundred guests. To my right and left, another group was raising crisp white tents that would serve as the food and drink stations. At the base of the terrace, still more were hammering down an enormous parquet dance floor. A canopy of tiny white lights hovered above. In the midst of the organized chaos, Chloe patrolled the grounds. A dark tailored business suit clung to her lithe form and her white-blond ponytail snaked down her back in a long shiny coil. As she surveyed the crew's progress, she methodically checked off items on her clipboard and barked orders into a walkie-talkie.

I spotted Graham and Peter huddled over by one of the tents. Graham gestured animatedly while Peter nodded thoughtfully. Spotting Chloe, Graham called her over. She briskly strode in their direction and then, strangely, faltered. Over the last few months, I'd never seen Chloe do anything that wasn't deliberate and organized. She seemed more machine than human. After the misstep, Chloe righted herself and made her way to Graham and Peter. She quickly spoke to Graham, and then she laid her hand on Peter's arm. She kept it there a good eight seconds longer than necessary (by my count, anyway). My stomach tilted. Chloe was an inhuman tyrant, but she was also exceedingly pretty. Sophisticated, chic, and worst of all, thin, Chloe had an air about her that made me feel as if my ancestors had only recently started walking upright. Graham said something and Chloe was forced to remove her talons from Peter's arm so she could take notes. Graham's gestures intensified and Chloe scribbled on her clipboard and spoke rapidly into her walkie-talkie. Peter's shoulders shifted uneasily and he shoved his hands into his pockets and glanced around. I recognized that stance; he wanted out of the conversation. I wanted him out of it, too, for that matter. Women like Chloe had been ruining my love life as far back as I could remember. Jutting out my chin in an imitation of my boss when she asks me to pick up her dry cleaning, I walked along the terrace, intent on rescuing Peter. As I passed the French doors leading to the study, a low voice inside caught my attention. The syrupy floral scent told me it was Roni. I peeked around the door frame. Her back was to me and she was talking to someone on her cell phone.

"I know, sweetie. I miss you, too," she purred, "but I have to stay here this weekend." I froze. My brain shouted at me to keep walking, but somehow my feet didn't have the same moral integrity. "Yes," she continued, "I think he's going to sell. What? No. Don't come here. It isn't safe. Just trust me, okay?" She paused. Her voice rose petulantly. "I'm not going to doublecross you, honey! Look, I'll see you Monday, okay? Just calm down—it'll be fine. Wait, I think I hear somebody coming. I have to go." With a soft click, she snapped the phone shut. Just as she turned to move toward the terrace, I ducked through the doors leading into the living room. Hidden behind the heavy curtains, I watched Roni walk out onto the terrace. Pausing, she reached inside her purse and pulled out a cigarette. With shaking hands, she lit it. Taking a deep drag, she moved forward and disappeared down the stairs. Before I could process what I'd heard, I became aware of rapidly retreating footsteps behind me. Turning in that direction, I peered across the living room but saw no one. The footsteps headed for the long hallway that led to the staircase, but by the time I got there, whoever it was, was gone. Walking back through the living room, I passed by the door to the study. It was slightly ajar.

Someone else had overheard Roni's conversation. The question was, who?

SEVEN

How was the wedding?
Brief, to the point, and not unduly musical.
—Noël Coward

AT FIVE O'CLOCK SHARP, we were standing in the vestibule of St. Paul's Episcopal Church. The richly detailed Greek Revival church dated back to 1845 and had been the Matthews family's place of worship for almost as long. And although that worship was infrequent at best, it nevertheless was the chosen site for the Matthewses' and other established Richmond families' marriages, baptisms, and funerals. Especially funerals, according to Harry, who liked to say that St. Paul's was "where those in Richmond go, when they go."

In spite of Bridget's dire premonitions, the wedding ceremony went off with only one minor mishap. Ashley, Bridget's flower girl, took one look at the long church aisle, chucked her specially ordered rose-filled flower basket, and fled. Her parents spent the remaining part of the ceremony soothing her "shattered nerves" with copious amounts of candy and kisses. Not surprisingly, as soon as she'd consumed one piece of candy, she would burst into tears all over again until another was produced. After twenty minutes or so, it became mildly annoying, but given the intensity of Bridget's fears, it was not the Greek tragedy I half expected.

Back at Barton Landing, the cocktail portion of the

reception was now under way. From the main terrace the band played a sedate selection of classical compositions while below, waiters in starched white coats circulated with assorted trays of hors d'oeuvres and champagne. The staff appeared passionately dedicated to their jobs. As soon as a shrimp puff or a glass of champagne was consumed, it was immediately replaced with another. At the current rate of consumption, I calculated the entire party would be full and/or drunk by the time dinner was served.

I stood on the side terrace with Bridget and Colin and the rest of their families, waiting to have our pictures taken. We were grouped in front of the enormous rose-covered wooden trellis that ran up the side of the house. The vibrant pink roses stood out full and lush, a glowing testament to Elsie's green thumb.

I shifted uncomfortably. As predicted, the sun's heat was intense and I stared longingly toward the refreshment tents, where there was the promise of shade and cold drinks. Chloe stood off to Bridget's left, impatiently tapping a manicured fingernail against her ever-present clipboard. Even though she was wearing a black sheath dress—a color most Southern women avoid on hot, sunny days—she looked cool and professional. I, on the other hand, felt like an overdone strand of spaghetti in my yellow dress. I was pale, sticky, and limp.

Catching my eye, Chloe moved in my direction. "Goodness, but you look hot, Elizabeth," she said sweetly.

I took that to mean that I looked like crap, but I nodded good-naturedly. "I am. I'm looking forward to getting under one of those tents and getting something cold to drink."

"Can't someone get you something? Where's Peter?"

She looked vaguely around before turning back to me. "I guess he's wandered off. Same old Peter," she added, giving me a knowing smile.

Same old Peter? I had assumed that Chloe had only met Peter this morning when he was outside with Graham, hardly enough time to start referencing him as "same old Peter." Something about her smile coupled with the way she pronounced Peter's name—slowly, intimately—sent a finger of unease sliding down my back.

"You know Peter?"

From the way her smile increased, I gathered she found the question amusing. The amusement was purely one-sided. For the first time, I noticed that her teeth were a brilliant white, a shade normally limited to toothpaste ads—or piranhas. The feeling of unease was gone. It had been replaced by a swelling panic. Please God, I begged, please don't let this paragon of cool perfection be an ex-girlfriend of Peter's. Please, let her be a cousin or, at the very least, an old friend. I amended the last part to an old friend who was a dedicated lesbian.

"You mean he didn't tell you?" She let out a small giggle, the source of which was not readily apparent to me. I could forgive much, but not that giggle. "He can be so ridiculous sometimes with his old-fashioned ideas of discretion." She fell silent for a moment as if lost in fond memories. "But, yes," she said finally, "I do know Peter. We go way back. We were about to take our own stroll down the aisle ourselves, oh, I guess it was about five years ago. But I was so young. I wasn't sure if I was ready for marriage and a family. We agreed that it made sense for each of us, me, especially, to experience life a bit—you know, date around." She considered me with a complacent smirk, which I interpreted as satisfaction that Peter's latest dating "experience" was a sticky, limp thing in a yellow dress. "Anyway," she continued, "it's been so great to catch up with him. I gather you two are old friends?"

Old friends? Catch up with him? When the hell had Peter been catching up with Chloe? And why the hell did she think Peter and I were just friends?

"Um…yes, I guess you could call us that," I began. "But then actually—"

"Have you met his mother, Jane, yet?"

I longed to say that I had. I longed even more to say that not only had I met her *and* Peter's father, but that they'd already told me all about Chloe. Then I'd duck my head as if embarrassed, and mumble how "they were very unkind—but I won't say any of that to *you*."

But the sad fact remained that I had *not* met Peter's parents. While Peter and I had known each other as kids, it was because we had both been staying with Aunt Winnie. Our own parents had been elsewhere. Since we had begun dating, I had spoken to Jane on the phone a few times, but both she and Peter's father, Patrick, had been so busy with their business that a proper meeting had yet to happen. However, I was damned if I was going to mention this to Chloe. I struggled to answer in such a way as to not give this fact away. Apparently, I needn't have bothered; my face did it for me.

"Oh, so you *haven't* met her then!" cried Chloe in a voice that sounded suspiciously like crowing to my ears. "She is quite a character. And while I absolutely adore Jane, she is very particular when it comes to Peter. God, I watched her give so much hell to Peter's girlfriends over the years."

"But not to you, I expect," I said, hoping my smile hid my sarcasm.

Chloe glanced down as if overcome with modesty. "Well, no, *we've* always gotten along just fine."

Honestly. If it weren't for the proximity of the wedding photographer, I really think I might have mashed my bouquet into her smug, perfect face. Inner poise, I sternly reminded myself, inner poise.

Ashley skipped up to us just then, singing loudly and pretending to casually swing her flower-girl basket in an overly cutesy manner. In reality, she was taking turns whacking us in the rear with it.

"What a cutie!" Chloe exclaimed after receiving her whack. Catching Bridget's eye, she added, "Your cousin is adorable, Bridget!"

Bridget was silent. It was impossible for her to say what she did not feel, however trivial the matter. The photographer called to her and she turned in his direction.

As soon as Bridget turned away, Ashley whacked Chloe again with the basket. Chloe's smile dimmed, but she responded only by saying, "She's certainly full of spirit today!"

"Ashley!" I said firmly. "Stop hitting people with your basket. It's rude."

"I'm not hitting people on purpose," she replied with complete and utter insincerity.

"Ashley," I began sternly. Hearing her daughter's name uttered in a tone that indicated imminent reprimand, Karen suddenly materialized.

"What's going on, pumpkin?" she asked brightly. Ashley used her mother's presence to full advantage.

Letting her basket drop forlornly by her side to the ground, she pushed out her lower lip. "Mother," she whined, "I was just swinging my basket—honest! But now everyone's mad at me." She glanced accusingly up at me from underneath her lashes. For once, Karen did not automatically jump to her daughter's aid. She studied Ashley's face for traces of deception. Sensing that her mother was not going to rise up in her usual lioness defense, Ashley upped the ante. Flopping her slight body onto the ground, she buried her face in her hands and began to cry. "It's because I'm little," she moaned. "Everyone thinks I'm a pain! Nobody likes me!"

Karen's earlier hesitation vanished in a flash. "Oh, my poor baby," she crooned, bending down to sooth Ashley's huddled form.

Chloe followed suit. "Don't cry, honey," she purred, as she crouched over the girl. "No one is mad at you! Why, how could they be? You are probably the sweetest little flower girl I've ever seen—and I go to tons of weddings! I don't think I've ever seen one as pretty as you!"

Ashley shifted her arms slightly and peeked out doubtfully at Chloe. "You really think I'm the prettiest?"

I rolled my eyes, but Chloe carried on. "Of course! No question! Now don't you worry about anyone being mad at you!"

"But Elizabeth was," she said, glancing in my direction.

Before I could open my mouth to defend myself, Chloe jumped in, "No, she's not, honey. It's just this awful heat." She lowered her voice to a conspiring whisper. "It makes some people grumpy."

While I tried to digest that without obvious rancor, Ashley smiled coyly at Chloe. "You don't seem grumpy. You seem real nice."

Chloe winked at her. "Well, thank you, Ashley. I think you're really nice, too. Now why don't we see if we can't get you something to drink?"

"I'll get you something, pumpkin," Karen said, pulling Ashley to an upright position again. "Thanks very much," Karen added with a grateful smile to Chloe before moving away. I received only a cool nod.

Chloe stood up in one graceful move and smoothed away nonexistent wrinkles from her dress. Catching sight of my annoyed expression, she smiled sheepishly. "I guess I'm just a sucker for kids," she said.

"So I gather."

Chloe glanced carefully around before continuing. Was she making sure her next words were not overheard—or just the opposite? "I can see how you might think she's a bit spoiled, and I grant you that you may have a point. But who could resist that face? She's so cute! I know I'd always be indulging my kids—should I ever be lucky enough to have any, of course. Besides," she added with a glance in Ashley's direction, "I've always had a soft spot for the kids who have a bit of the devil in them. I much prefer them to the polite, well-mannered ones."

"Really?" I couldn't resist, so added, "I confess, every time I see Ashley, I never think of polite, well-mannered children with any abhorrence."

Before Chloe could respond, Mr. Keys, the photographer, anxiously clapped his hands to get our attention. "I need the bride's family now!" he called.

I focused on him rather than on Chloe's obvious ploy to demonstrate to everyone within earshot that she was quite ready to be a mother to Peter's children. Everything about Mr. Keys was round. He had round, wire-rimmed glasses, a round, soft-looking body, a round, pink mouth, and a round balding head. In his right hand, he clutched one of those large white linen handkerchiefs that were popular in the early 1900s. Peering thoughtfully at our group, he alternately coughed into the handkerchief and mopped his head with it. Peer, cough, mop. Peer, cough, mop. We stood patiently while he did this. Mr. Keys might be eccentric, but he was also talented. Finally, a gleam of inspiration replaced the peering. The coughing and mopping stopped and he methodically arranged us according to some unknown master plan. In the midst of the shuffling, Avery called out, "Wait! Where's Megan?" We looked around, and realizing that she wasn't nearby, began to call her name. Within seconds she appeared from the terrace, flushed and apologetic.

"Sorry, I was just listening to the band," she said. "They're really good."

As Mr. Keys crankily reshuffled the rest of us to create a spot for Megan, Roni eyed her daughter critically. "Megan," said Roni, "is that the dress you wore to the church?"

Megan glanced warily down at her outfit before answering. The full-skirted silk dress of midnight blue was sophisticated and flattering. She looked lovely. Still, Megan tensed. "Yes," she finally said suspiciously. "Why?"

With a perplexed expression, Roni shook her head. "Where did you get it?"

Megan threw her head back and stared defiantly at Roni. "I bought it."

Roni's winged eyebrows lifted a fraction of an inch. "Really?" Her eyes flickered disparagingly at the dress. As she turned to face Mr. Keys, I heard her add under her breath, "From whom? Omar the tentmaker?" I wasn't the only one who heard the vicious remark. Megan bit her lip and looked away. Behind me I heard a sharp intake of breath, while another low voice muttered, "That bitch." The camera flashed just then, forever capturing the moment: Roni smiling obliviously, Megan's head ducked in embarrassment, Harry's mouth a hard, thin line of anger, Elsie's eyes narrowed and focused on Roni, and Avery with his eyes closed. Around them, everyone else wore bright, painfully artificial smiles. They say a picture is worth a thousand words. This one was worth twice that.

By EIGHT O'CLOCK the reception was in full swing. The band, abandoning its earlier serene melodies, was now blasting out "Mack the Knife." Guests packed the dance floor and gyrated in inverse proportion to their skill level. The air was filled with the smell of muted sweat underneath expensive perfume. Peter and I briefly joined the fray, but the onslaught of flailing arms and sharp elbows proved too much for us. After a particularly painful jab to my upper arm, I gave up. Deftly avoiding a twirling woman in a fuchsia dress, Peter led me off the dance floor and toward one of the refreshment tents. After getting me a glass of wine and a beer for himself, Peter shifted uneasily on his feet. "Elizabeth?" he said. "There's something I need to tell you."

My stomach flipped sickeningly and my body temperature instantly rose ten degrees. This is it, I thought. He's going to tell me about Chloe. I had refused to bring up the matter myself with the knowledge that to do so would only make me appear petty and jealous. I had been down this road too many times before and had finally learned my lesson. I would stay calm and cool. I would be—to coin a phrase—mistress of myself.

Taking a deep breath, I put my wineglass down before my shaking hands spilled it down my dress and looked at him. However, his next words were interrupted by the arrival of Harry. As he saw us, Harry's face split into a lopsided grin.

"How come you two aren't dancing?" he asked.

"I forgot to bring my body armor," I said, rubbing my still-tender arm.

"Well, it's a take-no-prisoners kind of crowd. We Southerners take our dancing very seriously," he replied.

"I notice *you're* not out there," I said pointedly.

Harry took a sip of his beer before answering. "We Southerners also take our drinking very seriously."

"No point in spreading yourself too thin," said Peter with mock seriousness.

"Exactly." Harry nodded, clinking his beer bottle against Peter's.

I rolled my eyes. A woman in a powder-blue linen suit moved past Harry and then stopped and looked up at him. "Hello, Harry," she said quietly.

At the sound of her voice, Harry whirled around and stared down at her. She was a plump woman in her late fifties with chestnut brown hair, light green eyes, and an open, kind face. When he saw her, Harry's demeanor changed. The sardonic façade vanished, his mouth lost its ironic twist, and the mocking glint faded from his eyes. Without a word he wrapped his long arms around the woman and enveloped her in a giant bear hug.

"Julia!" he said, once he had released her. "How are you?"

"I'm fine, kiddo. I saw you in town today, but I guess you didn't see me."

"Really?" said Harry flushing, "I don't think I—"

"Don't worry about it. You were in a rush, no doubt getting ready for the wedding. How are you? Have you lost weight? You look tired," she said, giving him a motherly pat on the cheek.

"Really? Shoot. I thought I looked debonair. Oh, well. Story of my life." Turning back to Peter and me, he said, "Elizabeth? You remember Julia, don't you?"

I smiled and extended my hand. "Hi, Julia. I'm Elizabeth Parker, Bridget's friend…"

Julia smiled and took my hand. "Of course, I remember you, Elizabeth. It's lovely to see you again. I was so sorry to hear about your father's passing. How is your mother doing?"

"She's fine, thanks. She's actually dating someone now," I said.

"Really?" Julia said. Julia worked as a family therapist. Something in my voice must have aroused her professional instinct. With a slight tilt of her head, she asked, "How do you feel about that?"

My mother is an English professor with a passion for Victorian literature. Her boyfriend, George, is a man heavy on the brawn and light on the brains, who labors under the illusion that George Eliot was really a man. He's a nice enough guy, but as Dorothy Parker once said about someone, "His ignorance was an Empire State Building of ignorance. You had to admire it for its size."

I waved my hands, at a loss for words. "Whatever makes her happy, I guess," I said finally.

"Loss is hard. It's a good sign that she's moving on," Julia replied.

There was a hint of sadness in Julia's voice as she said this, and I was sharply reminded that Julia had had her own share of loss. Her daughter, Becky, had died tragically some years back.

Becky was Julia's only child. As kids, Harry, Bridget, and I played with her, although she and Harry were the closest. Becky's father, Tom, was an alcoholic who took his anger at his own failings out on his wife and child. I'm not sure when Becky started using drugs and alcohol to numb the demons that plagued her, but by her eighteenth birthday, she had a serious problem. After being told that she was a worthless waste of space almost daily by her father, it was hard for Becky not to believe that on some level it was true. Julia did everything she could to help her daughter, but nothing worked. After attending a party one night, Becky showed up at Harry's bedroom window, high and drunk. Harry wanted to take her home, but she begged Harry to let her sleep in his room, saying that if her parents saw her in her current condition, her father would kill her. Harry relented and snuck her into his room. But Becky was drunker than Harry realized, and sometime during the night, she slipped into a coma. She never came out of it and died two days later. Julia was devastated.

Julia's eyes now slid to Peter, and I quickly introduced them. From there we all fell into easy conversation. Harry was regaling Julia with exaggerated stories of his past exploits when raised voices to our left caught our attention. Not ten feet from us stood Roni and Megan. Megan's back was to us; Roni's was not. Her artfully made-up face contorted in anger, she leaned in close to Megan, her face mere centimeters away, and gripped Megan's arm with such force that her nails made angry red marks. Roni's next words floated clearly to our ears. "I'm not going to tell you again," she hissed. "You're making a fool of yourself out there. Stop gawking at the boys in the band. They are not interested in you, nor are they likely to ever be. Men are not interested in obvious girls. Especially obvious *overweight* girls."

Megan yanked her arm free of her mother's grip.

"I hate you!" she spat out before whirling around and pushing blindly past us.

Roni took a half step in Megan's direction, then seemed to rethink the move. Instead, she pulled out a cigarette, lit it, and walked off in the opposite direction.

Julia's hand flew to her mouth. "Oh, my God," she whispered. "She's just—"

"A real bitch," finished Harry succinctly. Julia raised confused eyes to his but said no more. "I'll go after her," Harry said.

"No," I said suddenly. "Let me go. She'll be even more embarrassed talking to you about it."

"Are you sure?" Harry asked.

"Yes. Peter, I'll be back in a little bit."

"Okay," he said. "I'll wait for you here."

The band launched into the first few chords of "I Could Write a Book." As I turned back to wave goodbye to Peter, I saw Harry offer his arm to Julia. "How about a dance, Julia?"

Taking his arm, she walked silently away with him. When they were well out of earshot, they turned toward each other and began to talk, earnestly and passionately.

IT DIDN'T TAKE ME long to find Megan. She was in the summer-house, the little cottagelike structure that sat on the edge of Elsie's property. Marianne Dashwood would have found it sadly defective. The building was regular, the window shutters were not painted green, nor were the walls covered with honeysuckles. It was used mainly to store boating supplies, but there were a few chairs and a cot, as well. Bridget and I had used it as a place to sneak cigarettes when we were younger.

Megan was sitting with her back to me, her shoulders hunched. On the floor next to her, I saw a beer bottle.

I considered saying something about it but dismissed the idea. When I was seventeen, I'd snuck a few beers myself now and again. Megan's rebellious behavior was the least of her worries. "Megan?" I said softly. "Are you okay?"

She nodded her head but didn't turn around. "I'll be fine," she answered in a choked voice.

I pulled up one of the folding chairs and sat down next to her. She kept her head averted.

"Megan, I don't want to sound like a cliché, but, trust me, it does get better."

"The only way it will get better will be if she drops dead," she said bitterly.

"I know how you feel. I really do. Being a teenager is hard enough, and when you don't look like a Barbie doll, it's all the worse. When I was your age, I had to wear these horribly thick glasses, I had a retainer, and looked like I was in training to become a sumo wrestler."

She looked at me, her eyes red and puffy. "You're just saying that. I can't believe you were ever fat."

"My nickname was Cocoa Puff because I ate that stupid cereal day and night."

"Really? You're not kidding?"

"Nope."

She looked down again. "Well, that may be so, but I bet you didn't have a mom who made you feel worthless. You should have heard her tonight. She actually compared me to that stick woman, Chloe, saying that's the kind of figure I have to have if I ever want a boyfriend. She wouldn't shut up about her. I bet your mom never did anything like that to you."

My dislike of Chloe only increased at the news that Roni liked her. Viewed in a certain light, however, they did seem a perfect match. Unbidden, Austen's words came to mind, "There was a kind of coldhearted self-ishness on both sides, which mutually attracted them; and they sympathized with each other in an insipid propriety of demeanor, and a general want of understanding." Maybe I *had* been immersing myself in *Sense and Sensibility* a tad too much lately. "No, you're right," I admitted, after a moment. "My mom never made me feel worthless." I gave a little laugh. "The creeps I dated in high school did that."

Megan sighed. "She won't even *let* me date, so I wouldn't know about that." Shaking her head, she continued. "You know, if it weren't for Harry, I don't know what I'd do. He's been so nice to me. Did you know he takes me out almost every weekend?" she asked me with a small smile. "We go to the movies or to lunch—basically anyplace that's out of the house. I mean, Avery is great, too, and it really meant a lot to me when he officially adopted me last year, but he's so infatuated with *her* that he can't see what she's *really* like."

"I'm sorry, Megan. I won't pretend that this isn't hellish for you right now. All I'm trying to say is that there *is* life after your teen years. And there will be life after your mother. You're a smart, nice girl. You'll go off to college next year and start a new life and you'll see. It gets better."

She sighed and stared at her lap. "I guess it has to, right? But still, there are times when I really wish she would just disappear."

"I know." I put my arms around her and hugged her. From what I could see, Megan wasn't the only one who held that sentiment.

I LEFT MEGAN shortly after. She wanted to stay at the summer-house a while longer. It was hard to see Megan so miserable. I just hoped that she'd heard me when I said that it gets better. But when you're a teenager, it's hard to see beyond next week.

As I walked back, I saw Elsie standing at one of the tables. With a furtive glance around, she pulled something small out of the pocket of her peacock blue silk gown. Looking around one last time, she reached down and opened a bright pink clutch purse on the table and dropped whatever it was she was holding inside. Closing the purse again, she turned my way. When she saw me, surprise registered on her face, and she made her way over.

"Hello, Elizabeth," she said. "Enjoying the party?"

"I am," I said. I didn't tell her about Megan's fight with Roni. It would only upset her, and there was nothing anyone could do about it now. "Everything turned out perfect. This is such a beautiful place for a wedding."

"I'd love to host yours when the time comes," she said. With a broad wink, she added, "If I were you, I'd start making plans."

Embarrassed, I ducked my head. "Well, I don't think I'm going to need to do that soon."

"Oh, posh! But, I will grant you this—the boy won't have a chance to ask you unless you're with him. Now, why don't you go and ask him to dance?"

"Oh, I…"

"No excuses, now. Go grab your man and dance! The band's playing a slow one. Those are the best songs for proposals. Now scat! Peter's under the drink tent over there," she said, using her cane to point me in the right direction.

"Elsie, really…"

"Oh! There's Annabel Martin," she said, indicating a

petite woman wearing horn-rimmed glasses and a bright yellow gown. "Excuse me, Elizabeth, I haven't said hello to her yet." She quickly made her way across the lawn.

I walked over to Peter and told him about my conversation with Megan. Then, taking Elsie's advice, we braved the dance floor once again, but by the time we did the band had launched into another fast number. After a few futile attempts, we gave up and opted to watch from the safety of a nearby table. Once I was seated, Peter went off to get us some water. Although it was long past sunset, the heat of the day was still strong. After a few minutes, Avery and Roni approached.

"Elizabeth," said Avery, "may we join you?"

"Of course," I answered. "Peter's just gone to get us something to drink." While they settled in at the table, I eyed Roni thoughtfully. Throughout the day, I had seen her receive several more calls on her cell phone. However, each time she had immediately hung up, claiming it was a "crank" or "wrong number." I didn't believe her for a minute, suspecting that she merely didn't want to take the call while someone was in earshot. I now searched for something to say. Unfortunately, the only things that sprang to mind were "How's the affair?" and "So, have you verbally abused Megan enough for one day?" Finally, I settled on, "I can't believe it's still so hot." Mundane, yes, but not toxic.

"I know," said Avery, "but a storm is coming. This heat will break soon." After delivering this bland observation, Avery's face underwent a startling transformation. His eyes widened, his mouth parted in surprise, and two bright spots of color formed on his pallid cheeks. I assumed that this reaction was due not to a sudden fear of storms on Avery's part but to whatever it was that he was gaping at over my shoulder. I glanced behind me. It was Julia.

She stared at Avery, a small sad smile hovering on her lips. "Hello, Avery," she said.

Some of Avery's stupor faded and in a voice heavy with emotion, he said, "Julia! How are you? You look wonderful!"

The low timbre of Avery's voice caught Roni's attention. Narrowing her eyes, she studied Julia, while Avery continued to gush his excitement. I smothered a smile as her brows wrinkled in perplexity. To a woman like Roni, Julia's attraction would be an eternal mystery. Roni could no more understand the importance of warmth, humor, and intelligence than a rattlesnake could understand the importance of comfortable shoes. However, while she may not have understood the attraction, she clearly sensed it.

Roni eyed both Avery and Julia as she carefully arranged her necklace. Concocted of delicately spun platinum and glittering diamonds, it was Avery's latest and most extravagant gift to Roni yet. Reflecting the vibrant pink of her dress, the diamonds blazed in a rosy fire. Once satisfied that it was properly displayed on her chest, she turned her eyes on Avery.

"Avery, honey," she purred, "aren't you going to introduce me to your friend?"

A startled expression crossed Avery's face at the sound of Roni's voice. I wondered if he'd forgotten that she was there.

"Oh, of course, excuse me," he said quickly. "Roni, this is Julia Fitzpatrick. Julia, this is…my wife, Roni."

Roni curled her body into Avery's. "It's nice to meet you, Julia," she said, her long fingers still toying with the necklace.

"I've heard a lot about you," Julia replied, a tight smile on her lips. Roni took this as a compliment and smiled, but I suspected that Julia's words held a far different meaning. "That's a lovely necklace," Julia added.

Roni's full lips pulled up into a smug smile. "Isn't it? It's a gift from Avery. He's so thoughtful."

Julia's glance flickered to Avery, and I noticed a faint blush creep up his neck. "You're a very lucky woman" was her only reply. "Well, it was wonderful to see you again, Avery," she said, as she moved away from the table. "Nice to meet you, Roni," she added. Giving me a discreet wink, Julia disappeared into the crowd and was gone.

"Didn't you used to date her?" Roni asked.

Avery was staring at the place where Julia had stood. "Mmmm," he said, nodding his head.

"She's not very pretty, is she?"

Neither Avery nor I responded. Roni eyed Avery suspiciously, seemingly unsure what his silence meant. Pulling her coordinating clutch toward her, she pulled out a lipstick. After applying the glossy red sheen liberally to her full mouth, she re-capped the gold tube and dropped it back into her bag.

Her task complete, she turned my way. "So, Elizabeth, tell me all about you and Peter. How long have you two been dating?"

"Since January," I replied.

"That's nice." She twirled a long strand of her raven hair around her finger. From the way she covertly studied Avery from beneath her long lashes, I suspected that her words were mechanical and her mind was actually miles away from the conversation. "Are you two talking about marriage yet?" She patted Avery's hand and continued. "I can tell you, once you find the right man, it's wonderful."

Avery seemed not to have heard. Staring off in the distance, his face wan and drawn, he didn't look like the poster child for a promarriage campaign. Roni noted her husband's silence and her brow furrowed as she twisted in her seat to peer at his face. "Avery? Honey, are you all right?"

At the sound of her voice, he jumped slightly and raised vague eyes to hers. "I'm sorry, dear, did you say something?"

"I was just telling Elizabeth how wonderful marriage can be with the right person." She smiled expectantly at him.

Avery turned back to me. "Yes," he said slowly, "that's true. Whatever you do, make sure you find the right person. It can make all the difference." From underneath her long lashes, Roni shot him an uneasy look and let out a nervous trill of laughter. "Avery! You sound so dire! Goodness, what's gotten into you tonight?"

Avery shook his head and gave her a half smile. "I'm sorry, dear. I guess I'm a little more tired than I realized." At these words, Roni cooed and fussed over him. She was certainly playing the part of the dedicated wife, I thought, but as her phone call earlier had made clear, it was just that—a part. While it would be gratifying to see Roni unmasked, I couldn't reveal what I'd heard. Telling Avery would be akin to kicking a puppy, and telling either Bridget or Elsie would be akin to dropping a match into a bucket of gasoline. All things considered, silence seemed my best option. Someone else had heard Roni's conversation on her phone earlier. I wondered if that person planned on spilling the beans. My ruminations were interrupted by the arrival of Millie. In her starched uniform, she was the only woman other than Bridget wearing white. She stuck out like a luminous moth. She bent low and quietly whispered something to Avery. He looked at his watch and nodded his head. "Okay, Millie. I guess you're right. I am tired. I must have overdone it today." Patting Roni on the arm, he said, "I'm going to turn in now."

"Oh," she replied, her eyes wide. Her voice hesitated slightly as she added, "Do you want me to come, too?"

"No. There's no need for you to miss out on the fun. I'll see you later."

Roni smiled and jumped up from her seat. Carefully running her hands over her shapely hips to smooth out the folds of her snug pink dress, she kissed him lightly on his cheek and said, "I won't be long. I think I'll just go and see where Megan is. I'll pop in and say good night to you when I get in." I wondered at this. Given her earlier poisonous exchange with Megan, I doubted that she was really interested in finding her. So where was she going? Was she going to make another phone call to her "love"?

Turning to Millie, Roni added, "Millie, I leave him in your capable hands. Make sure you take good care of him for me!" Blowing an airy kiss to Avery, she sashayed toward the dance floor, gliding across the lawn like a pink snake. She passed near Claire. Claire hesitated a moment and then turned to follow her. Reaching out, she grabbed Roni's shoulder and whirled her around. I couldn't hear what they were saying, but their body language spoke volumes. Claire's back was to me, but from her stiff posture and jerky movements, it was clear she was angry. Roni, however, was not. She listened to Claire with a mocking smile and laughed at something Claire said. Claire raised her hand and I had a sudden thought that she meant to strike Roni. A couple danced between us, obscuring my line of vision. When they moved out of the way, Claire and Roni were gone.

Next to me, I noticed Avery and Millie staring out at the spot where the two women had been. Avery's face was pained; Millie's was etched with disgust. Wondering if it could have been Millie's footsteps I'd heard earlier today in the hallway, I snuck a quick look at her shoes: white with rubber soles. I doubted they had made the loud footsteps.

Giving me little more than a mechanical good night, Avery signaled to Millie that he was ready to leave. I sat at the empty table for another five minutes before pushing my chair back and going in search of Peter. Heading toward the closest drink tent, I craned my neck over the thick crowd. I soon found him. He was standing away from the tent, partially hidden by the loping branches of a large magnolia tree. Chloe stood next to him. To steal a quote from Groucho Marx, if she were standing any closer, she'd be behind him. Peter said something and Chloe let out a peal of laughter. Gently placing a slender hand on his chest, she leaned in to whisper something in his ear and he laughed in response.

My mind reeled. The summer I was twelve, my parents enrolled me in a soccer camp, ostensibly because studies had shown that girls who participated in sports did better in school. The real reason, however, was I was overweight due to the recent acquisition of an Easy-Bake Oven, which I liberally used to sooth myself about two other recent acquisitions: thick glasses and a mouthful of braces. During one of the camp's torture sessions, also known as scrimmages, I fell and was kicked in the stomach. Painful as a pair of cleats smashing into your gut can be, it was nothing to how I felt seeing Chloe lean in toward Peter, her hand on his broad chest.

Suddenly aware that I was gawking like a wounded school-girl, I quickly turned and headed back for the table before they saw me. I know I should have calmly joined Peter and Chloe, but I simply couldn't. There was no way I could trust my emotions. I had a long, painful history with cheating boyfriends. The last guy I'd dated had been seeing at least two other women behind my back. I had been made a fool of too many times before to be calm now.

Thankfully, Harry grabbed me just then for a dance, saving me from having to sit at the table alone and brood. But as much as I enjoyed both Harry's conversation and dancing, it did not escape my notice that we had danced three songs before Peter finally reappeared.

THE LAST GUEST LEFT just before one a.m. Exhausted and yet radiant, Bridget and Colin disappeared soon after to their room downtown at the Jefferson Hotel. Colin's parents left a few minutes later. They were staying at the same hotel but wanted to give Colin and Bridget their privacy.

Inside the house, I sank into one of the couches in the living room and pried my shoes off my swollen feet. Claire and David were also in the room. From the looks of it, Claire was trying—without much success—to get David to go to bed. She shot me a distracted smile before turning her attention back to David.

Peter came in and sat down next to me. "Has something happened? You seem upset," he said in a low voice.

I turned to face him, firmly reminding myself of my resolve to remain composed. "Upset? Me? What a funny question. Why should I be upset? Is there any reason I should be upset?" I abruptly snapped my mouth closed. I can be really smooth sometimes.

He opened his mouth, looked at me closely, and then shut it. Glancing over at Claire and David, he said, "I don't know. You just seem upset."

I didn't want to talk anymore. I wanted to crawl into bed and try to block out what I'd seen. "I'm just tired, I guess," I said, making an excuse for disappearing upstairs. "It's been a long day. I don't think I'll have any trouble sleeping to night," I added with a forced yawn.

"Really?" said Peter. "I'm having the opposite problem. I'm completely wired. I must have had too much coffee."

Harry stumbled into the room. From the bottle of beer clutched in his hand, it was clear why his balance was off. From the mud stains on his pants, it was also clear that this wasn't his first stumble of the night. "Whoopsie," he said with a sheepish grin. Spying us on the couch, he flopped down next to Peter. "That was a fun party," he said. At least, that's what I think he said. It might have been, "Hats are sun hardy." Harry's balance wasn't the only thing that was off.

"Have a nice time?" Peter asked mildly.

"Yep," Harry said, draining the rest of his beer. He stared sadly at the empty bottle. "Time for a beer run. Pete, you wan' one?"

Peter shook his head and reached out his hand to stop Harry from getting up. "You'd better switch to water, Harry."

"Don' be silly. I'm fine." Harry pulled himself unsteadily to his feet. For a second it looked as if he was going to come back down in a hurry. Once he stopped swaying, he grinned proudly at us. "See? Fine."

The doors from the terrace opened again and in

walked Roni. So much for getting back to Avery early, I thought. Looking at us, she said, "Have any of you seen Megan? I can't find her anywhere."

Peter and I shook our heads, as did Claire and David. Megan had spent most of the night watching the band, but once they stopped playing, I hadn't seen her. Harry glared at Roni and took an unsteady step toward her. "If anything happens to her, it's your fault," he said with slow deliberation.

Roni narrowed her eyes. "What's that supposed to mean?"

Harry leaned in close to her and jabbed her shoulder with his forefinger. "It means you're a terrible mother, Roni. It means you ran your daughter off."

Roni took a step back, her expression disdainful. She sniffed. "You're drunk."

Harry nodded his head vigorously, sending his blond hair falling into his eyes. "That I am," he agreed. "But in the morning, I'll be sober. You'll still be a bitch."

Without a word, Roni's tanned arm swung up and she slapped him across the face. Claire let out a gasp. David sat still and stared bug-eyed. Peter and I jumped to our feet. Harry pulled his hand back to retaliate, but Peter grabbed it and pushed it back down. "Whoa!" Peter said. "Let's everyone calm down." But Harry wasn't listening. "You're a bitch," he repeated. "You ruin everything you touch: Megan, my dad, everything. Someday you'll get yours. And I hope I'm the one who gives it to you." He pulled against Peter's arm, but Peter held firm.

Roni's face was white under her tan, but she held her ground. "You think I ruin things? Well, in your case you just might be right. After this, I'm going to make sure that your father cuts you off completely. You are done, Harry. Do you hear me?" Her voice rose an oc-

tave. "Done! You can bet on that." She whirled around
and marched back out to the terrace, slamming the door
behind her. In the darkness outside, I saw a flash of red
as the ember of a cigarette was lit.

Peter released his hold, and Harry fell back onto the
couch. Peter and I stared down at him. "Are you okay,
Harry?" I asked.

He nodded, rubbing the red mark on his cheek. "Yep.
Except…"

"Except, what?"

"Except, I think I'm going to be sick."

Peter and I quickly yanked Harry to his feet. Pro-
pelling him up the stairs to the bathroom with lightning speed, we deposited him in front of the toilet and
quickly backed out into the hall. "Thanks, guys," he
said thickly, before kicking the door shut. Through the
door, I heard him begin to retch. After a minute, he
called out, "Guys?"

"Still here, Harry," I said. "Can I get you anything?"

"Better judgment would be nice. Think I'm going to
take a quick shower."

Peter, who was sharing a room with Harry, called
out, "Good idea. We'll wait for you."

Hearing the shower turn on, Peter and I sat down
on the top steps of the staircase. He wrapped his arm
around me. Closing my eyes, I breathed in his familiar
scent and leaned my head against his shoulder. For a
moment, my anxiety about Chloe vanished and all was
right with my world. Somewhere down the hall, I heard
one of the bedroom doors open and shut.

"Poor guy," said Peter with a shake of his head. "I
wonder if he'll remember any of this in the morning."

"Well, if he doesn't, Roni certainly will."

Peter grimaced. "I gotta tell you. I debated not pulling his hand back. That woman is vile. What do you think she'll do to Harry?"

"I don't know. But Avery is putty in her hands. I can only imagine what she'll say or suggest as punishment. But one thing is for sure, Harry's in a world of trouble."

We both fell silent and sat listening to the steady stream of water from the shower. After ten minutes or so, Harry emerged wearing a towel, appearing chagrined but more coherent. Peter and I pulled apart and stood up. "Sorry about that, guys," said Harry. "I feel like a real ass."

"Don't be silly, Harry," I said. "You lost your temper, that's all."

Harry looked down at his feet. "That's not all I've lost, I think." Shaking his head, he slowly walked down the hall to his room.

"He'll be okay, right?" I asked Peter.

"Yeah. I'll keep an eye on him. But I think the worst is over. Except for his headache tomorrow morning."

We said a quick good night. I know the kiss I gave Peter was tempered by my insecurity at seeing him with Chloe. Was it my imagination, or was Peter's kiss tempered as well?

I headed for my room. Opening the door, I fumbled with the wall light switch before remembering that it didn't work. As Bridget was at a hotel tonight, Megan had been moved into my room. Switching on the nightstand lamp, I was relieved to see that Megan wasn't there. I wasn't up to making small talk. I wanted to get my thoughts in order. Quickly changing into my pajamas, I wearily crawled into bed. Peter was not the kind of man to cheat or lie, I told myself. Granted, as a child he'd been a creep, but he'd outgrown that. I mentally listed all the reasons why I could trust Peter and sternly

reminded myself that he was not like my other boyfriends. Besides, after tomorrow, Chloe would be gone,
along with all the tables and chairs and other parapher-
nalia of the wedding. Peter and I were headed for Cape
Cod to visit my Aunt Winnie and spend some much
needed time together before Peter left for London. He
was leaving next week and would be gone for almost
three months helping his parents open another hotel. It
would be a long separation, but everything would be
okay. I tried to ignore the nasty little voice that mocked
this assumption. After twenty minutes of these mental
gymnastics, I reached over and turned out the light.
Megan still wasn't back. I glanced at the clock. It was
two thirty. Unconcerned, I shrugged mentally and rolled
over. I had been seventeen once, too.

EIGHT

Death...a melancholy and shocking extremity.
　　　　　—Jane Austen, *Sense and Sensibility*

A LOUD RUMBLE woke me. I lay curled into my pillow for several seconds, disorientated at not being in my own bed. The rumbling continued and I reluctantly lifted my head. The movement sent waves of pain across my skull. Through the soft white curtains I could see heavy, fat clouds thundering across a bleak gray sky. Some people get a twinge in their joints before a storm; I get a migraine.

The storm's real action hadn't started yet, but it was clearly only a matter of time. The digital clock next to my bed read seven a.m. Brunch wasn't scheduled until noon, so I laid my throbbing head carefully down onto my pillow, intent on going back to sleep. The problem was, I couldn't.

I rolled over, remembering a recent article I'd read touting the healing benefits of deep breathing and soothing thoughts. While methodically forcing air in and out of my lungs, I congratulated myself on surviving Bridget's wedding. I had not had a nervous breakdown or taken up smoking. Granted, I'd devoured enough hors d'oeuvres, petits fours, and tea sandwiches over the last few months to last me a lifetime, but that was rectifiable with a few serious weeks at the gym. The thought of physical activity set off new stabs of pain, so I shifted gears. In just a few hours Peter and I would leave for Aunt Winnie's B and B on the Cape. However, thinking of Peter stirred up another memory. Viewed in the cool light of day, most late-night melodrama looks silly. Unfortunately, from the way my stomach twisted at the memory of Peter and Chloe standing close together, it was obvious that it would take more than the light of day—cool or otherwise—to banish my insecurities.

Deciding that the deep-breathing-think-happy-thoughts method of pain reduction was a load of bunk, I opted for the tried-and-true means of aspirin and coffee. Pushing aside the bedcovers, I sat up, held my head against the sudden throbbing, and looked around. The bed where Megan should have been sleeping was empty. From the look of the neat, smooth sheets, it had been empty all night.

Gulping down three aspirin with a mouthful of water, I pulled on jeans and a T-shirt and quietly padded downstairs. From the silence, I gathered I was the only one up. I slipped into the kitchen in search of coffee. Sadly, there was a decided lack of that healing odor. I started a pot, then I poked around until I found the bagels. Minutes later, with a large mug of steaming coffee and a toasted bagel in tow, I headed for the dining room, only to come to a sudden halt in the doorway; the room was set for the brunch. The table was overflowing with elaborate flower arrangements, sparkling crystal, delicate china, and gleaming silverware. All that was missing was a large plaque reading DO NOT TOUCH. I backed out slowly, deciding the terrace was a safer option.

Outside, the air was thick with the impending deluge. Overnight, the temperature had dropped and the leaves on the magnolia tress danced and swayed to the wind's increasing tempo. Below me, the catering crew scrambled about, folding up the chairs, tables, and tents, working quickly to get everything stored away before the rain started. Inadvertently, my eyes searched the grounds for Chloe. My search was rewarded, if that's the right word. She stood off to the left of the house, barking orders into her walkie-talkie and checking her clipboard as usual. Her silky hair was pulled back into her trademark ponytail and she was wearing another one of her perfectly tailored suits. Although I couldn't actually see from where I was standing, I was ninety-nine percent sure her teeth were gleaming and her skin was dewy fresh. She'd also probably risen at dawn, eaten a handful of nuts and berries, and gone for a six-mile run.

Conscious of my ratty jeans, unwashed hair, and non-dewy everything, I opted to drink my coffee and eat my calorie-packed bagel slathered with cream cheese in the privacy of the side terrace. Out of view, out of mind, I told myself.

Several chairs and chaise longues were arranged in front of the rose trellis. Settling into one of the cushioned chairs, I saw that I was not alone after all. On another chaise, a recumbent figure lay under one of the wool quilts Elise kept outside for chilly nights. Was this where Megan had spent the night?

Fat drops of rain splattered onto the patio, slowly at first and then increasing in tempo. A bolt of lightning crackled against the dark sky. It was going to be a hell of a storm. I gathered my coffee and bagel and stood up.

"Megan?" I called out. "You've got to wake up. It's starting to rain. What are you doing out here, anyway?"

When I didn't receive an answer, I reluctantly put my coffee and bagel back on the side table and walked toward her. As I neared the chair, my foot kicked something. Stooping down to pick it up, I saw that it was a white plastic hotel key card. I raised my voice and tried again. "Megan? Are you okay? Come on, we need to go inside now." Again there was no response. I reached out to nudge her, gently pulling back the blanket. Staring down in astonishment, I saw that I was wrong on both counts. It was not Megan and she wasn't asleep. It was Roni, and unless I was very much mistaken, she was dead.

She was lying on her side, her beautiful eyes wide and staring. The silent grimace of her lips reminded me of Edvard Munch's painting *The Scream.* Except Roni's hands weren't clutching her head; they were frozen, clawlike, at the place in her chest where a large kitchen knife protruded.

I must have started screaming, but I don't really remember. I found myself at the other end of the terrace surrounded by the catering staff and soaked from the rain.

"Hey, lady," said a man with arms roughly the size of my thighs. His blue catering T-shirt stretched tight across his chest. "Are you all right?"

I shook my head and silently pointed at Roni's body. I couldn't find my voice. Mr. Big Arms shot me a funny look and walked over to where Roni lay. I dragged my eyes away from the horrific sight of Roni sprawled on the chaise, fighting the waves of nausea rolling through my stomach, and forced myself to concentrate on the rose-covered trellis. But there was no relief to be found there. All my eyes could see were those roses that were now wilted and dying, their delicate petals edged in brown. Death, it seemed, was all around me.

The other staff stood protectively around me, making assorted calming noises. Someone opened an umbrella and held it over my head. Mr. Big Arms looked down at

the body. "Jesus!" he said, staring back at me in astonishment. "This woman's dead!" The other members of
the staff abandoned their attempts to comfort me and
quickly edged over to get a look, taking the umbrella
with them. Ghouls. Mr. Big Arms looked at me again,
a wary expression now on his face. "Did you do this?"

My voice came back in a rush. "*No!* Of course not!
I just found her. Oh, God. We need to call the police.
I've got to tell the family!" I looked around anxiously.
Chloe was just coming up the terrace steps. "Elizabeth?" she said. "Is something wrong?" Just as I had
suspected, she was dewy fresh. "Roni's dead!" I said in
a jumble. "Over there." I pointed behind me to where a
rapidly growing crowd of men in blue T-shirts grouped
around the chaise.

Chloe's eyes slid to where I pointed. "Eric! What's
going on?"

Eric, aka Mr. Big Arms, popped his head up. "She's
right, Ms. Jenkins. There's a body here."

I pushed past Chloe. "Call the police," I yelled at her
over my shoulder. I bolted into the house, and taking the
stairs two at a time, dripping and sobbing, ran straight to
Peter's room. I pounded frantically on his door until he
opened it. "Elizabeth?" he said, as I fell into his arms.
"What's going on? You're sopping wet."

I buried my head in his chest. "It's Roni. I found her
outside. She's dead."

Peter grabbed both of my arms and eased me back.
"Dead? Are you sure?"

The horrible image of Roni's dead, staring eyes came
back to me and I pushed his hands away. "Yes, I'm sure.
I'm not a medical expert, but usually when someone
has blank, staring eyes and a large kitchen knife stick-

ing out of her chest, it's a pretty safe bet that she's not coming back."

"Christ! Are you okay?"

I covered my face with my hands and realized that I was still clutching the hotel key. "No. I'm sorry. I didn't mean to snap at you. It's just…it's just so awful. She's lying out there…dead!" I looked down at the plastic card. It was from the Jefferson Hotel.

"What's that?" Peter asked. Silently, I handed him the key. Confusion registered in his eyes.

"Where did you get this?" he asked.

"It was outside. By…by the body." My legs turned to jelly. I must have swayed because Peter suddenly caught me and pulled me close. "Jesus. This is unbelievable," he murmured.

Behind him, I could see Harry sprawled across his bed. He was snoring.

"Have you called the police?" Peter asked.

"No. I asked Chloe to do it."

"Chloe's here?" Peter asked with surprise.

My stomach lurched at the sound of his voice saying her name, but now didn't seem the time to address the matter. "Yes," I said, pulling away. I peeked up at him. He looked terrible. His face was haggard and his eyes bleary. "She and the crew were out back taking down all the chairs and stuff. They all ran over when I started screaming."

"I guess we'd better let everyone here know what's happened. Before the police arrive."

We both turned and looked at Harry. He let out another loud snore. "He did that all night," said Peter wearily, running his hand through his hair. "For some reason, I couldn't get to sleep last night. I read until around three and even after that I didn't sleep very well. I doubt I slept more than two hours."

"Well, we'd better wake him," I said. "I think he should be the one to break the news to Avery."

Waking Harry and telling him that Roni was dead was not easy. Not because Harry was upset or anything. He was just extremely hungover. For the first five minutes, he swatted at Peter and me as if we were nothing more than bothersome flies. For the next five minutes, he seemed to think we were playing a prank on him. It was only when he heard the sirens screaming up the driveway that he took us seriously.

WITHIN A HALF HOUR the whole house was up and gathered in the living room under the watchful eye of one Detective Paul Grant. He was probably only in his early fifties, but his sun-ravaged face and prematurely gray hair made him appear older. With his wide, solid body, blunt features, and crooked nose, he looked like an ex-boxer. Dressed expensively in a tailored gray pinstriped suit, crisp white linen shirt, and red-and-cream-striped silk tie, he looked like an ex-boxer who had done very well for himself. From the way he studied us with hooded gray eyes, he also looked as if he didn't like us very much.

I can't say that I blamed him. We didn't present a particularly caring picture. Harry had to excuse himself twice to throw up. By comparison, David looked almost healthy. Claire stared bleakly out the terrace window, methodically chewing her fingernails. Blythe sat woodenly on the sofa, repeatedly offering to get breakfast started. It was an offer no one took her up on. Behind her, Graham paced up and down the carpet, trying to reach Bridget on her cell phone. Elsie sat in her usual high-backed chair. She watched Detective Grant with a thoughtful expression. Anna lay at her feet, alert and watchful. The only one who showed any real emotion over Roni's death was Avery. After telling Detective Grant that he'd gone straight to bed after leaving the reception and had slept through the night, he'd fallen into a zombielike silence. He sat off to one side, slumped over in his chair, his head buried in his hands. Next to him, Millie stood with her arms firmly crossed over her massive chest, watching her patient with worried eyes.

A soft tapping at the French doors caught my attention, and everyone else's for that matter. It was Chloe. She stood uncertainly on the threshold between the patio and the living room, her perfectly manicured hands still on the door, the heavy rain providing an almost Wuthering Heights–like backdrop for her beautiful image. Next to me, Peter stiffened. Just what the hell was the attraction with her, anyway? I mean, other than the fact that she was beautiful…and thin…and talented…and…I stopped. Not because I'd run out of things to list, unfortunately, but because the potential length of the list was making me nauseous.

"Excuse me?" Chloe said. "I was told that a Detective Grant wanted to see me."

"Are you Chloe Jenkins?" Detective Grant asked. His appraising glance took in her snug little black gabardine suit, still crisp and clean despite the torrential rain outside. Even her black leather boots were spotless. Detective Grant tipped his head forward infinitesimally in a nod of approval. So she's pretty and dresses nicely, I wanted to sneer. What kind of idiot wears leather boots—*Prada* leather boots, no less—during a rain-storm?

"I'm Chloe," she answered. "Are you Detective Grant?"

"Yes. Please come in. I understand that you were on-site when Ms. Parker discovered the body?"

"Yes, sir," Chloe answered, her eyes flickering in my direction. But her gaze did not rest on me. Instead, it landed slightly to my right, where Peter sat. I suppressed a childish urge to frantically wave my hand and call out, "Over here, dear!"

"I see. Please take a seat, Ms....." Detective Grant looked down at his notebook bound in glossy black leather and paused. "Is it Miss or Mrs. Jenkins?" he asked politely. Again Chloe's gaze briefly landed on Peter before she answered wistfully, "It's *Miss*."

Was she kidding? She couldn't have been more obvious if she'd wrapped her bra around her house key and flung it at Peter's head. I looked about the room at everyone else to gauge their reactions to this gaudy spectacle, but no one had seemed to notice. Their eyes were all steadily focused on Detective Grant.

He cleared his throat. "I will need to take a statement from everyone. Is there somewhere private I can do that?" His voice was surprisingly soft, completely at odds with his appearance.

"I think the study will suit your needs admirably," Elsie said. She rose gracefully from her chair and walked past Detective Grant. "If you will just follow me."

Detective Grant turned and followed her. Pausing at the study's doorway, she politely ushered him inside. "Would you care for any coffee or tea while you work?" she asked.

"Coffee would be fine."

"Cream? Sugar?"

"No, thank you."

"Are you hungry? Can I get you something to eat? I'm sure we have plenty."

"No, thank you," he repeated firmly.

Elsie nodded her head briskly. "Coffee it is then. Black. I'll just be a moment. Whom shall I send in first?" Elsie's solicitous tone and conversation seemed to catch Detective Grant off guard. As I'm sure Elsie intended.

Detective Grant squared his shoulders in an attempt to regain control of the conversation. "I'd like to talk to the young lady who discovered the body." He flipped through his notebook and read, "Ms. Elizabeth Parker."

At the sound of my name, my headache, which had started to subside, came back in full force. I stood up on shaky legs. "That's me," I said in a voice that was more of a squeak. Next to me, Peter grabbed my hand and gave it a reassuring squeeze.

Detective Grant's eyes locked on mine. I had the sensation that he was searching my soul—and didn't like what he'd found. As he had done with Chloe, his eyes quickly took in my outfit, touching briefly on my old flip-flops. Just as quickly, he looked away, as if offended by what he saw. There would be no nod of approval for me, I thought. After a brief pause, he gave a curt dip of his head and disappeared into the study. I took an unsteady step in his direction. Elsie reached out and grabbed my arm.

Leaning in close, she whispered fiercely, "Delay him all you can, Elizabeth. We've got to find Megan before that man realizes she's missing!"

Delay him? Me? Was she kidding? I had been known to freeze up when a cute guy asked me what time it was. Did Elsie really think I had the wherewithal to battle wits with the likes of Detective Grant?

My ineffectual sputterings of reluctance were ignored. Still holding tightly on to my arm, she marched me toward the study. Rapping her knuckles briskly on the open door, she thrust me inside. "Here she is, Detective Grant," she said brightly. "Now, I'll just go and get that coffee."

With one last meaningful look at me, she shut the door firmly behind her. I turned back to Detective Grant. His blunt features were bunched in a ferocious scowl. Not at me, but at the door where Elsie had just stood.

Outside, heavy rain splattered against the terrace doors. Thunder and lightning blasted across the black sky. The overhead chandelier flickered, sending dark shadows across Detective Grant's unsmiling face.

And I was supposed to stay in this room with him as long as I could. The story of Daniel and the lions came to mind. All things being equal, I think I would have preferred the lions.

NINE

Surprises are foolish things. The pleasure is not enhanced, and the inconvenience is often considerable.

—Jane Austen, *Emma*

I SAT DOWN IN the leather club chair opposite the desk. After a brief glance in my direction, Detective Grant turned his back to me and stared out the window. Neither of us spoke. The only sound came from the rain pelting the windows and the grandfather clock's swinging pendulum.

Sadly enough, this wasn't the first time I had been interviewed by a detective in a murder investigation. While I was visiting my Aunt Winnie's B and B last New Year's, one of her guests was murdered. I spent the majority of New Year's Day being interrogated by a humorless detective by the name of Aloysius Stewart. That in and of itself says a great deal about the man. I mean, if you had been named after the teddy bear in *Brideshead Revisited,* you would think you would have developed *some* kind of a sense of humor.

I watched Detective Grant warily from my chair. While this kind of interview wasn't new to me, it was still nerve-racking. A thin sheen of sweat covered my palms, and the vein next to my left eye throbbed spasmodically. The only thing that could make my appearance any more suspicious would be the sudden manifestation of a facial tic.

After an interminable pause, Detective Grant turned back to face me. With rapid-fire intensity, he asked me all of the regular questions, my name, age, and relationship with the family. Finished, he strode around to the front of the heavy mahogany desk. Leaning back on its scalloped edge, he crossed his arms over his chest and simply said, "So, tell me about Megan."

Shit. I felt a facial tic coming. Too late, I slapped my hand up to hide the twitching of my cheek. My heart jumped thickly in my chest. I'm quite sure I looked like a page in the police academy's textbook training manual, the page labeled "example of a witness with something to hide." Plus, I was wearing ratty flip-flops.

"Um," I finally mumbled, "she's Roni's daughter."

"And where is she?"

"I don't know."

He stared at me unblinkingly, his expression non-judgmental. I wasn't fooled. "I haven't seen her since last night," I went on, my voice unfortunately again beginning to squeak. "She never came to her bed last night."

That made him blink. Reaching behind him, he picked up his leather notebook from the desk and, with a click of his gold-plated pen, scribbled something before turning his attention back to me. "How was her relationship with her mother?"

I didn't want to answer that. Megan was already under suspicion because of her absence. I didn't want to push her farther under the bus.

"Well…" A roll of thunder sounded. If it was a sign from above on how I should continue, I missed it. Detective Grant waited patiently. "You know how teenagers can be," I said feebly.

"Actually, I don't," he said curtly. "I don't have kids. Enlighten me."

Great. "Oh, you know, they all fight with their parents."

"I see. And did Megan fight with her mother?"

Considering that Elsie asked me to stall this conversation for Megan's sake, I was doing a doozy of a job. "Um, yeah, a little, I guess." Megan's enraged face last night as she spit out, "I hate you!" to Roni swam before my eyes. Why was I lying for a girl I hardly knew? But I already knew the answer. There was something about Megan that made me feel protective. Probably because she reminded me of myself at that age: overweight, insecure, and desperate to belong.

Detective Grant was watching me. From his expression, I wondered if he knew what I was thinking. I've never been very good at hiding my feelings. I've been told that my face gives me away every time. Running his blunt fingers through his short gray hair, he said only, "I see. Why don't we come back to Megan later? Tell me about finding the body."

Relieved not to have to rat out Megan any more, I launched into my tale, numbly reciting my quest for coffee, my assumption that the body was Megan's, Mr. Big Arms, and telling Chloe to call the police. I briefly toyed with the idea of suggesting that Chloe might have something to hide but quickly dismissed the idea as childish—satisfying, but childish.

As I spoke, Detective Grant nodded and added, "Yes, well, that fits. The knife used is a standard kitchen knife. I doubt if we'll ever be able to determine if it came from here."

"Oh!" I said suddenly. "I almost forgot! I also found a key."

Detective Grant's head snapped up at this. "A key? What kind of key?"

Reaching into my pocket, I drew out the item. "This was lying next to Roni on the ground—" Detective Grant's giant paw of a hand shot out and snatched it from me before I could finish.

His lips pulled down into a tight frown. "Where was this again, Ms. Parker?" he asked, his tone ominous.

I squirmed in the chair. "Um…by the body?" I said. Then, realizing that I sounded like a schoolgirl caught passing notes in class, I forced myself to sit up straighter. "It was by the body," I repeated in a firmer voice. "That's why I'm giving it to you. I think it's obvious that it's a clue and—"

Again he cut me off. "Why don't you let *me* decide what is obvious and what isn't," he said. "However, I must say I find it strange that you are just giving it to me now."

"There's nothing strange about it. With all the commotion, I just…forgot." Damn it, he was right. It did sound strange. Detective Grant said nothing but continued to stare at me, his gray eyes inscrutable. Then he rapidly scribbled away in his little black notebook, no doubt adding other various comments about my evasive and suspicious nature.

When the scratching of his pen on the paper subsided, he looked up at me, his cold eyes boring into mine. "Did you happen to see anything else, Ms. Parker?"

"No, just the key."

"I see," he said. After a moment's hesitation, he pulled what looked like a sandwich baggie from a folder in front of him. Inside was a note written on heavy white paper. "Any idea what this might mean?" he asked, handing me the letter.

Across the top was the logo for the Jefferson Hotel. Below that ran the message. In thick black words, it read, **"MEET ME OUTSIDE THE SIDE TERRACE AT 2 A.M. OR I TELL ALL!"** It was written in all capitals; there was no signature.

I looked back up to find Detective Grant studying me intensely. I handed him back the letter. "Where did you find that?" I asked.

"Inside the deceased's purse. Any ideas?"

"Well, it would seem that someone who was staying at the Jefferson wanted to meet Roni at two a.m. And based on the room key I found, it would appear she kept the appointment."

"Quite a lot left behind at the scene, I'd say," he said.

"I suppose."

He eyed me in silence before continuing on a different track. "How was the deceased's behavior during the wedding? Did she seem upset? Nervous?"

"No, she seemed fine." I paused, thinking back. "I sat with her and Avery for a while, and then Avery said he was tired and wanted to go to bed early. Roni said that she'd be along shortly to say good night to him, but she stayed at the reception. I remember because she came inside a few minutes after I did, and I remember...feeling sorry for Avery."

"Wait a minute. She stated she was going to say good night to her husband when she got in? Weren't they sharing a room?"

"No. Avery recently had a stroke. He said he'd been having trouble sleeping lately and didn't like keeping Roni up. He has a room here on the first floor. Roni has—had—a room upstairs."

A faint line formed between Detective Grant's eyebrows. He flipped through his notebook until he found what he was looking for. "I have here"—he tapped the page with his pen—"that Mr. Matthews stated he slept through the night last night." He looked up at me.

I shrugged. "I didn't say it was true that he was having trouble sleeping, I just said that was the reason given for the separate rooms."

"Ah, I see." He closed the notebook and drummed his fingers on the desktop. "So you saw Mrs. Matthews at the end of the night. What time was this?"

"Around one thirty, I guess."

"That is interesting." It was? My heart beat faster. Not to be outdone, my head picked up the thumping beat. Great. I had a band of pain pulsating through my body.

"Why is that interesting?" I asked.

"The coroner places the time of death between one and three a.m."

"Really? Well, then that means that the note was probably from the killer!" I said excitedly. "They met at two and…" Seeing Detective Grant's exasperated expression, my face flushed. I shifted gears. "Right. Well, you probably already figured that out for yourself," I said, trying to undo the damage.

"Yes, my brain was actually able to make that rather astounding leap of logic," he said. "But thanks for the tip."

As there seemed to be no intelligent response to this, I remained silent: I wished I would stay that way, but experience assured me that in mere moments I would again be saying something stupid.

"Quite a bit of luck for the family, you finding this key and us finding the note, wouldn't you say?"

From his tone, I gathered that he meant anything but that. "What do you mean?" I asked warily.

"Just that this note, written on hotel stationery," he said, giving it an accusatory shake, "and this key left at the scene, sure do point to someone outside the Matthews family committing this crime, now don't they?"

"Well, maybe that's because someone outside the family *did* commit the crime," I shot back.

He shrugged his large shoulders, the action sending a wave of movement across the expensive fabric of his suit. "Maybe. But it's a rather neat little find you made, wouldn't you say?"

I wouldn't. I stared back at him with what I hoped was a look of sublime innocence at his sordid meaning.

After a beat, he smirked. "Let's get back to last night. You said you last saw Mrs. Matthews around one-thirty. Was anyone else with you?"

"Oh, yes!" I replied, glad to prove that I hadn't been alone with Roni. "My boyfriend, Peter, was with me. And Claire and David were in the room. And Harry was there, too…" I came to an abrupt stop before I chucked Harry under the bus next to where I'd thrown Megan. If Detective Grant noticed my sudden cessation of speech, he didn't say. Instead, he looked at his notebook—for a very long time, it seemed to me. Finally, he looked back at me. "How would you describe the deceased?" he said.

"How would I describe her?" I repeated, startled by his abrupt change of subject. Was he trying to catch me off guard, hoping I'd say something stupid? I debated telling him that if this were the case, he needn't bother. I was quite capable of saying something stupid without any help from him.

"Yes. What kind of person was she?"

Was he kidding? She was an egotistical bitch, but

I couldn't very well come out and say that. He might *really* start to think I killed her. "I didn't know her very well, so—"

"Don't give me that crap. You are a longtime friend of this family. You strike me as a moderately intelligent young woman. Surely you must have formed some kind of an opinion about the woman. Was she well liked?"

I bristled. "*Moderately* intelligent?"

His lips curved into a malicious smile. "Well, let's see how you answer my questions before we upgrade that assessment, shall we? Now, why don't we try this again? Was she well liked?"

"Her husband loved her," I said, still stalling for time. I knew that he would eventually discover that most of the Matthews family hated Roni. I just didn't want it to be from me.

"Okay," said Detective Grant, with exaggerated slowness. "But that leaves"—he silently counted on his fingers—"at least eight other people I need to know about. Can you enlighten me on *them*? Ever overhear any of them talking about her?"

At the word *overhear,* the memory of Roni on the phone slipped into focus. Glad to have something to give the detective that wasn't related to the Matthewses, I sat up straighter in my chair. "Wait a minute," I said. "I did overhear something yesterday. It was in this room, actually. Roni was in here alone. She was talking on her cell phone about her efforts to get Avery to sell the family's landscaping business." I tried to glide over the part where I stood outside and blatantly eavesdropped, fearing it might suggest nasty things about my basic character. "From her end of the conversation, it sounded not only as if she was working with the person at the other end but that she was also having an affair with him. Maybe *he* was the one who sent her the note and dropped the key!"

Detective Grant stared at me. I don't know for how long exactly, but long enough for my upper lip to start twitching.

Pushing himself off the desk, he strode around to the other side and sat down heavily in the chair. Muttering something about the stupidity of people withholding important evidence, he grabbed his pen again and furiously scratched in his notebook. I had a sneaking suspicion that my "moderate" rating had slipped a notch.

"Start at the beginning," he said. "What's this about the family business being sold?"

I took a deep breath. "From some conversations last night, I gather that Avery—he's president of the Garden—received a buyout offer. He was mulling it over and was going to get input from the whole family before making a decision, but it was clear that Roni wanted him to sell."

"Did she say why she wanted him to sell?"

"Avery is a workaholic. He had a stroke last year and a lot of us thought his work habits were to blame. Roni said she was worried about his health and wanted him to retire."

"And what did you think?"

I shrugged. "The Garden is worth a lot of money. Avery would be very wealthy if he sold it."

"Could you tell what Avery thought about the deal?"

I hesitated. "I think he wanted to get the family's opinion first. After all, Elsie's father started the business. Selling it would have to be a family decision."

Detective Grant wrote something down. Tapping his gold pen thoughtfully on the desk, he asked, "But Mrs.

Matthews—Roni—thought she could convince her husband to sell?"

"Well, from what little I heard of the phone conversation, she did seem pretty confident, yes."

"And you've no idea who she was talking to?"

"No, she never said his name."

"But you assumed it was a man?"

"I did, yes." He wrote something again and I thought about his question. The phone conversation had been loverlike, but Roni a lesbian? I dismissed the idea. I had never seen her look twice at a woman and I had seen the way she looked at men. No, it had to be a man on the other end of that phone call.

"Okay, so you said it sounded as if this person wanted to meet her but she said no?"

I thought back. It had all happened so fast. What *had* Roni said? "She told the person not to come and meet her, that it wouldn't be safe. Whoever it was must have gotten angry because Roni got upset and said that she wasn't going to double-cross them."

"Double-cross them," he repeated. "Did she use those exact words?"

"Yes."

"Did she say anything about a meeting later?"

"No."

"Did you happen to"—he paused significantly—"*accidentally* overhear any other phone calls?"

I flushed. "No, but I noticed Roni did receive several more during the day. I happened to be nearby when some of them came in, but she didn't take the calls. She kept hanging up, claiming that it was either a wrong number or a crank call."

"But you don't believe this was the case?"

"Not really. I guess because of what I'd overheard

earlier, I just assumed that the person from before was calling again and she didn't want to take the call."

"Did anyone else overhear this first conversation?"

I hesitated. All I had was a suspicion. And that suspicion could potentially implicate someone in Bridget's family.

"I can see from the expression on your face that the answer is yes. By the way, if you don't already know this, let me offer you a word of advice—never play poker. Now, who else overheard this conversation?"

"I don't know for sure. When Roni left the study, she went out to the terrace to have a cigarette. Through there." I pointed to the French doors behind him. "She smoked when she got upset and I didn't want to bother her just then," I continued in a rush, not caring for the knowing smirk Detective Grant directed my way. "I stepped back inside the house through the French doors leading to the living room. It was then that I heard the footsteps. I followed them but didn't see anyone. When I came back, I saw that the door to the study was open a crack."

"Meaning someone could have been listening."

"I guess so. But as I said, I didn't see anyone."

"And where did these footsteps go?"

"Down the hallway, toward the upstairs staircase."

"Describe the footsteps. Were they heavy, light, lumbering?"

I thought back. "They were rapid and loud, as if someone was wearing a hard-heeled shoe."

"High heels?"

"No. At least, I don't think so."

The sound of footsteps rapidly approaching the door caught my attention. Detective Grant stared at me. "Were they like those?"

They were, but I couldn't bring myself to answer. As it turned out, I needn't have bothered. Detective Grant took one look at my face and knew the answer as surely as if I'd screamed it at him.

In silence we watched as the door swung open and the owner of the footsteps entered. It was Elsie. She was bearing an elaborately set tray, with a coffeepot, cups, a pitcher of cream, and sugar, as well as a plate of assorted tea cookies. I noticed that the coffee service was her best set. She was certainly pulling out all the stops.

Placing the tray in front of Detective Grant, she said, "Your coffee, Detective. May I pour you a cup?"

Detective Grant leaned back in the leather chair, the movement making a soft creaking noise, and casually crossed his arms across his chest. "Yes, thank you, Mrs. Matthews. And then perhaps you can tell me if you've had any success locating Megan."

If his question rattled Elsie, she did an excellent job of hiding it. Calmly pouring out a cup of rich, hot coffee, she handed it to him before answering. "Well, no, Detective. We haven't found her yet. I'm sure she'll turn up soon. This is such a dreadful business. Megan will be just devastated. She's a good girl, really, but you know how teenagers can be."

"Actually, as I told Ms. Parker here," he said, with a brief nod in my direction, "I don't have any kids. How would you describe teenagers?"

Elsie studied him with a level look. "Well, Detective, I don't think one necessarily needs to have teenagers to understand them. For instance, you were a teenager once, correct? Or did you just skip all that and spring to your current age?"

I winced. Elsie's family and friends had grown accustomed to her outspokenness. At times it could be endearing. I suspected from the way Detective Grant's gray eyes glittered that this was not one of those times.

"Surprisingly enough, Mrs. Matthews, I was indeed a teenager—a very long time ago. And I think I remember how it feels to not get along with a parent, which, from what you two are *not* telling me, seems to be the case with Megan. Now, why don't you tell me exactly why Megan and her mother didn't get along?"

Elsie ignored his question and instead pounced on something else. "You didn't get along with your parents? Whyever not? An upstanding man like yourself? I find that hard to believe."

Detective Grant glared at Elsie. "This conversation isn't about me, it's about Megan."

"Of course, but I'd feel better knowing that I'm talking to someone who might actually understand our Megan. Megan is a special girl, but that fact seems to have escaped her mother."

Was Elsie completely off her rocker? She was telling the detective in charge of the case to open up about himself before she told him about Megan. I braced myself for the explosion.

Surprisingly, Detective Grant did not leap to his feet and place Elsie into custody. Shifting in his seat, he merely said, "I wanted to be a dancer. Like Gene Kelly. However, my father had very definite ideas about my career, and being a dancer wasn't on the list."

While I struggled not to gasp in astonishment at the image of Detective Grant deftly swinging from a lamppost, Elsie contemplated him with serious eyes. "So you just gave it up?" she asked.

"No. I kept at it for a while, actually. But in the end, I just didn't have the talent to make a career out if it. But it was a rough time for me and my dad. So in answer to your question, yes, I think I can view a rocky parent-child relationship with an open mind. Now, why don't you tell me about Megan?"

After a moment, Elsie gave a sharp nod of her head. "Megan doesn't look like a Barbie doll and she has a brain. In short, she is the complete opposite of her mother." With a twist of her mouth, she added, "May she rest in peace."

"Mrs. Matthews," Detective Grant said with slow deliberation, "a murder was committed here last night. Not only that, but the victim was your daughter-in-law. She was brutally stabbed not fifty feet outside these doors behind me. I would think that given the circumstances, you would be a little more…*enthusiastic* in helping the police catch her killer."

Elsie placed both of her hands palm down on the desk and leaned forward. "Oh, don't misunderstand me, Detective Grant. I am *extremely* enthusiastic about helping the police find the killer. But what I want to make very sure *doesn't* happen is that the police focus on the wrong person. I know my family. They are not murderers. I saw how you looked at everyone. You saw a group of people, very few of whom seemed upset by Roni's death. May I speak freely, Detective?"

"It seems inconceivable to me that you would do otherwise."

"My daughter-in-law was not a very nice person. She was vain, shallow, and greedy. And I don't think she particularly cared for my son. But she had a life outside of this family. I just want to make sure that the police focus on *that* life and not just our limited interactions with her. We may not have liked her, but we certainly didn't kill her."

Detective Grant tasted his coffee. "For your sake, I hope you're right, Mrs. Matthews."

So did I, I thought, staring at Elsie's shoes.

TEN

A COMMOTION IN THE living room ended the ensuing
stare down between Detective Grant and Elsie. Striding briskly to the door, Elsie yanked it open. "Oh, thank
God!" she said, placing her hand on her chest. "Megan!"

At that, both Detective Grant and I leaped out of
our seats and dashed for the door. As Elsie had indicated, Megan stood, dazed, in the middle of the living
room. Her upsweep was undone, leaving her hair hanging around her face. She was still wearing the dress
she'd worn to the wedding. Harry stood with his arms
wrapped around her, whispering in her ear. I saw her
eyes widen at his message. Avery rolled his chair up
next to her and grabbed one of her hands. "Oh, Megan,"
he said, "thank God, you're all right."

My eyes sought out Peter's, and to my sharp dismay
I saw that while I was in with Detective Grant, Chloe
had co-opted my seat. She sat snuggled in next to Peter.
My mind quickly noted the depressing fact that Chloe's
silky blond hair and lithe frame and Peter's dark curls
and athletic build made the two of them look like something out of a catalog for shiny happy people. I, on the
other hand, with my humidity-induced frizzy hair and

nonathletic, nonlithe anything, presented an image more appropriate for the before segment on an episode of *What Not to Wear*. My stomach tightened.

Next to me, Detective Grant stepped forward. "Megan Matthews?" he said, his voice ominous.

Megan turned confused eyes in his direction. "Yes. What's going on? What's happened?"

Detective Grant paused. "Why don't you sit down." He indicated one of the club chairs. With an apprehensive glance at Harry, Megan detached herself from his arms and sank into the chair. Avery rolled his chair next to hers and gently took her hands in his. Shooting Detective Grant a quelling look, he said, "Megan, I don't know how to tell you this, but it's about your mother."

Megan stared at Avery, her round face white and frightened. Taking a deep breath, Avery continued. "She's dead, honey. Someone…someone killed her last night." Avery's voice broke and he lowered his head, still clinging to Megan's hands.

Megan stared at Avery's bowed head. Slowly, she raised her eyes and sought out Detective Grant's. "Someone killed my mother?" she asked in a small voice.

"I'm afraid so," Detective Grant replied.

"But why?" asked Megan, looking back to Avery.

"That's what we're trying to find out. Do you know of anyone who wished her harm?" asked Detective Grant.

Megan's eyes snapped back to Detective Grant's. I saw wariness in their depths as she answered. "My mother is…um…was…um…a difficult woman at times." She glanced back to Avery as if afraid of offending him. "But I can't imagine someone killing her because of that."

Detective Grant nodded. "I have to ask you about your whereabouts last night."

Before he could finish, Elsie stepped forward. "I'm going to have to insist that that question wait, Detective. As anyone can see, Megan is in shock. She needs some time to process this before she answers. You can interview the rest of us while Megan gets herself together. Elizabeth, please take Megan upstairs to your room." Elsie turned to Blythe. "Blythe, why don't you get Megan a cup of hot tea? I think that might help." Blythe nodded her head, rose briskly from the couch, and started for the kitchen.

I walked forward and extended my hand to Megan. "Come on, sweetie." I hoped she would take my hand and leave before Detective Grant thought better of Elsie's decree. Luckily, Megan seemed to be on the same wavelength. She nodded and quickly rose from her chair. With a brief backward glance at Avery, she crossed the room with me and headed for the stairs. I didn't look directly at Detective Grant as we exited the room, but I did catch a glimpse of him out of the corner of my eye as we rushed past. He looked as if he were about to object, then suddenly stepped back and nodded for us to continue.

In our room, I shut the door. Megan sank down on her bed, staring numbly at the floor. Now, alone with her, I had no idea what to say. I crossed to my bed and sat down opposite her.

"Somebody actually killed her," she said. It was more of a statement than a question, so I didn't answer.

She looked up at me. "Why don't I feel anything?" She dropped her head in her hands, her brown hair spilling all over. "My mother is dead and I don't feel anything! What kind of monster am I?"

I quickly moved off the bed and knelt in front of her. "Megan, you are not a monster! You're in shock."

She moved her hands away from her face and stared at me. Her eyes were dry and clear. "No, you don't understand. I really don't feel anything! She was a bitch and I'm glad she's dead! You've no idea the living hell she made my life!"

"Megan, I know living with her must have been hard, but—"

"But nothing, Elizabeth! You don't know the half of it! When I was twelve, my father divorced her. I remembered wishing *I* could divorce her, too. My father realized what kind of woman she was and he had had enough. He wanted custody of me because he loved me. *She* wanted custody because she knew it would hurt him and because she wanted the child support money." Megan's voice grew increasingly agitated. "The judge said that I was old enough to choose which one of them I wanted to live with and so, of course, I picked my father. I got up on that stand and told the judge that I wanted to live with my father. I told him why, too." Her mouth twisted at the memory. "She hated me for that. Really hated me. I embarrassed her and ruined her plans. All I cared about was that I was going to live with my dad and not have to deal with her anymore. Six months later, my dad died in a car accident. Can you believe that? I had to go live with her again!" she cried indignantly. "You can't imagine…" Her voice failed. "Of course, it was worse than ever. She punished me for choosing him over her—every single day. I hated her! I'm glad she's dead!" Tears washed down her face and her breath came in ragged gulps. "Oh! I wish my dad was here now! I miss him so much!"

Sobs racked her body and she curled up on her bed,

burying her face in her pillow. A soft knock sounded at the door. It was Blythe. She held a steaming mug of tea. Looking over to the bed, she saw Megan. "Poor thing!" she whispered. "She's really taking Roni's death hard, isn't she?"

TWENTY MINUTES LATER, Megan, if not calm, was at least calmer. She had finished the tea and was sitting on her bed, her back pressed against the wall and her arms wrapped tightly around her knees. Blythe and I sat opposite her on my bed.

"Do you want to tell us where you've been all night, honey?" Blythe said.

Megan stared at the tops of her knees. "Not really," she answered with a shy smile. "It figures that the first time I stay out with a boy, I come home to find the cops waiting for me."

Megan had stayed out with a boy? I don't know why, but I was shocked. Other than a slight stiffening of her spine, Blythe took this statement in relative stride. She'd probably heard all sorts of stories in her years as headmistress.

"Are you all right?" she asked gently.

Megan looked up at the question. "Oh, yeah. Oh, God! I mean, yeah, I stayed out, but not like *that*."

"Then like what, dear?" Blythe asked. There was a hint of an edge to her voice.

Megan sighed and pushed a wayward strand of hair behind her ear. "I got to talking to one of the guys in the band—Bobby. He's the drummer."

I nodded with understanding. In bands, it was always the drummer.

Megan continued. "Anyway, he was really nice. Then *she* saw us and made this huge scene about what a fool

I was making of myself." Neither Blythe nor I needed to ask whom Megan meant by "she." "After that I ran off," Megan continued. "When their set was over, Bobby found me. He had seen everything. He was really sweet. We started talking and, well, I didn't want to go home. Bobby and I went to the summer-house."

Blythe made a noise, a cross between a groan and a sigh. Megan looked at her. "I told you, it wasn't like that. We just talked."

Blythe seemed unconvinced. Peering at Megan over her glasses, she asked, "How old is Bobby?"

"Twenty," replied Megan. "He's a sophomore at the college down here. He's only in the band part-time."

I don't know about Blythe, but I sure as hell was relieved to hear this. I had a horrible vision of Bobby being some aging pot-head lothario who liked young girls. A twenty-year-old, part-time band member, full-time student was a much better scenario.

"So you spent the entire night there?"

"Yes. We stayed up late talking. Then Bobby said he was going to head home. I don't know what time it was. I didn't want to go back to the house yet, so after he left, I went to sleep. When I woke up, I came back and, well, you know the rest."

"So you stayed in the summer house?" I asked.

"Yeah," said Megan.

Blythe glanced at me. I knew she was thinking the same thing I was.

Megan didn't have an alibi.

Before I could process this latest twist, the door opened. With an impatient yelp, Anna burst through the doorway and leaped onto my bed; specifically, she leaped onto me. Thrusting her furry face into mine, she licked my neck with an enthusiasm that made me rethink my perfume choice. A second later, Elsie's head popped around the corner, her face lined with worry. "Megan, honey? How are you?" Not waiting for an answer, she moved into the room and pushed onto the bed next to Megan. "Would you rather have a glass of wine than tea? I have a bottle of an excellent Shiraz downstairs—it was Walter's favorite, actually. He always drank a glass when his sciatica acted up."

Megan rejected the offer with a shake of her head, while I wondered at the vastly different complaints for which Shiraz could be recommended.

Pulling Megan into a hug, Elsie continued. "Sorry I didn't come up sooner, but I had to make a few phone calls about Detective Grant and call in some favors from a few friends. I told them that I wanted this cleared up as soon as possible and I didn't want our family to be the sole focus of the investigation. But in the meantime, we do need to give him our statements. Do you think you're ready to talk to him now, Megan? If you're not, just say so. I'm more than happy to tell him to go cool his heels for a while longer."

Megan shook her head. "No, I'll be okay."

Elsie nodded and opened her mouth to speak, as Megan continued with a sigh, "Besides, I can't put this off any longer."

Megan's words had an odd effect on Elsie. Her mouth still open, she gave Megan a searching look, seeming to rethink whatever it was that she was going to say. In a soft voice, she said, "Whatever you think is best."

Megan looked at Elsie, her expression firm. "Let's go," she said.

Not without difficulty, I pushed Anna off me and we followed Megan downstairs in uneasy silence. Everyone was still in the living room. I noticed that Peter and

Chloe stood together by the window, a little distance off from the rest of the group. Detective Grant stood stiffly near the room's doorway, his mouth set in a hard line. Seeing Megan's red-rimmed eyes and blotchy skin, his expression softened. "I know this is a hard time for you, Miss Matthews," he said quietly. "I'll make this as brief as possible."

It was a good thing that he didn't know that Megan's tears were for her father and not Roni. Otherwise, I suspect his generous treatment of her would come to a screeching halt.

Megan sat down in a chair next to Avery and grabbed his hand. Taking a steadying breath, she said, "I expect you want to know where I was last night."

Detective Grant tipped his gray head in acknowledgment. Megan took another breath and closed her eyes. "I stayed out with Bobby, one of the boys in the band," she said in a rush. "We sat talking at one of the tables and then went to the summer house. He left around dawn, but I…I didn't want to go back to the house. I stayed in the summer house and went to sleep on one of the cots."

A long, uncomfortable pause followed these words. Surprisingly, Detective Grant did not follow up with this line of questioning. Instead, switching gears, he asked, "How was your relationship with your mother?"

Megan's eyes slid to mine. They were followed by Detective Grant's. I met his gaze with what I hoped was an expression of concerned innocence, but I suspected I probably only looked constipated. Megan focused again on Detective Grant. "It wasn't very good. She didn't like me much and—"

Avery interrupted. "Now, Megan. That isn't true. She adored you. I know you two had your differences, but—"

Megan turned to him. "No, Avery. She hated me. And…and I hated her."

"Megan!" Avery burst out. "That simply isn't true! None of it is true! Roni wanted only the best for you!"

Megan shook her head and looked sadly at Avery. "No. She didn't. I'm sorry. I know that you loved her, but she didn't love me."

"Megan…"

"No!" Megan stood up, roughly jerking her hand from his grasp. "Please! This is hard enough without you pretending that we were one big happy family! She never forgave me for wanting to live with my dad and not her. She never even wanted me in the first place— didn't she ever tell you that? Because she sure told me enough times! She did everything she could to make me miserable. I hated her! I hated her so much I don't even know if I *care* that she's dead!" A half sob, half laugh escaped her lips. "Hell, I really don't know if I care *who* did it!"

"Megan!" Elsie snapped, her tone commanding. "Stop this nonsense right now. You're hysterical. You've no idea what you're saying."

At the sound of Elsie's voice, Megan jerked and faced Elsie. Seeing Elsie's stern expression, her shoulders slumped and she covered her face with her hands.

Detective Grant continued to watch her, his hooded eyes appraising. After a minute, Megan spoke again, her voice calmer. "I'm sorry. I don't know what I'm saying. You all must think I'm a terrible person." Pulling her hands away, she met Detective Grant's level gaze. "I had a horrible relationship with my mother, Detective. But I didn't kill her. I hated her, but then so did most everyone else."

"Everyone else?" prompted Detective Grant in a silky

voice. Megan paled with the realization that she'd said more than she intended.

"Miss Matthews?" continued Detective Grant. "Who exactly is everyone else?"

Megan gulped. "Well, David for one," she said, with a feeble gesture in his direction.

At the sound of his name, David tensed and sputtered loud denials.

"I'll get to you in a minute, Mr. Cook," Detective Grant said curtly. "Why do you think David hated your mother, Megan?"

Megan paused. "I heard them fighting yesterday before breakfast."

"About?"

Megan stared at the carpet. "About money, I think. David wanted money and my mom laughed at him. He was mad. Really mad."

Detective Grant's gaze slid toward David. "Is this true, Mr. Cook?"

David struggled to regain his composure. Giving a small shrug, he said, "It was a minor disagreement, that's all. I assure you, nothing more. You know how children exaggerate things," he added with a patronizing smile.

"You called her a hateful bitch," countered Megan.

David flushed as heads turned his way. "This is ridiculous," he said. "I had no reason to kill Roni!" No one spoke. Seeing the doubt on our faces, something akin to fear crept into David's eyes. "I didn't do it!" His eyes darted around the room in panic. Then he met Harry's gaze. Like a rat backed into a corner, he attacked. Desperately pointing his finger at Harry, he yelled, "Why don't you ask Harry about killing Roni? After all, he's the one who threatened to do just that!"

ELEVEN

*Something unpleasant is coming when men are
anxious to tell the truth.*

—Benjamin Disraeli

THE ROOM FELL SILENT at David's accusation. Next to him,
Claire gasped. "David!" she cried in dismay.

"Shut up, Claire. It's the truth and you know it." Turning to Detective Grant, he continued. "Harry threatened
Roni last night in this very room."

"That's bullshit!" Harry shouted. Seeming to forget
his epic hangover, he jumped out of his chair. The sudden movement cost him and he swayed slightly. Stretch-
ing his hand out, he grabbed the back of the chair. His
face was pale and his frame seemed as if it might collapse in on itself. "That's bullshit," he repeated, in a
quieter, less sure voice.

"No, it's not!" David replied, his voice rising. "Harry
got stinking drunk last night. Claire and I were getting
ready to go to bed when he came lurching in, slurring
his words, completely belligerent. Then Roni came in
looking for Megan and Harry went crazy. He started
screaming at her. Not only did he threaten her, but he
tried to hit her! If we hadn't restrained him, I don't know
what would have happened."

"We?" I blurted. "Peter stopped him. You had nothing to do with it!" Too late, I snapped my mouth shut,
but the damage was done.

His cold eyes bearing down on me with laserlike intensity, Detective Grant cleared his throat. "You were here for this altercation, as well? How interesting. Exactly how many interviews do I need to conduct with you before I get the whole story?"

I assumed that this was one of those snarky, rhetorical questions and so did not answer. I was right. He continued without missing a beat. "Perhaps you could be so kind as to tell me your version of events, Ms. Parker." He made no attempt to downplay the anger in his voice.

I looked over at Harry's curiously blank face and I wondered how much of the exchange he even remembered.

"Well, um." I glanced to where Peter stood with Chloe by the window. He moved away from them both and stood by my side. "We were talking to Harry when Roni came in."

Detective Grant cut in. "Who is 'we'?"

I gestured to Peter. "Peter," I said feebly.

Detective Grant's eyes slid to Peter. "I see. Go on."

"Well, we were talking with Harry, who was a little drunk, but I wouldn't call him belligerent. It was only when Roni came in looking for Megan that he got upset. We'd seen Roni yelling at Megan earlier, and it was pretty brutal." I paused, hoping I could stop there, but Detective Grant nodded at me to continue. Great. "Harry told Roni that he didn't like how she treated Megan." From the corner of my eye, I saw Megan raise her head and face Harry. "Roni got mad and said that it was none of Harry's business. Words were exchanged, but it was Roni who slapped Harry. Just to make sure that the argument didn't escalate further, Peter pulled Harry away. But Harry didn't threaten Roni. Not really. If anything, it was Roni who threatened Harry."

"How so?"

"She said that she was going to tell Avery and…" Crap, now what was I doing? I was getting Harry into deeper trouble.

"She said she was going to tell Avery and make sure that Avery cut Harry off," David finished.

"This is preposterous!" Avery bellowed, glaring at David. "I know my son, David. How dare you insinuate that he would hurt Roni! What would you know, anyway? You go through life half drunk! Asking you to recall anything past your first drink of the night is a waste of time!"

David's complexion, normally mottled, became one solid blotch of red. "If you don't believe me, ask Claire. She was there, too," he shot back.

Detective Grant turned to Claire. "Yes, Mrs. Cook. We haven't heard from you yet. Please give us your version of events."

Claire closed her eyes and sighed. She'd always had a soft spot for Harry, doting on him like a son. She sat fidgeting—a trapped animal. Would she back up David's version of events or would she try to soften the blow? David shifted in his chair and stared at her. I couldn't see his face from where I sat, but his posture was nothing short of aggressive. He leaned in close, his shoulders hunched forward. I thought he whispered something to her, but I wasn't sure.

I tried to catch Claire's eye, but she averted her glance. I knew that she'd made her decision.

"Harry was drunk," she said, her voice miserable. She didn't look at Harry or anyone else. She squeezed her eyes shut as if to block out what she was saying. "He called Roni a bitch and she slapped him. Hard. I thought that Harry was going to strike her as well, but

Peter grabbed Harry's hand. That's when Roni said that she'd ruin Harry. She was going to tell Avery what had happened and make sure that Harry was cut off."

"I see," said Detective Grant, sizing up Harry with obvious interest. "Is this true?"

Harry glanced uneasily at Avery before answering. "I'm not going to lie to you, Detective," he said. "I didn't like Roni and I didn't like the way she treated Megan. She was particularly nasty to her this weekend. Last night, I had too much to drink and said some things I shouldn't have. I'm not sure of all the details, but I know I told Roni that she was hurting Megan."

"Did you threaten her?"

Harry spread his hands out. "I honestly don't know. If they say I did, then I guess I did."

Claire cleared her throat—twice. We all looked at her. "There's something else you should know," she said.

"I'm listening," replied Detective Grant.

Taking a deep breath, Claire said, "After Roni's fight with Harry, I took David upstairs and put him to bed." She glanced briefly at David with an oddly challenging look. "I was…upset. I didn't like the way Roni was behaving and I didn't think she was being…fair to Harry." Claire seemed to be choosing her words with care. "I went back downstairs to talk to Avery. I thought he should hear what had happened and not just from Roni."

"I see," said Detective Grant. "And did you talk to Mr. Matthews?"

Claire glanced nervously at Avery. "No. I knocked on his door but there was no answer. I opened it up and peeked inside. I saw that Avery was asleep and decided not to wake him. I thought I would tell him in the morning."

"What time was this?"

"Around two."

"Did anyone see you?"

Claire nodded toward Chloe. "Yes, Chloe did. I came down the back stairs, the ones that go to the kitchen. Chloe was there."

Detective Grant looked at Chloe for affirmation. "Is this true, Miss Jenkins?"

Chloe nodded, her mouth turned up into what I considered an obsequious smile. "Yes. I saw Mrs. Matthews come downstairs around then. I was in the kitchen getting everything ready for the brunch."

"You work late hours," Detective Grant said with a note of admiration in his voice.

Chloe tipped her glossy head in acknowledgment. "I do what ever it takes to ensure that my events run smoothly," she replied, feigning modesty. Honestly, I wanted to smack her.

Detective Grant turned back to Claire. "So you went to talk to your brother but decided not to wake him after all. What did you do then?"

"I heard a thump. It sounded like it came from upstairs. I rushed back upstairs, worried that David had… had fallen," Claire finished diplomatically.

Detective Grant looked at David. "Had you fallen, Mr. Cook?"

"Of course not! I can't imagine why anyone would think I would have," David replied indignantly.

Detective Grant made no response. Turning again to Claire, he asked, "Did you go back upstairs through the kitchen?"

"Yes."

Detective Grant turned his head to Chloe for her to verify this, but Chloe only shrugged her graceful shoulders. "I didn't see her, Detective." An uncomfortable pause followed as we all struggled with the implication that Claire might be lying. Perhaps sensing the impact of her words, Chloe hurried on. "But I was also moving back and forth between the kitchen and the dining room, so I could have easily missed her. For what it's worth, I also heard a thump."

Detective Grant stared down at his notebook, tapping it lightly with his pen. He read a few pages before raising his eyes to where Megan sat slumped in her chair. "I'd like to go back to your night, Miss Matthews," he said. "You say that you and Bobby went to the summer house. What time was that?"

"I'm not sure. It was late."

"Did you see anyone? Did anyone see you?"

"I thought I saw someone on the terrace. To be honest, I was trying not to be seen. I...I really wasn't up for my family just then."

What? I sat up straighter in my chair. Megan had seen someone on the terrace? Had she seen Roni or Roni's killer? An airless silence filled the room and we all stared bug-eyed at Megan. Detective Grant took a small step forward. "Who did you see on the terrace, Miss Mathews?" His voice was bland but his expression was not. His jaw was tense, the muscle twitching.

"I don't know. It was dark. But..."

"Yes? Who did you see on the terrace?"

Her eyes flickered to the expansive couch where David, Claire, Elsie, and Harry sat. "I...I don't know," she said. "I just saw a figure."

"A man or a woman?"

"A man...I think. I don't know. I really couldn't say one way or another."

Detective Grant gripped his pen so hard his fingers showed white. "What was this figure doing?"

"Standing by one of the patio chairs."

Somebody gasped. Megan looked at us with confused eyes. We hadn't told her yet that Roni's body had been found on one of the patio chairs. Her eyes widened as she made the obvious connection.

"I'm going to ask you again, Miss Matthews," Detective Grant said in a low voice. "This is very important. Do you have any idea who it was that you saw?"

Megan's eyes flickered toward the window. She paused a little too long before answering. "No," she said in a firm voice. "It was too dark. I'm sorry."

"What time was this again? Think carefully."

Megan considered before shaking her head. "I'm sorry, I don't know. I didn't think to look at my watch."

I could see from Detective Grant's expression that we were thinking exactly the same thing.

Megan was lying.

A uniformed policeman entered the room from the terrace. Rain dripped off his black plastic parka, leaving tiny pools of water in his wake. Elsie glared at him. "Young man! I would ask that you please not drip water all over my carpet."

The policeman, a young man with flaming red hair and no discernible chin, ducked his head. "Yes, ma'am," he said politely. He carefully skirted the perimeter of the room where the carpet did not reach, until he stood next to Detective Grant. Having watched this progress with an expression of bemusement mixed with annoyance, Detective Grant gave an audible sigh. "Yes, Johnson?"

Officer Johnson leaned forward in an attempt to keep his message private and muttered in Detective Grant's ear.

Elsie rapped her cane sharply on the floor. "Didn't

anyone ever tell you that it's not polite to whisper?" she burst out.

With deliberate slowness, Detective Grant turned his head to face Elsie. He reminded me of a sleek panther about to spring. "Didn't anyone ever tell you it's not polite to stick your nose in where it doesn't belong?" he retorted.

Elsie's chin jutted out. "Not to my face."

"Then consider this the first time."

Elsie's eyes narrowed. "Inasmuch as a murder has taken place in my house, I think I have a right to know what is going on."

"Correction. You have the right to know what *I* deem necessary." Before Elsie could respond to this, Detective Grant turned to Avery. "Mr. Matthews. The coroner has finished and is getting ready to leave. Would you like a moment before he does?"

Avery's face sagged. He gave a feeble nod.

"If you'll follow me, sir," Detective Grant said, gesturing toward the terrace. Avery exited the room, heading toward the makeshift tent erected by the police. Millie followed him at a respectful distance. Turning back, Detective Grant looked at Megan. "Miss Matthews, would you like a moment as well?"

Megan did not immediately respond. Raising her head, she met Detective Grant's eyes. "No," she said. "No, I don't think I can do that."

Detective Grant nodded and stepped out onto the terrace, shutting the door behind him.

There was a two-second pause before all hell broke loose. Elsie led the charge. "You ridiculous buffoon!" she hissed at David. "I knew you were a wretched person, but I didn't know *how* wretched until now."

"Me? I'm the bad guy?" David spit out indignantly.

"*I* didn't do anything! That detective wants the truth. If we try to hide facts, then we'll only bring his wrath down on all of us."

"Have something to hide, do you, David?" said Graham from his chair.

"Me? Hiding something? Don't be stupid," David snapped back.

"I don't know. You seemed in a pretty big rush to direct the detective's attention to Harry. Why is that?" Graham's voice was deceptively calm. If you ever wanted a read on Graham's emotions, you watched his eyebrows. They were a barometer of his emotions. Right now they were bristling. When Bridget and I were little, bristling eyebrows meant it was time to run for cover.

David's own brows pulled together ominously and he aggressively shifted his shoulders. "I'm not trying to direct anything. I'm only trying to help."

In a deceivingly casual move, Graham stretched his long legs out in front of him and stood up. Next to him, Blythe tensed. "Graham…" she warned.

"No, I'm interested in hearing about how David wants to help." He crossed the room and stood directly in front of David's chair. Graham moved so quickly that David had no time to react. He sat pressed against the back of his chair, forced to stare up into Graham's face.

"For instance," Graham went on, "when you get blind stinking drunk, how are you helping? When you verbally abuse my sister, how exactly are you helping?"

"Graham, please," said Claire.

"Now listen here," David barked, but Graham wasn't listening.

"And when you stupidly try and pin this tragedy on Harry, how the *hell* do you think you are helping?"

These last words were shouted, and David shoved

his large frame out of his chair and faced Graham. His body was trembling and his hands were balled into fists. "You know what?" he hissed menacingly. "I don't care what you think of me because I know that I'm innocent. I was with Claire all night. I have an alibi. Do you?" He turned to the rest of us and sneered threateningly. "Do any of you?"

A soft cry escaped from Megan, and David's eyes landed on her. Strangely, upon seeing her pinched expression, his face blanched with regret. "Megan," he said, his voice oddly constrained, "I am so sorry about... about all of this. If there is anything I can do..."

"Anything *you* can do!" Megan shot back. "Just what do you think you can do, David? From what I've seen, *you've* done quite enough!"

"From what you've..." He stopped abruptly. "Megan, I know you're...upset. But I'd like to help."

"Help," Megan scoffed. "Here's an idea, David—how about you do the right thing? For once, why don't you just do the right thing?"

"I—" David began.

"Leave it. I can't deal with you now," said Megan quietly.

"Megan?" began David.

Graham cut him off. "David! Shut the hell up! Can't you see that every time you open your mouth you only make things worse?" Graham's eyebrows were now standing straight out and I looked for a place to seek shelter. Before I could find one, the terrace doors swung open, letting in a chilly gust of rain and wind and Avery.

"It's gone," Avery gasped.

"What's gone?" Elsie said.

"The necklace, Roni's necklace. The one she was wearing last night. The one I gave her. It's gone!"

We looked mutely at one another.

"Someone killed her for her necklace?" asked Elsie. Her voice held a tinge of hope. If Roni had been killed for the necklace, then the realm of potential suspects would widen considerably. Right now, it was decidedly claustrophobic.

Detective Grant stepped into view behind Avery. "We haven't come to any conclusions yet," he said, "but I'd like a guest list from last night's reception."

Elsie nodded and hurried off to the study.

"How much was that necklace worth?" asked Blythe.

"I just had it appraised for two hundred thousand dollars," came the reply.

Someone gave a low whistle. My sentiments exactly.

TWELVE

Anything that begins "I don't know how to tell you this" is never good news.

        —Ruth Gordon

STILL STUNNED by this latest development, we all heard the front door slam and Bridget's voice carry into the living room. "Mom?" she yelled. "Dad?"

"We're in here, honey," Blythe responded.

Bridget rushed into the room and ran straight to her parents. Bridget and Colin were booked to go to Bermuda for their honeymoon and Bridget was clearly dressed for the trip. She was wearing neon yellow Bermuda shorts, a blue-and-green-striped tank top, lace-up espadrilles that added a solid three inches to her height, and what appeared to be a small frog on her right shoulder blade.

With a mother's instinct, Blythe's eyes homed in on the mark. It was a tattoo. Bridget had told me that she was planning on getting one. From the "Oh, shit," expression on her face now, it was clear that she hadn't planned on sharing this acquisition with Blythe. Colin saw Blythe's expression and quickly draped his arm over Bridget's shoulder, blocking the tattoo from view.

"We came as quickly as we could, Mrs. Matthews," said Colin smoothly. "What's going on?"

"It's about Roni," said Graham, his eyes darting to where Avery sat. "She's dead. Murdered."

Bridget let out an exclamation. It would have earned her few points with her new mother-in-law, but it managed to accurately sum up the general mood.

Graham nodded his head. "Exactly. Elizabeth found her this morning." Bridget's eyes flew to mine. I could see her thoughts taking shape and knew what she was going to say. The only problem was, I couldn't stop her.

"*You* found her! Jesus! Not again! Christ, what are the odds?"

"I'm sorry," interrupted Detective Grant, his voice ominous. "What are the odds about what?"

I winced. Bridget answered breathlessly, "Elizabeth found a body before. Last New Year's…" Belatedly, she saw the dark suspicion building in Detective Grant's eyes. "Oh, I mean, Elizabeth had nothing to do with it, of course. She just happened to find the…um…body."

Detective Grant turned and stared at me. For a long time. I tried to calm my shattered nerves by thinking of Detective Grant as a kind of modern-day singing detective, but it was no good. My nerves won out. Unfortunately, when I get nervous I tend to ramble. I did so now in rather spectacular fashion.

"That was different," I said. "I mean, yes, I found a body. She'd been beaten, though, not stabbed. Not that any of that *matters,* of course. But I didn't have anything to do with it. I mean, I did, kind of. I helped the police find the killer. Not that I'm saying you need any help, of course…"

Peter moved next to me and squeezed my hand—hard. With relief, I realized that I had finally stopped talking. "What Elizabeth is trying to say, Detective," Peter said calmly, "is that she found a body this past New Year's. There was a murder at her aunt's inn and Elizabeth was instrumental in finding the killer. I can put you in touch with the detective in charge of the case, if you have any questions."

Detective Grant's cold eyes never left my face. "Oh, I'm going to have questions," he said. "I can promise you that."

From the corner of my eye, I noticed Chloe openly studying me. I didn't need a translator to interpret the faintly raised eyebrows and the tiny line of confusion etched between them. She was wondering how Peter had ever gotten involved with someone like me. I quickly re-arranged my face into an expression I hoped suggested fierce intelligence and a brilliant wit.

Elsie returned from the study clutching a thick sheaf of paper. "Here's the list of wedding guests, Detective." Seeing Bridget and Colin, she stopped. "Hello, dears. I didn't hear you come in." Kissing them both on the cheek, she sadly shook her head from side to side. "I see you've heard. It's all very shocking. Detective Grant here." She paused, raising a quizzical eyebrow. "I'm sorry, have you been introduced? Bridget, Colin, this is Detective Paul Grant. He's been put in charge here. Detective Grant, this is my granddaughter Bridget and her husband, Colin Delaney."

Bridget, Colin, and Detective Grant nodded at each other. "We were just talking," Bridget said with an apologetic glance in my direction.

"Apparently, Roni's necklace is missing. Detective Grant thinks it might be related to her mur...death," Elsie said, with a sideways glance at Avery.

"I never said that, Mrs. Matthews," protested Detective Grant, but Elsie wasn't listening. Like Blythe, she had homed in on the mark on Bridget's shoulder. "Is that a tattoo, Bridget?"

Bridget sighed and rolled her eyes. "Yes. Okay? I got a tattoo. It's no big deal."

Blythe stepped forward. "I knew it!" she said. Pushing her glasses firmly up on the bridge of her nose, she turned Bridget around and peered at the mark.

"Good God," she said. "A tattoo. Whyever did you get a tattoo? And of a frog, no less."

Bridget craned her neck, staring at her shoulder. "It's not a frog," she said defensively, roughly pulling back and facing Blythe. "It's a shamrock."

"It doesn't look like a shamrock to me. It looks like a frog. Doesn't it look like a frog?" Blythe asked, addressing the rest of us.

We all stared at it in silence. Even Detective Grant silently considered it. I had to admit it looked like a frog.

"For God's sake, why do you have a tattoo of a frog on your shoulder?" asked Blythe.

"Shamrock," interjected Bridget.

"Whatever," Blythe replied. "You're not even Irish!"

Bridget lifted her chin. "No, but Colin is. I got the shamrock as a wedding present for him."

Blythe stared at her in open-mouthed amazement. "A tattoo? You got him a tattoo for a wedding present? Who does that? What's wrong with a nice watch?"

Detective Grant stepped forward. "Excuse me, ladies, but I am trying to conduct a murder investigation. Could we discuss the frog tattoo another time?"

Blythe and Bridget fell silent and nodded, although I saw Bridget mouth *shamrock*.

"I'm sorry, Detective," Blythe said, shaking her head apologetically. "Forgive us. We're really not as callous as we appear. I think we're all anxious to focus on anything other than the tragedy at hand."

Elsie stepped forward and thrust the list at Detective Grant. "That's everyone who attended last night," she said. "Phone numbers and addresses are included."

Detective Grant took the thick stack of paper and idly thumbed through it. "Thank you," he said.

As the meaning of this exchange dawned on Bridget, her jaw fell open. "Wait a minute! You can't possibly think that one of our guests had anything to do with this!"

"I understand your concern, Mrs. Delaney. But it's a possibility that we need to take into consideration." From his tone, I suspected he considered it to be only a faint possibility. "There was a key found near the body, found by your friend Ms. Parker," he said with a nod in my direction. "It is from the Jefferson Hotel. Additionally, we found an anonymous note in the deceased's purse. It demanded a meeting at two a.m."

"Yes, but that doesn't mean…" Bridget began.

"It was written on stationery also from the Jefferson," Detective Grant added.

Bridget's mouth snapped shut. All of the out-of-town wedding guests had stayed at the Jefferson.

A sudden chirping noise broke the uncomfortable silence that followed this statement. Glancing down at the silver beeper on his belt, Detective Grant pushed a button and silenced the machine. "Excuse me a moment," he said, turning back toward the study. "I need to make a phone call. I'll be right back."

No one spoke until the study door shut behind him. Bridget whirled around and faced her parents. "He really thinks one of our guests killed Roni? This is absurd. We're… we're nice people! Our friends are nice people. None of them could have done this. It's not possible!"

Blythe stepped forward and wrapped her arm around Bridget's shoulder. "I know, dear, but—"

Before she could continue, David interrupted, "But the alternative is an even less attractive possibility."

"What do you mean?" asked Bridget.

"I mean, that if one of *them* didn't do it, then one of *you* did," David said.

"David!" gasped Claire. "How can you even think that?"

"Because, unlike some people, I have half a brain."

"Yes, but we've never actually held that against you, David," said Elsie, her voice tight with anger. "Although, if you keep talking like this, we might have to revisit that decision."

Elsie was one of the few members of the Matthews family who weren't afraid of David's unpredictable temper. She considered him nothing more than a bully and firmly believed that when dealing with bullies, you had to push them harder than they pushed you. I admired her courage: David, angry, made me just want to run like hell.

He ignored her. The rest of us held our breath as we watched their showdown.

"I don't recall you having any kind words for her when you realized she wanted Avery to sell the Garden," Elsie continued.

"That's different!"

"Is it? I don't see how."

Elsie took another step closer to David. She gripped the cane in her right hand, and for a wild moment I thought she was going to bash David over the head with it. Whether she would have or not, I don't know because Millie suddenly yelled out, "Mr. Matthews! Avery! Oh, dear God! Avery!"

At the sound of the panic in her voice, I jerked my head in her direction and saw Avery slumped in his chair. His face was a sickly shade of gray and his breathing labored. After her moment of panic, Millie transformed back into her role of efficient nurse. Leaning over his recumbent form, she grabbed his wrist and closed her eyes in concentration.

"Dad!" Harry said, crossing the room in a few steps to Avery's side.

"Avery? Can you hear me? Are you ill, dear?" Elsie asked.

Avery answered weakly, "Just a little dizzy."

Millie shook her head. "You need to rest. Now. This is too much for you. I won't risk you relapsing." Her voice rose in agitation. She took a breath to calm herself and continued. "I'm taking you to your room," she said decidedly. Briskly stepping behind Avery's chair, she pushed him from the room. Harry followed, his face a mask of worry.

Elsie watched them leave, a pensive expression on her face, before turning again to David. Squaring her shoulders, she tilted her head back and glared at him. "I will not have you throwing about your asinine accusations," she said in clipped tones. "You obviously have no idea of the damage they can do."

"All I've done is tell the truth. You all hated her. It's only a matter of time before the police find out."

"Oh, I think it's safe to say that the police already know that," said a deep voice to my left. I didn't need to look to know who it was.

THIRTEEN

Cheer up! The worst is yet to come!
                              —Philander Chase Johnson

FROM THE DOORWAY, Detective Grant contemplated us, his wide face carefully devoid of emotion. That's not to say, however, that his mood was indefinite. Far from it, in fact. He angrily drummed his gold pen against his gray pant leg in a manner that suggested that he was either highly annoyed or horribly strung out on caffeine.

Suddenly, he took a step toward us, his movement graceful, like a panther about to pounce. His expression was ominous. It took all of my self-control not to take an equally large step back. "Let me make myself clear," he said with deliberation. "I do not like games." He paused. "I do not like people who play games. I do not like people who withhold vital information." He paused again. "A woman was murdered here last night. It's my job to find out who did it. If you know something, then you will tell me. It's as simple as that. And if you don't..." He shrugged expressively. "Well, let's hope it doesn't get that far, but in the meantime, I'm going to ask that none of you leave town."

"What?" yelped Bridget. "But what about our honeymoon? We're scheduled to leave today! I mean, I don't want to sound insensitive, but..." She paused. After a moment she ducked her head and muttered, "Never mind. I already *am* sounding insensitive."

Graham stepped forward. "How long are we to stay here?" he asked.

"Until I say so."

Graham's eyebrows bristled ominously and Blythe quickly moved in front of Graham, putting a restraining hand on his arm.

"Detective Grant," she said smoothly, "I can assure you that we will cooperate with your investigation. *All* of us," she added with a quelling glance at Graham. "Like most families, we have our fair share of infighting, although I'm sorry you had to witness it. We're all tired and in shock and clearly not at our best. But I can assure you that despite how anyone might have felt about Roni, she was a part of our family and we will all do all we possibly can to help you."

"Yes. I know you will," said Detective Grant. This avowal was clearly more of a statement of fact than an acknowledgment of Blythe's offer of assistance. "I understand that this is a terrible situation for you, but I am here to do a job, and that job is to find out who killed Mrs. Matthews. As uncomfortable as it may be for you, I have to consider all possibilities." His eyes moved to Elsie, and his next words seemed directed especially to her. "Even those that include a family member."

I wondered at the meaning of his words until I remembered that Elsie said she'd called in some favors from influential friends. I wondered if Detective Grant's beeper message had something to do with that. If it had, it would certainly account for his annoyed expression as he faced Elsie.

Unaccountably, a chill that had nothing to do with the outside temperature overtook me. I considered the Matthews family to be an extension of my own. Suddenly, I knew that Roni's death would have far-reaching consequences and the Matthewses would never be the same again.

"I have a few more phone calls to make," continued Detective Grant. "But then I think I'll talk with you, Mr. Cook. In private, if you don't mind."

David nodded, an obsequious smile pasted on his thick lips. "Of course, Detective," he said in an oily voice. "I'd be happy to tell you everything I know."

"I'm pleased to hear it. Meet me back here in fifteen minutes."

David nodded again and ducked out of the room, no doubt having no desire to stay in the same room with Elsie.

Just as Detective Grant disappeared back into the study, the red-haired policeman returned. Studiously not stepping on the carpet, he politely coughed and said, "Mrs. Matthews? There's a Mrs. Julia Fitzpatrick out front who says she's a friend of the family—"

The officer got no farther. With a yelp, Elsie burst out, "Oh, dear God! Julia! The brunch! We forgot to cancel the brunch!" She stopped, a confused expression on her face. "Wait. Julia wasn't invited to the brunch. Oh, never mind. I've got to call everyone!" Turning to Chloe, she said, "I'll need your help, Chloe."

"Of course, Mrs. Matthews," she responded, her face flushed at this evidence of her imperfection, and hurried from the room. I was surprised at Chloe's oversight—she was normally almost robotic in her catering perfection. But, I amended, most bookings probably didn't include a murder. Elsie trailed after her, calling over her shoulder as she did, "Let Julia in, Officer. I'll be right back."

The officer left and moments later returned with Julia in tow. The change in her appearance was startling. Her hair, normally neat and tidy, now hung wet and limp around her pale face. Her clothes, too, were altered. Instead of one of her usual expensively tailored outfits she was wearing old paint-splattered jeans and a scruffy sweatshirt. By comparison, my ensemble looked almost couture. Seeing us, she nervously asked, "What's going on? Why are the police here?" Her green eyes widening in fear, she said, "Oh, my God! Is Avery all right? Nothing has happened to him, has it?"

Blythe stepped forward. "Julia, Avery is fine. But I'm afraid there's been a...well, Roni's dead. She was killed last night."

Although a soft cry escaped from Julia's throat and her slender hands fluttered in front of her ashen face, I noticed that her eyes did not seem surprised. Instead, they sought out Megan's before quickly focusing again on Blythe. "Do...do the police know who did it?" she asked, her voice shaky.

Blythe shook her head. "Not yet. They're going over the guest list from last night."

Harry returned to the room. "Dad's all right now. Millie gave him something and is going to stay with him for a while." He pulled up short upon seeing Julia. "What are you doing...I mean...Why are you...?" He stopped, gave himself a shake, and pulled Julia into a hug. "Sorry. Hi, Julia."

Julia gripped Harry's arm tightly. "How's your dad?"

Harry's brow creased and his eyes shifted questioningly to Blythe, seeming to ask if Julia had been told about Roni. Blythe nodded. "He's pretty upset," said Harry. "But Millie is taking care of him. I think he'll be okay."

Julia's shoulders sagged in relief. "Do you think I can see him?" she asked, her voice small.

Harry paused, running his hand through his tousled hair. "I'm sure he'd like that, Julia, but I don't think it's such a good idea right now. He's resting."

Julia swallowed hard and looked up at Harry. After a moment she said, "Will you please tell him that I came by?"

Harry's eyebrows pulled in concern. "Sure I will," he said. "Julia? Are you feeling all right? Is there something I can do?"

Julia looked around uncertainly. "I..." she started, but her words died upon Elsie's entrance.

"Well, I was able to get ahold of Joan Cumberland," said Elsie. "Between her and Chloe, they should be able to get hold of everyone in time." Seeing Julia, Elsie stopped. "Hello, Julia. I gather you've heard our terrible news."

Julia nodded. "Yes, Blythe's just told me. I'm simply...stunned. Do the police have any ideas who did it?"

"Oh, they have ideas," said Elsie. "I'm just not sure if they're the right ideas. Apparently, Roni was wearing an expensive necklace that has gone missing, and among other things, the detective in charge wants to interview the guests from last night. And, of course, he"—she nodded toward the study—"wants to interview us. So, Julia, what can we do for you?"

Taking a deep breath, Julia said, "I...I wanted to see Avery. I needed to talk to him about...I didn't realize..."

Elsie's eyes flickered toward Blythe. Blythe caught the glance and shrugged slightly in response.

"I'm so sorry," Julia continued. "If there's anything I can do..." Her eyes slid to Megan, slumped zombie-like in her chair.

Elsie followed Julia's gaze. Glancing back at her,

she asked, "Julia, have you met Megan?" Julia shook her head.

At the sound of her name, Megan raised dull eyes.

"Megan?" said Elsie in a soft voice, "I'd like you to meet an old friend of our family. Julia, this is Megan, Avery's stepdaughter. Megan, this is Julia Fitzpatrick."

Megan rose from her chair and held out her hand. "Pleased to meet you," she said mechanically.

Julia took Megan's hand, holding it tightly in her own. "Hello, Megan. Harry's told me a lot about you. You sound like a very special young lady." Shifting her shoulders slightly, Julia fell into her professional mode of counselor. "This must be a very difficult time," she added, "but I hope you know that you are surrounded by people who love you."

I noticed that Julia hadn't gone with any of the standard proclamations of sympathy. No "I'm sorry for your loss" or "This is such a tragedy." Julia either knew or sensed that such expressions would be wasted on Megan.

At Julia's words, Megan ducked her head, but not before I saw that her eyes were glistening with unshed tears. Without a word, Julia pulled Megan into a maternal hug. "It'll be okay, trust me. Everything will be all right," she whispered. Megan rested her head on Julia's shoulder. I had a feeling that it had been a long time since anyone had hugged Megan like that. I certainly doubted that Roni ever had. Watching them, I had a peculiar sensation of discord. Something was missing or not right, but before I could put my finger on it, the feeling slipped from my grasp.

"Harry," said Elsie with brisk authority, "why don't you take Julia and Megan into the kitchen and make them some tea?"

"Of course," said Harry. "Follow me, ladies." Julia released Megan from the hug but still held her hand. The two of them followed Harry to the kitchen.

After their departure, Colin sighed and turned to Bridget. "Guess I'd better call the airlines and see what I can do about our tickets. I should probably call my parents, too." He glanced at his watch. "I think they've already left for home, though."

Bridget made no response. She stared at the carpet, her face scrunched in confusion.

"Bridget?" he repeated. "I'm going to see about our tickets and call my parents."

With a small start, Bridget's focused her eyes on Colin. "I'm sorry, Colin. Did you say something?"

"I said that I was going to call my parents and the airline and see what our options are."

"Oh, yeah. Okay."

Stooping his tall frame down to Bridget's eye level, Colin peered at her in concern. "Bridge?"

Bridget waved away his unasked question. "I'm fine. I'm just thinking."

Colin kissed her lightly on her head before moving to leave the room.

I turned to Peter. "We should call Aunt Winnie and tell her that we'll be a bit delayed."

Peter nodded. "Yeah, you're right. I'll do it. You stay with Bridget. Wait up, Colin," said Peter. "I'll walk out with you."

Graham left with them, saying that he needed to call his office.

Beside me, Bridget continued to stare at the floor. "Hey," I said softly, giving her arm a gentle squeeze. "Are you okay?"

Bridget turned her eyes to me. Before she spoke,

something over my shoulder caught her attention. Turning, I saw that Claire was still in the room. Sitting perfectly still on the couch, Claire stared anxiously at the study door while systematically gnawing what was left of her fingernails. I doubted if she was even aware of our presence.

Bridget pulled on my sleeve and jerked her head in the direction of the foyer. I followed her. "What's going on?" I said.

"Keep your voice down. Let's go to your room."

I followed her in silence until we got to my room. Inside, she shut the door.

"What?" I asked.

"*What? Are you serious? Roni was murdered! That's what! And at my *wedding,* no less! That's what's going on! I feel like I've missed the first act of the play. I can tell by your face that you know more than you're telling me. So give. Just what the hell has been going on here? And just what the hell has gotten into David?"

I wasn't looking forward to this conversation, but there was no way I could avoid it. Knowing Bridget's volatile temper and vivid imagination, she could take the news of what I had seen and heard over the last twenty-four hours in any number of ways, very few of them productive.

Taking a deep breath, I quickly and without elaboration brought her up to date on Harry's fight with Roni, Megan's outing with the kid from the band, and my gruesome discovery of the body.

"Holy shit!" she cried. "What a mess."

"Keep your voice down. You're right. It is a mess. But, unfortunately, there's more," I said. "Yesterday, I overheard Roni on her cell phone. From the sound of it, she was having an affair with someone, someone who was also hoping that Avery would sell the Garden."

Bridget's eyes narrowed to malachite slits. "That bitch," she muttered, slapping her hand against her thigh. I agreed, although I was glad Detective Grant wasn't nearby to hear the venom in her voice. There were enough suspects in the Matthews family already, I thought, remembering the rest of what I'd seen and heard. Bridget glanced at my face. I quickly tried to think of something neutral, but having never actually been to Switzerland, I failed.

"Okay, but what about David? I can tell by your face, there's more. Out with it."

I sighed. "Not really. I mean, I don't know what it means—"

Bridget reached out and gripped my arm. "Spill."

"Okay, okay. I saw David storm out of Roni's bedroom yesterday morning. Megan must have seen it, too. David was furious. He was asking her for money she'd apparently promised him, but she told him to get lost. Also, she was laughing at him. I don't know, but the whole thing seemed weird. And then last night during the reception, I saw Claire confront Roni. I was too far away to hear what she was saying, but Claire was livid."

Bridget rubbed her eyes in concentration. "Roni seemed to have that effect on a lot of people." Bridget looked at me with something like astonishment. "And you didn't tell me any of this! I can't believe you!"

"It was your wedding day."

"But—"

"No buts. It was your wedding day," I repeated firmly.

"Okay." She paused. "But the key and that note— they seem to point to someone outside the family as

having killed Roni, right? Such as one of the guests?"
I decided not to point out that this was the very scenario that she had just hotly denied to Detective Grant.

"It would *seem* so."

She heard the hesitation in my voice. "But that detective doesn't believe that, does he? He thinks one of us did it."

"I honestly don't know, Bridge. But I think it's a possibility."

"This is insane. I'm supposed to be on my way to Bermuda now! I should be sitting on a plane drinking from tiny little bottles, not in the middle of a murder investigation!" She paused in front of the dresser and stared at her reflection in the heavy wood-framed mirror. Twisting her shoulders, she leaned closer and carefully inspected her image. "Does this really look like a frog?" she asked.

I didn't answer. I sat down on my bed. Reaching over to the nightstand, I idly picked up Megan's pile of books and spread them out on my lap. My stomach jerked and tightened. Every one was a pulp fiction novel set in the 1940s. Each seemed to follow a rough, foul-mouthed detective who solved violent crimes involving beautiful, voluptuous women. On one cover, a man's dark shadow lurked ominously in an empty alleyway. On another, a man's dead body lay sprawled at the feet of a hard-looking blonde in a tight red gown. But it was the cover of the third book, the one that was worn from obvious frequent readings, that made my insides curl. A woman lay dead, her black hair spilling out in an inky puddle underneath her. Her blue eyes stared blankly at the knife protruding from her generous chest. I closed my eyes and saw Roni's dead face all over again. Bile rose in my throat. The book slipped from my grasp and fell to the floor. From inside the book, something fell out. I picked it up. It was a packet of rolling papers. Crap. No one but hippies rolled their own cigarettes if they were just smoking tobacco. I wondered if Megan was doing anything else besides pot.

Holding the book and the rolling papers, I stood up. "Bridget!" I whispered.

"Elizabeth!" she said simultaneously.

She turned to face me and I held up the book, showing her the cover and the packet of rolling papers. Her eyes grew wide.

So did mine. In her outstretched hand she held Roni's necklace.

Our eyes locked.

"Where did you find that?" I asked. "In Megan's bureau?"

Bridget swallowed before answering. "No. In yours."

One of us said, "Holy shit!"

I think it was me.

FOURTEEN

*It is always the best policy to tell the truth, unless,
of course, you are an exceptionally good liar.*
                                        —Jerome K. Jerome

"WHAT DO YOU MEAN, you found it in my bureau?" I sputtered. "That's impossible!"

"I know," Bridget replied, shaking her head in disbelief, "but I did. I noticed one of the drawers was open a little. When I went to shut it, I saw something glittery inside."

I stared horrified at the shimmering necklace dangling from her hand. "But how did it get there? I certainly didn't put it there!"

"Well, I know *that*. The question is, who did?"

I gaped at the coil of diamonds, my mind decidedly blank. I looked to Bridget for an explanation, but the puzzled expression on her face told me that she was equally dumbfounded.

"What are we going to do?" she whispered.

Before I could answer, Colin hurried into the room. "There you are! I've been looking everywhere for you! Mom and Dad said to tell you…" He pulled up short when he saw the necklace. "Is that…?"

"Yes," said Bridget.

"…Roni's necklace?" he finished unnecessarily. "Where did you find it?"

Bridget jerked her head in my direction. "Someone put it in Elizabeth's bureau."

My stomach lurched and my legs morphed into jelly. I sank heavily onto the bed and stared at the floor. My headache returned in spectacular fashion. First I had found the key. Then I stumbled upon Roni's body. Now her necklace had been tucked in among my possessions. It was nothing more than a sick coincidence. Unfortunately, Detective Grant didn't strike me as a man who believed in coincidences—sick or healthy.

I looked up at Colin and Bridget. Bridget still held the necklace in her outstretched hand; its pendulous movement had slowed to a standstill. So, too, had my brain. How had the necklace gotten here—with my underwear, of all places?

Bridget spoke. "We'll just say that we found it... on the floor. There's no need to say that we found it in your bureau."

The barest wisp of my mental fog lifted and I shook my head. "No, Bridget. That won't work and you know it. Where are we going to say that we found it, anyway? The hall? Too many people can contradict that." Pointing at the necklace, I said, "There's no way that anyone would have missed *that* on the hallway floor."

Bridget opened her mouth to argue, but I cut her short. "No," I said, pulling myself up to a standing position. "We have to tell Detective Grant the truth and hope that he has enough sense to realize that I didn't have anything to do with Roni's murder." I grabbed the necklace from Bridget's hand. As I felt its cool weight, my confidence wavered. People had killed for far less than what I now cradled in my palm. Before my cowardly side could overtake me, I squared my shoulders, turned, and marched out of the room. Bridget and Colin followed close on my heels.

In the living room, the family was still in attendance. Elsie stood with her back to the room, looking out the windows at the terrace. Anna lay curled at her feet. Blythe and Graham occupied two of the overstuffed chairs, leaning their heads close together to converse quietly. Megan sat alone on the couch, staring into space. Someone had started a fire in the fireplace. The gold-and-blue flames crackled and danced in the cobalt-and-white-tiled hearth.

It looked like a normal family tableau, but I eyed them again critically. Could one of these people have slipped that necklace into my bureau? And if so, why? To my far left was Detective Grant. My step faltered. The reason for this misstep, however, was not the sight of Detective Grant's dour face, although that was a reason in and of itself to fall to the ground and assume the fetal position. No, the reason for my stumble was the sight *behind* Detective Grant. Peter and Chloe stood huddled together in an obviously private conversation. Chloe's body language reminded me of a cat's eyeing a bowl of cream.

A surge of anger overtook me. Perfect. Someone stuffs a $200,000 bauble in my drawer—a bauble stolen from a dead woman, no less—and where is my shining knight when I need him most? Chatting up the gorgeous blonde in the $2,000 suit.

Although I wasn't aware of having made any noise, Chloe abruptly pivoted in my direction, the sudden movement causing her ponytail to swing out behind her like a silken rope. It reminded me of a snake, a beautiful but deadly snake that you'd see featured on the Nature

Channel. The kind that makes you cheer when a grizzly trods upon it.

Something in my expression must have alerted Peter to my mood, because his brows pulled together and he moved my way. Giving him what I hoped was a look of icy disdain, I marched over to Detective Grant and thrust out my hand. The necklace caught the firelight and glittered forth like a loop of flames. Around me, I heard gasps. The only discernible reaction in Detective Grant was an instant shrinking of his pupils into hard, cold dots of black. It took every ounce of courage not to throw the necklace at his feet and make a mad break for the door. Peter stood next to me and wrapped an arm protectively around my shoulder. I was torn between leaning into his warm strength and angrily slapping his hand away.

"This was in my bureau," I said loudly. "We just found it."

Detective Grant stepped forward and took the necklace from me. I was glad to let it go. Holding it up so that it hung in one shining rope, he shifted his gaze from it to me and asked simply, "Who, may I ask, is 'we'?"

"Bridget." I pointed in her direction.

Detective Grant's gaze slid to Bridget. "Which of you found it?"

"I did," said Bridget, with a nervous glance in my direction.

"I see," he intoned. He dipped his large hand into his suit pocket and retrieved a plastic bag. Slipping the necklace inside, he then took out his notebook and pen. "Tell me how."

"Elizabeth and I were in her room talking when I noticed something shiny in the top drawer of her bureau. I looked inside and saw the necklace."

"I see. And what was Ms. Parker's reaction to this?"

Bridget lifted her chin. "Elizabeth took the necklace from me and immediately came down to give it to you, of course! I can't imagine what *else* you think she would do!"

Yeah, Bridget!

Detective Grant seemed unimpressed by this assertion of my good character and resumed his stony-eyed appraisal of me.

"Detective Grant, I'm not sure I like where you're going with this," said Peter. "Elizabeth is an honest person. To state otherwise is ridiculous."

"Mr. McGowan, I'm sure your loyalty does you credit, but I don't believe that I've officially stated anything, ridiculous or otherwise."

Peter tensed in anger, while I tried not to scoff at Detective Grant's use of the word *loyalty.* Ignoring Peter's look of annoyance, Detective Grant continued. "Interesting coincidence, though, wouldn't you say, Ms. Parker? First you find the *body,* then you find the all-important *key* that suggests an outsider committed this crime, and now you find the *necklace.*" He tapped his pen on the notebook for emphasis.

"I don't think it's a coincidence…" I sputtered.

This was greeted with a tight smile. "Well, now that's something we can agree on, because neither do I. Who shares that room with you?"

My eyes flew to Megan. She was still sitting on the couch. Before I could answer, she stood up on trembling legs and said, "I do. I share the room."

When he saw her pale face and large frightened eyes, Detective Grant's hard expression softened. "When did you last see your mother's necklace?"

"Last night," said Megan. "She was wearing it during the reception."

"Did you know that it was in your room?"

"No, of course not!" Her hands shook and she swayed slightly. Looking wildly around, she cried out, "I didn't kill my mother! And I didn't take her necklace! I swear I didn't!" Her voice was unsteady and her eyes looked glassy. I peered closer at her, wondering if she'd already been smoking this morning.

In two quick moves Detective Grant was at her side. Gently taking her hand, he helped her back onto the couch. While I appreciated Detective Grant's sensitive treatment of Megan, I briefly wondered why I didn't warrant the same handling. After all, I was upset, too. Before my mind could provide the obvious answer, I forced it to focus on something else.

Seeing Megan's dazed face, a wave of protectiveness overcame me. If she had been smoking, she'd probably still reek of it. The last thing she needed was for Detective Grant to smell it. I cleared my throat and said, "Detective Grant, perhaps you should continue the rest of your interview with me in private."

He turned to face me. I couldn't read his expression, but instinct assured me that it wasn't good.

"Yes," he said, with a sidelong glance at Megan. "Perhaps that would be best—"

Before he could finish, Claire and David entered the room. Claire entered first and David shuffled in behind her, warily eyeing the rest of us.

Seeing Detective Grant's ominous expression, Claire hesitated. "What's going on?" she asked.

"Mrs. Matthews's necklace has been recovered," Detective Grant answered.

"What!" cried David. "How?"

"It was found in Ms. Parker's bureau," came the answer.

Claire and David turned to me, their faces wearing identical expressions of shock. "In *Elizabeth's* bureau?" David said. "But..."

"But why would Elizabeth have it?" Claire finished, her eyes wide.

"That's what I propose to find out," said Detective Grant calmly. "Now, if you'll excuse us, I'd like to speak to Ms. Parker in private." Turning to Elsie, he said, "May I use your study again, Mrs. Matthews?"

Elsie answered him with a curt nod. Crossing the room to me, she laid a hand on my shoulder. "Elizabeth, dear," she said in a low voice, "you know you have our full support. I don't know how Roni's necklace ended up in your room, but don't worry. No one could possibly think you had anything to do with this." Looking into her face, I wished I shared her confidence. Peter gave my arm a reassuring squeeze as I silently followed Detective Grant into the study.

As before, I settled into the leather chair opposite the desk. Leaning against its heavy mahogany frame, Detective Grant opened his notebook and looked at me, his gray eyes inscrutable. He said nothing.

I refused to act intimidated. I forced myself to think of him in tap shoes dancing like Gene Kelly and singing "Gotta dance, gottaaaa dance!" Strangely enough, it helped calm my nerves. "I was under the impression that you wanted to *speak* to me," I said.

He tipped his head in tacit acknowledgment. "So, you found the necklace," he said. It wasn't a question.

"Actually, Bridget found the necklace."

"Yes, but it was found in *your* bureau. Any idea how it got there?"

"None," I said, sticking out my chin. "As I said before, I had nothing to do with this awful incident. And neither did Harry. No one here did. I don't know why you insist on looking at the Matthews family. Roni obviously received a note from someone staying at the Jefferson! Plus there was the key! Can't you find out registration information from the key?"

"No." Detective Grant said. "Whoever used the room checked out. Once checkout is complete the keys are useless; they contain no personal information."

"But nevertheless, it still proves someone outside the family killed Roni!"

"Ah, yes, your all-too-pat outsider theory."

"It's not *my* theory!"

"Isn't it?"

"That note isn't a theory!"

"No," he said with a smile that made me uneasy, "I definitely wouldn't call it *that*."

I pressed on, deciding it was best not to ask what he meant. "And what about the phone call I overheard? Have you forgotten that? Now, there's someone you might want to track down. For all you know, the call could have come from the Jefferson!"

"Actually, I did look into the call. And while several calls came into Mrs. Matthews's cell phone from the Jefferson, they were all of a duration of five seconds or less. The call you overheard was from a 'gentleman'— and I use that term loosely—in New York by the name of Jimmy Michaels. From what I have been able to learn, he and the late Mrs. Matthews were indeed romantically involved."

"Well, there you have it!" I cried excitedly. "It's not

as if New York is on the other side of the world. Who's to say that this Jimmy Michaels didn't come down here to confront Roni and booked himself a room at the Jefferson?"

"I say he didn't."

"You say? How do you know?"

"Because Mr. Michaels has an alibi for the time of the murder. He was with his wife."

I considered this news and quickly dismissed it. "So what? Lots of wives lie to protect their husbands. She probably didn't know that he and Roni were lovers."

"Oh, I'm fairly certain that she did *not* know that fact. However, I'm still inclined to believe the young woman."

"And why is that?"

"Because she was giving birth to their fifth child at the time in question and Mr. Michaels was at her side the whole time playing the role of the devoted husband."

I made a noise.

Detective Grant nodded. "Yes, I would tend to agree with you there. But the fact remains that he has an alibi. I'm sorry, but with your discovery of the necklace it's clear the 'outsider theory' is nothing more than someone's clever diversion. Unless, of course, you are proposing that the murderer, overcome with remorse, snuck back into the house and planted the necklace in your bureau."

Put that way, I had to admit it did sound kind of stupid.

"But there was a note and a key. *Both* from the Jefferson," I argued stubbornly.

"True," he conceded. "Someone, perhaps, who wanted us to believe that this crime was committed by someone *outside* the family."

I shook my head in denial at this scenario, but on a certain level, I knew what he was saying had to be the truth.

"Are you sure there's nothing else you want to tell me?" he asked in an oddly gentle voice. "You wouldn't be the first person to try and help out after the fact, you know."

"What are you suggesting?"

"I'm not suggesting anything. I just know from experience that strange things happen in a murder investigation."

Was he kidding? Did he really think I was somehow involved? All of my pent-up emotions of the last few hours boiled over. I was still reeling from the horror of finding Roni's body, my frustration at the line of inquiry the police were taking, and my dread of Peter's apparent infatuation with Chloe.

"This is absurd!" I said, roughly pushing myself out of the chair. "I didn't take the damn necklace and I most certainly did not kill Roni!" Stomping up and down the width of the study, I jabbed the air with my finger as I rattled off my grievances. "I don't know who did kill her or why the damn thing landed in my drawer, but I will not be made someone's patsy! For Christ's sake, I barely knew the woman! Yes, she was horrible to Megan and Harry, and probably to Avery, as well. I didn't like her. But that doesn't mean any of them killed her, and it certainly doesn't mean *I* killed her!"

Other than a slight tensing of his broad shoulders when I burst out of my chair, Detective Grant did not move. He merely watched me, his hooded eyes alert and appraising. More than ever, he resembled a boxer sizing up his opponent.

"While you may not have known *her* very well, you

do know this family quite well. In fact, some might even consider you a part of this family."

"What the hell does that have to do with anything?" I snapped. I knew I wasn't making any points with him by losing my temper, but I couldn't stop. My mind had rejected Elinor as a role model; it had instead chosen Marianne.

"It means that you might want to do them a favor, perhaps? Get rid of the thorn in their side for them. Stranger things have happened, you know," he added conversationally. "Sometimes, people just snap."

That stopped me. I froze, letting his words sink in. Blindly, I reached out and grabbed the back of the chair. Easing myself into it, I attempted to undo the damage of my outburst.

"Some people may snap and kill someone," I said with as much dignity as I could muster, which, granted, was precious little, "but I am not one of those people. I just snap and then usually make an ass of myself."

I thought I saw a ghost of a smile at this admission, but I couldn't be sure. A loud electronic peal broke the silence. Detective Grant looked down at his cell phone and grimaced at the readout. Looking at me, he said, "Excuse me, I need to take this."

Flipping open the phone, he turned his back to me. "Grant here," he said.

As he listened in silence to the caller, his shoulders bunched and tightened. "Yes, sir, I understand, sir…"

I tried to listen without appearing to be doing just that. Shifting my gaze to the wall of bookcases that ran the length of the room, I stared at them as if just noticing their existence.

"Yes, sir, I understand you want this settled soon and I am doing my best, but…"

Crap, I knew it. Elsie's behind-the-scenes machinations were backfiring. What she had hoped would be pressure to make Detective Grant look at suspects outside the family had merely become pressure to wrap up this case fast. With the discovery of the necklace, the easy solution was no longer that an outsider had committed this crime. The easy solution was that one of us had. Given David's wild accusations earlier, I had a horrible feeling I knew who was about to become suspect number one.

Detective Grant's next words confirmed my worst fears. Hanging up the phone, he turned to me.

"I think it's time I had a chat with Mr. Harry Matthews," he said.

FIFTEEN

The more I see of the world, the more am I dissat-
isfied with it; and every day confirms my belief
of the inconsistency of all human characters, and
of the little dependence that can be placed on the
appearance of either merit or sense.
—Jane Austen, *Pride and Prejudice*

A HALF HOUR LATER, Harry was still in the study with
Detective Grant. I had to admit, it didn't look good.
Bridget, Colin, Peter, and I sat in my bedroom, awaiting any news. A loud rap on the door jolted us out of
our silence. It was Elsie. Her face drawn and tight, she
looked, for once, her full age.

"Where's your father?" she demanded crisply of
Bridget.

"I don't know. I think he went to make some phone
calls. Why? What's wrong?"

"I just heard raised voices in the study. Harry was
yelling at that detective. I don't like it. I have a bad
feeling. God only knows what David said to Detective
Grant during his interview. I need your father. He'll
know what to do."

Bridget's face lost color. She pressed her hand to her
chest. "You think Harry needs a lawyer?"

Elsie nodded. "Knowing David, I think we all do. I
had thought that we would be fine having Graham here,
but now I'm wondering if we need additional backup."

Elsie swept away in search of Graham.

Bridget leaped to her feet. "Come on!" she said.

"Where are we going?" I asked.

"Out. We need a plan and fast."

Minutes later, we were in Colin's car and headed for downtown Richmond, where Bridget reasoned we could talk in private. "On to Richmond!" the battle cry of the Federal troops during the Civil War, reverberated in my head as the car brought us closer to the capital. But while the pithy saying might have raised the sprits of the boys in blue, it was doing nothing for mine.

After hearing of Elsie's suspicion, Bridget cast herself into the role of amateur sleuth, resulting in a bizarre behavior combination of Lucy Ricardo and Nancy Drew. Colin had to make a few more calls regarding their canceled trip and it was proof of his extreme distraction that he had asked Bridget to drive.

Peter and I huddled quietly in the backseat while she tore south along I-95 in Colin's BMW. If that suggests a certain peacefulness to our outing, let me rephrase. My back was pressed firmly against the leather seat. My right foot desperately sought out an imaginary brake. With one hand I clung to the door handle in a white-knuckled grip and with the other I clasped tightly to Peter's. Peter's posture was a little more blasé, although I heard him mutter, "Oh, sweet Jesus," more than once.

As she drove, Bridget outlined all the reasons we needed to save Harry. While I agreed with them all, I wished she didn't feel the need to elucidate each point with a raised finger. If anyone needed both hands on the steering wheel, it was Bridget.

"Reason number five. Do you remember the time Harry saved Queen Mab?"

"Who is Queen Mab?" asked Peter.

"More like *what* was Queen Mab," I mumbled beside him.

"I heard that!" Bridget yelled with mock indignation. The subject of Queen Mab had been good-naturedly debated between us for years. Each of us thought the other was dead wrong, of course, but we didn't take it personally. Turning around to continue her defense of Queen Mab, she also turned the steering wheel. The red Jeep next to us honked frantically as we slid into its lane. "For the love of God, Bridget! Watch the road!" I yelled, as the side of the Jeep loomed terrifyingly closer. I braced myself for death or, at the very least, a nasty injury.

Bridget wrenched the steering wheel back before either happened. The owner of the red Jeep flashed Bridget a gesture I wholeheartedly agreed with before speeding away from us.

"Hey!" Bridget cried indignantly. "That guy just flipped me off."

"Just be grateful he didn't have a gun," I muttered.

"Whatever. Where was I?" she asked, ignoring me.

"Queen Mab," Peter replied in an odd voice. I eyed him carefully for signs of shock.

"Right, Queen Mab," Bridget replied, her voice growing misty with memory. "Queen Mab was my dog. I got her for my twelfth birthday. She was the cutest little thing."

Inadvertently, I made a rude noise. Seeing Bridget's body begin to turn again, I yelled out, "For God's sake, don't turn around again! I'm sorry! I'm sorry!"

"What kind of dog was Queen Mab?" Peter asked.

"A miniature poodle," Bridget replied. "Elizabeth didn't like her."

"No one liked her," I replied. "She tried to attack everyone but you!"

In the rearview mirror, I saw Bridget's lips curve in fond memory. "She just thought she was protecting me, that's all."

"Protecting you!" I sputtered. "What about that time she attacked me when I was in a dead sleep! What exactly did she think I was going to do to you?"

"I don't know! Maybe you were snoring or something! She probably just wanted to make sure you didn't wake me."

"Oh, that's brilliant," I replied. "First of all, I don't snore, and second, even if I did, I would like you to explain how my terrified screaming as I tried to fend of that crazed dog in the middle of the night is preferable to my snoring—which I don't do in the first place?"

"You do too snore, and if you ever heard it, you would already know the answer to that," she replied loftily. "My point is, Queen Mab loved me and I loved her. But remember that weekend when we were all down visiting Elsie when Queen Mab got out and followed us to the boat house?"

I did. It was winter and the temperature had dipped below freezing. Harry, Bridget, and I snuck out to the boat house knowing the cold would prevent any of the adults from following us. Bridget and I were about sixteen at the time and had just discovered the stupid pleasure of smoking behind our parents' backs. Huddled in the boat house, we puffed away, while Harry regaled us with stories from his first year of college. I don't remember which one of us first noticed Queen Mab wandering out onto the ice-covered James River, but one second she was there and the next she wasn't. Screaming hysterically, Bridget ran out after her, but Harry yanked her back before she flung herself into the frigid waters. Seeing Bridget become hysterical at the thought of her beloved dog drowning in the freezing water, Harry jumped in after Queen Mab. He emerged a heart-stopping minute later, shivering and faintly blue, but clutching a trembling and drenched Queen Mab. For his efforts, Harry landed in the hospital with hypothermia and three rather nasty bites from an incredibly ungrateful Queen Mab. But that was Harry; he was always trying to save everybody.

Wiping away tears of remembrance, Bridget finished her story. "Harry saved Queen Mab that day. Anyone who would jump into those freezing waters for a dog that he didn't even like could never be a murderer. He's just too much of a softie. They don't make guys like Harry anymore."

I nodded. While I didn't share her affection for Queen Mab, I did agree with her about Harry. He was a good guy. He'd spent the better part of his life trying to help others; the least we could do was try and help when he needed it. Next to me, Peter cleared his throat; he'd been doing that a lot today. I wondered if he was coming down with a cold.

Finally, we neared Capitol Square, normally an oasis of enormous trees and expansive green lawns and home to the State Capitol building. Today, however, thanks to the morning's unrelenting downpour, it was an oasis of slick leaves and muddy puddles. Even the crisp, white neoclassic angles of the State Capitol looked gray and lumpish through the watery haze.

With precious little warning, Bridget yanked the steering wheel viciously to the left and we skidded into a parking garage and into a vacant spot. Bridget switched off the ignition, and the car gave a pathetic shudder and fell quiet.

No one spoke, until Colin began to mumble, mantralike, "I will always drive. I will always drive. I will always drive."

Bridget turned in her seat. "What are you talking about?" she demanded indignantly. "There's absolutely nothing wrong with my driving! There's not a scratch on this car!"

Peter leaned forward and laid his hand on Bridget's shoulder. In a somber voice, he said, "Some scars are on the inside."

Bridget scoffed as she threw the car keys to Colin. "You guys are a bunch of babies."

"If by that you mean that your driving induces a lack of control of emotion and bladder, then I agree with you," I said, easing myself out of the car on rubbery legs.

"Whatever," Bridget said, tossing her head. "I didn't drag you three down here so you could make fun of my driving. We need to go someplace private and talk. What are we going to do about Harry?"

"Honey, nothing's *happened* to Harry. The police are just talking to him," said Colin. "And where are we going exactly?" He peered out from the garage doorway to the rain-soaked streets.

"The Slip," replied Bridget, referring to Shockoe Slip. The area had once been the city's largest commercial trading district and part of the city ravaged by fire during the Civil War. Now its remaining nineteenth-century warehouses boasted elegant restaurants, nightclubs, and shops. With a flick of her wrist, Bridget sprung open an enormous lemon-colored umbrella. Raised high above her head, it resembled a giant, merry toad-stool. Unfortunately, even though she held it as high as she could, the umbrella was still a good three inches below Colin's head. Good-naturedly taking the umbrella from Bridget, Colin wrapped his arm around her and the two proceeded out onto the sidewalk. Peter and I followed under my more sedate black umbrella. The temperature had dropped with the arrival of the storm. Huddled inside my jacket, I ducked and weaved along the sidewalk to avoid the traffic's watery shower.

"What is she planning on doing, anyway?" Peter asked me as we both danced to the right to avoid the spray from an on-coming minivan. Cold, dirty water nevertheless splattered across my khaki pants. I looked down at them in dismay. My attempts to spiff up my appearance had been for naught. Chloe wears leather Prada boots in a thunderstorm and doesn't get a drop on them. I wear khakis from the Gap and get drenched. That's justice for you.

"To steal a line from Daffy Duck, you've got pronoun trouble," I said. "It isn't what 'she' is planning on doing. It's what she's planning on 'us' doing."

"Oh, God," he moaned.

"Yeah," I said, "that about sums it up."

After a few minutes slogging through the water-logged streets, we arrived at the Tobacco Company, a warehouse restaurant that serves one of the best brunches in town. A soaring three-story atrium of brick and intricately carved wood paneling, it is crammed with antiques, stained glass, and nineteenth-century tobacco advertisements. Entering through the cocktail lounge, which was populated with patrons reclining on large red sofas, we took the exposed antique elevator to the dining floor above. The hostess quickly found us a table. I slid into my seat and clamped my arms around me to warm my damp skin.

The waitress, a perky young woman who cheerfully identified herself as Sandy, appeared seconds later to take our drinks order. Colin, in his role as designated driver for life, ordered coffee. The rest of us required something stronger. I only wondered if, after hearing Bridget's "plan," one would be enough.

"So," said Bridget, quickly surveying her menu, "we need to prove that Harry is innocent."

"And how are we going to do that?"

"It's simple. All we need to do is find the *real* killer."

"*All* we need to do?" sputtered Peter.

Colin shot Peter a quelling glance. "Bridget, honey," he said, "I understand that you want to help Harry, but I think we should leave it to the police."

"The police? Are you kidding? Did you see that detective? He hates us!"

"I don't think he hates us," I said slowly, pushing my menu away. "I think he's annoyed. Elsie told me that she called in a few favors to put pressure on him to wrap up the case quickly. I think she thought it would force him to focus on the outsider theory."

Bridget covered her face with her hands. "Oh, God! I know she means well, but the last thing we need is a detective who's in a rush to solve this case! He's going to fixate on Harry and arrest him merely to be done with it! I just know it! He's not even going to consider anyone else!"

"You don't know that for sure—"

She interrupted me, throwing her menu down on the table in frustration. "For Christ's sake, this is ridiculous! Why would Harry kill Roni? Why would any of us kill her? Please! The woman was a pain in the butt, but to brutally stab her in the chest like that suggests a level of hatred that goes *way* beyond mere annoyance."

I was spared a response by the return of Sandy. Hearing Bridget's last comment, the wattage of her smile dimmed significantly. She quickly distributed our drinks, took our orders, and scurried away.

Bridget didn't notice. "Elizabeth, you talked with Detective Grant. What did he say? Did you get any idea of what he thinks?"

I took a grateful mouthful of my Bloody Mary, then forced myself to put the heavy glass down before I drained it in one gulp. I took a bite of the celery stick before answering. "He didn't exactly confide his thought process to me. Somehow, I didn't get the impression that he liked me very much."

"As I said, I don't think he likes *any* of us. But what did he *say*?"

"Just that Roni was probably killed somewhere between one and three in the morning. They don't know for sure if the knife is from the kitchen. I don't know if there were any prints on it."

"And at around one-thirty Roni came in saying that she was looking for Megan?" asked Bridget.

"Yes," I said. "That's what she said, but I doubt she was telling the truth. It's more likely that she was trying to hide the fact that she was supposed to meet someone at two."

Bridget nodded in agreement. "Who else was there?"

"Just me, Elizabeth, Harry, David, and Claire," said Peter. I took another sip of my drink. "Both Harry and David were pretty bombed."

"And that's when Harry had the fight with Roni?" asked Colin.

I nodded. "Yes. It was awful. I really thought he was going to hit her."

"And David saw all this, right?" asked Bridget.

"Yes."

"Okay, wait a minute," said Bridget slowly, her eyes

closed in concentration. Finally, she gave a loud snap of her fingers. "David. It must have been David."

I eyed her doubtfully. "David?"

"Yes, David! Don't you see?"

I frowned. "Not really…"

"Think about it," she pressed. "It makes perfect sense." I silently questioned her use of the word *perfect,* but I knew better than to voice it. In an eager whisper, she continued. "What if David and Roni were having an affair and then he found out that Roni was not only seeing someone else but was plotting with this other person about selling the Garden? He'd be pretty mad. I mean, let's be honest, if Avery sells the Garden, David is out of a job."

"True," I conceded. "But why on earth do you think that David was having an affair with Roni?"

"Because it makes sense. You said yourself that he was in her bedroom. That's kind of odd, don't you think? And let's face it, David has never bothered being faithful to Claire. If Claire found out about the affair, it would explain the fight she had with Roni."

"So would at least three dozen other scenarios…"

"But this one makes the most sense."

Before I could argue the truth of this, she went on. "And we all know David has a terrible temper, especially when he's mad or drunk. And he was certainly drunk last night."

"True, but he's drunk nearly every night and so far he hasn't killed anyone."

"There's a first time for everything." Bridget looked meaningfully at me. "Think about it. Based on what you overheard between the two of them yesterday, we know that David needed money and Roni refused to give it to him. He's furious. He slips Roni the note, telling her to meet him outside. He's going to blackmail her into giving him the money. She either gives it to him, or he'll 'tell all.' But something goes wrong. Maybe he realizes that she's going to double-cross him."

I saw Sandy approaching with our food and tried to stop Bridget from continuing. "Bridget!" I hissed.

"Wait! I think I've got it," she said, shutting her eyes again. "Having just seen Harry threaten Roni, David decides to kill her, take her necklace, knowing he can probably shift suspicion to Harry given the fight they've just had. David grabs a knife from the kitchen and voilà! he stabs her in the chest."

From the sharp intake of breath to my right, I knew that Sandy had overheard. Glancing up, I saw that her earlier perkiness was gone. Her rosy complexion had paled, and her eyes were wide with horror. I gave her what I hoped was a reassuring smile and said, "It's a plot for a TV show."

From the way she quickly deposited our plates and bolted from our table, I don't think she believed me. I couldn't really blame her; I wouldn't have believed me, either.

Bridget went on, oblivious that the entire staff was probably being informed that crazy, homicidal people were eating at table ten. "That works," she said, slapping the table triumphantly. "David, drunk and angry that Roni has been playing him for a fool, kills her knowing that Harry will most likely be blamed. Plus, with her gone, his job is safe. I doubt Avery will sell the Garden now."

The image of Roni's body sprawled on the chaise longue, an enormous kitchen knife protruding from her bloodstained chest, swam before me. Bile rose in my throat and I pushed away my eggs Benedict. Losing the few pounds I'd gained over the past months would be easier than I'd thought.

"So how did the necklace end up in Elizabeth's drawer?" asked Peter.

"I haven't figured out that part of it yet," said Bridget with a casual wave of her hand. "Maybe he stashed it there and meant to get it later. We know he's in need of money. And if that necklace really *is* worth two hundred thousand dollars, then he'd definitely take it. Besides, it confuses the motive."

"Well, that works, then, because I'm definitely confused," agreed Peter. I kicked him under the table.

"Bridget, I'm not disagreeing with you," I said, "but there's so much that we don't know. If it really *was* David, then wouldn't Claire have noticed that he was gone? And why would David write a note on Jefferson stationery? He wasn't staying there…"

"That doesn't mean he didn't have a room there," she countered.

I shook my head. "Why on earth would he have a room there?"

"What about…" began Colin.

Bridget ignored him. "Oh, don't be so naïve! People having affairs need hotel rooms for their rendezvous!"

I sighed. "Bridget, you have got to stop reading those Harlequin novels."

"One thing we could do…" ventured Peter.

Bridget talked over him. "Whatever," she said, "we need to tell the police."

"Tell the police what?" I asked. "That you think David might have done it? We have no proof! I know you don't like David—I'm not fond of him, either. But just because you can't stand him doesn't mean he's the killer."

"Just because I can't stand him doesn't mean he *isn't* the killer, either," Bridget said with surprising logic.

"We have no evidence!" I insisted. "And besides, he's not the only one who had a reason to dislike Roni."

"So Peter, what do you think of the Colts' starting lineup?" Colin suddenly interjected.

"Not bad," said Peter. "Of course, I'm a Pats fan myself, but the Colts seem to be having a pretty good season so far."

"Did you see last week's game?"

"No, I missed it. They won, right?"

Bridget turned to stare disbelievingly at Colin. "How the hell can you jabber on about football at a time like this?" she burst out.

"Oh, I'm sorry," said Colin with mock surprise. "I didn't think you were interested in our opinions. You seemed to be handling everything just fine without our input."

Bridget tapped her fingers in annoyance on the table. "Okay, you've made your point. Can we move on now?"

"Absolutely," Colin agreed with a grin.

"So, who do you suggest, then?" asked Bridget.

"I'm not suggesting *anyone*," said Colin, "but I agree with Elizabeth. I don't think we can leap to David."

"Meaning you can't think of anyone else. And the reason you can't is because I'm right." Bridget smirked.

"No…" said Colin.

"Then tell me one other person who has motive."

The memory of Julia hugging Megan floated before my eyes and I realized the reason for my earlier feeling of discord. "Becky," I said to myself.

"Becky?" Bridget repeated in surprise, turning to me. "What are you talking about?"

"I just realized that when Julia hugged Megan, it reminded me of—"

"Becky!" Bridget finished, seeing my meaning.

"Becky's father was a lot like Roni," I said softly.

Bridget nodded, her spiky red bangs falling into her eyes. "Except for the tight dresses and the enormous breasts, he was exactly like Roni."

"Well, that's a big exception, but do you see my point?"

"Sort of, but—"

"Wait!" interrupted Peter. "Who is Becky?"

"Becky was Julia's daughter and a close friend of Harry's," I explained quickly. "She died of an alcohol and drug overdose a few years ago." Turning back to Bridget, I continued. "Julia may have thought she could prevent Megan from ending up like Becky," I said, re-membering the way Julia reacted to seeing Roni and Megan fight at the wedding. "Do you remember how devastated she was about Becky's death? She blamed herself for not preventing it. I don't think she ever for-gave her husband for his treatment of Becky. Remem-ber how when he died a few years later, she didn't seem that upset? And there's the fact that I think she's still in love with Avery."

"It's possible," Bridget conceded, mulling over this information. "But I just can't see Julia stabbing some-one. However, I *can* see David doing that."

"I really can't see Julia doing it, either. But you can make a case based on motive for just about anyone. Let's face it, Roni wasn't a popular woman. But until we have *proof,* we have nothing."

"That's just what I propose we get. I refuse to sit still and let the police think Harry did it." Bridget pointed a triangle of toast at me for emphasis. A yellow glob of egg yolk dripped off its corner and landed on her plate. "Maybe we can bug David's room."

"Bug his room?"

Bridget nodded eagerly. "Yes. If we work together, I know we can find out—"

"No," I said.

"No," Peter echoed.

She stared uncomprehendingly at me, as if I'd suddenly launched into a torrent of French. "What do you mean, no?"

"I mean, no." I spelled it for her to be extra clear. "I see no reason for us to get involved. Detective Grant seems capable. I'm sure he can handle this investigation just fine without our help. You may not like him—and I'll admit, he's not high on my list of People I Want to Spend More Time With—but he does seem competent. I don't think he'll bow to pressure from his bosses and rush an arrest. I'm sure that he can find Roni's killer without our help. And especially without us bugging David's room!"

"But you were so great helping Aunt Winnie last New Year's!"

"That was different! I got involved in that because the police suspected Aunt Winnie. I was trying to clear her name."

"Yes, but—"

"Bridget, wait! The police are still investigating. We don't even know for sure that they've focused on Harry! I'm not about to pull some Lucy-and-Ethel stunt with you simply for the hell of it!"

"This isn't for the hell of it! It's got to be David. I just know it. Didn't I tell you that something terrible was going to happen at my wedding? Well, something bad *did* happen. Roni was killed!" She slapped her hand on the table for emphasis.

"Bridget," I said slowly, "most brides are convinced something is going to go wrong on their wedding day."

Bridget's eyes narrowed underneath her spiky red bangs. "I am *not* most brides." She emphasized these words by jabbing her finger onto the table on each syllable. "You know that I've always been sensitive to things."

Sensitive. In the sixth grade, Bridget's "sensitivity" to the weather convinced me that there was no need to study for our upcoming math test because we were going to get a huge snowstorm that night. It rained. In high school, Bridget's sensitivity to my love life convinced me to buy a nonreturnable purple Calvin Klein dress because she was sure that Joe Cassidy was going to ask me to the homecoming dance. He didn't. Two years ago, her sensitivity to numbers convinced me to give her my grocery money to buy lottery tickets. We didn't have even one of the final numbers and we were forced to eat crackers and jelly all week. Now her sensitivity was telling her that David killed Roni. I bit my tongue. Hard.

She went on, outlining the need for our involvement, oblivious to my reservations. Which, in my opinion, showed a definite lack of sensitivity to anything.

When she finally finished, she saw my unmoved face and shifted her glance to Peter. Seeing his doubtful expression, she sighed and turned to Colin. "Colin? What do you think?" she asked.

He put his arm around her and hugged her close. "Bridget, I love you. I love your enthusiasm and your loyalty to your family, but in this case, I have to agree with Peter and Elizabeth. I think we should let the experts handle it."

She looked pleadingly into each of our faces one more time and, with a shrug, gave up. "Fine, but will you at least promise to help if things change?" she said to me.

"I promise," I said, hoping it was a promise I would never have to keep. Seeing that everyone was finished eating, I signaled for the check. Sandy practically threw it in my lap and ran off. I insisted on paying. "Think of it as another wedding gift," I said, pulling out my credit card. Besides, I wanted to give Sandy a hefty tip. We'd given her a hell of a morning.

THE RIDE BACK TO Barton Landing was quiet. Colin drove, and I was actually able to relax and enjoy the scenery. The rain had stopped and the sun looked as if it would soon break through the cold, gray clouds. Hope rose in my chest that it was a sign that all would turn out well.

We pulled into Barton Landing's drive. No sooner had we stepped out of the car than the front door burst open and Elsie ran out, Anna barking at her heels. "Oh, thank God you're here," she cried.

Bridget ran forward. "Why? What's wrong? What's happened?"

"It's that damn detective," Elsie said. "He's gone and taken Harry to the station!"

Bridget gasped and turned to me. She didn't need to say a word.

Somewhere, in the deep recesses of my brain, I heard a faint cry. "Luuuucy!" it called. "I'm home!"

SIXTEEN

Look for the ridiculous in everything and you will find it.

—Jules Renard

BEDLAM REIGNED INSIDE the house. Graham paced the length of the dining room, shouting into his cell phone about lawyers and Harry. At the long table, Blythe and Julia were trying to console Megan, as she sobbed uncontrollably. The only living being not animated was Anna. Her large brown eyes solemn, she curled up under the sideboard to watch the action.

Bridget and I pressed Elsie for details. "What happened exactly?" asked Bridget.

Elsie ran a shaking hand across her face before answering. "Well, as you know, after that detective finished his interview with David, he asked to see Harry. I should have guessed what David had said by the way he scurried out of here." She paused, shaking her head. "Anyway, Harry was in there a long time. Then the detective came out and told us that we should get a lawyer for Harry, a good one, as he was sending him downtown for further questioning."

"He said, 'a good one'?" asked Bridget.

"He did."

"Shit," Bridget whispered.

"At the very least," agreed Elsie, nodding.

"Is Detective Grant still here?" Bridget asked.

"He's in the study," said Elsie.

"So, wait," I said. "Was Harry arrested, or was he just taken in for further questioning?"

"Officially, it's just for questioning. But I saw the look in that detective's eyes. He's convinced that it's Harry. He's ready to call it a day on Roni's murder."

"Then we're not too late." Bridget exhaled with relief.

"Too late for what?" said Elsie.

"Too late for me and Elizabeth to find the real killer! Elizabeth promised to help!" said Bridget with giddy confidence.

Elsie turned to me for either confirmation or explanation. Unfortunately, inasmuch as my mouth was hanging open in shock, I doubt I was a reassuring sight. Not that it mattered, of course. Bridget kept going.

"Elizabeth has a knack for this sort of thing," she said. "You should have seen her last New Year's. Remember that horrible murder at Aunt Winnie's B and B? When the police suspected Aunt Winnie of being the killer, Elizabeth immediately began her own investigation. Elsie, she was amazing." Bridget beamed at me. "She not only figured out who the killer was, but overpowered her!"

Next to me, muffled choking sounds emerged from Peter. His eyes were suspiciously bright. And no wonder—he had been with me when I had "overpowered" the killer. As flattering as Bridget's version of events was, it was far from reality. The sad truth was that I had been kidnapped and held captive in a basement; I escaped from my bonds long enough to bash who I thought was my captor over the head with a flashlight. Only it was Peter's head that I bashed. And while the reasons for this slight goof on my part were completely understandable, they were nevertheless a constant source of teasing by Peter. I suspected that his portrayal of my detective skills would be vastly different from Bridget's.

"And," Bridget continued, "you yourself said that the whole experience was so exciting that you wouldn't mind getting involved in another investigation!"

My jaw dropped in astonishment. "I said no such thing!" I protested. "Don't palm your own absurd thoughts off onto me!"

"Bridget," said Colin, "I know you want to help, but maybe we should—"

"Should what?" Bridget demanded, hands on hips. "Let the police handle it? Well, we did that and look how *that* worked out!"

Elsie sighed and rubbed her eyes. "I have to agree with Bridget. I fear the police have made up their minds." Turning to me, her blue eyes grave and lined with worry, she grabbed my hand. There was a tremor in her normally firm grip. "Elizabeth," she said, "I don't know if you can help or not. But I'll be forever indebted to you if you can do anything for Harry."

All thoughts I had of protesting my ability to be of any real assistance died in my throat. I nodded. "Of course I'll help," I heard myself saying. I ignored the looks that Peter and Colin shot my way. Apparently, their opinions of my talents were not far from my own.

Bridget turned to me. "Okay, now that that's settled, here's what I had in mind. First, we need to get some electronic equipment…" The rest of her plan, which no doubt involved bugging bedrooms and God knows what else, was mercifully cut short by the arrival of Avery. Slumped low in his wheelchair, he stared at us with lackluster eyes. Behind him, Millie gently guided him to us. Her hair was still scraped off her face in a severe bun, and she still wore her starched nurse's uniform, but she was somehow different. I peered at her, trying to identify the change, when it hit me. Millie was wearing makeup. It wasn't obvious; only a slight addition of rouge, a touch of mascara, and a hint of eye shadow. However, given the stark plainness of her face, even these small changes made quite a difference.

Avery looked up at Elsie. Seeing the expression on her face, he simply asked, "What's happened?"

As if pulled by the same puppeteer's string, every head in the room swiveled in Elsie's direction to see how she was going to tell Avery that Harry was the lead suspect in Roni's death.

Elsie paused. It was enough to alert Avery that something was amiss. Elsie is many things, but she is rarely at a loss for words.

A wary expression crept into Avery's eyes. He sat up straighter in his chair and glanced around the room.

"Where's Harry?" he demanded.

Elsie's hands clenched. "Avery, I hate to tell you this, but the police are interviewing Harry downtown. Graham is getting a lawyer."

Avery turned to Graham, who put the mouthpiece of his phone to his chest and said, "I'm on the phone with Jake Martin now. He's one of the best defense lawyers in the state. Don't worry, we'll take care of this."

Avery shook his head in disbelief. "But I don't understand. Harry? Why do the police think Harry did it?"

Why would the police think Harry killed Roni? I silently echoed. Was he kidding? Given the kind of woman Roni was, it was more of a question of finding someone who *hadn't* wanted to kill her. I averted my eyes. I didn't want Avery reading my expression. I noticed I wasn't alone. Around me, numerous heads ducked low.

Elsie's did not. Staring calmly into Avery's questioning eyes, she said, "Because he didn't like her, Avery.
Unfortunately, someone made sure the police knew
that."

"But that's ridiculous," Avery began and then
stopped. Taking a deep breath, he nodded his head in silent acknowledgment that what Elsie had said was true.
Raising his eyes again, he asked, "Who told the police?"

No one answered. Again all eyes were on Elsie.
Squaring her shoulders, she answered him with one
curt word. "David."

Avery's complexion flared bright red and he gripped
the rails of his chair so tightly that the veins on the
backs of his hands popped forth in an angry blue maze.
I glanced at Millie in concern. Her eyes were riveted
on her patient.

At that moment, as though bidden by all thoughts in
the room, David himself wandered in. From the empty
cup clutched in his hand, I assumed he was in search
of more coffee. An uneasy silence prevailed as we all
stared at him. Pushing free of Millie's grip on his chair,
Avery angrily wheeled himself to where David stood.

"You," Avery spat out. "You fed the police your per-
verted theory that Harry killed Roni, didn't you?"

"Avery…" David said. I don't know what he planned
on saying in his defense because he got no farther.
Avery latched onto David's hand and viciously yanked
him down to his own eye level. David tried to pull away
but failed. Avery was holding on to David's arm with
a death grip. It was not without cost. Beads of sweat
broke out on Avery's pale forehead. "I'll see you rot in
hell, you bastard!" he hissed.

Heaving his body backward, David broke Avery's
grip. Avery struggled in his seat, intent on getting at

David. Stunned, I watched him plant his feet on the wheelchair's footrest and push himself forward. Millie saw the movement, too. Her face a mask of horror, she burst out, "Avery! No!" Rushing to him, she firmly pushed him back into his seat by the shoulders. "You must remain still. Please," she added in a lower voice. Turning his chair so that he no longer faced David, she said, "We must get you some orange juice. You need to get your blood sugar up." She quickly pushed him toward the kitchen. No one pointed out that there was a large pitcher of orange juice on the sideboard.

Once they were gone, Elsie rounded on David like an irate tiger. "Get out of here," she said, her voice shaking with anger.

David shifted his sizable bulk aggressively, but there was uncertainty in his eyes.

Elsie took a menacing step toward him. Through clenched teeth, she bit out, "I'm only going to *ask* you once." She took another step toward him, raising her cane high above David's head. Earlier, when Elsie had confronted David, I wondered if she was going to bash him over the head with her cane. This time, there was no doubt. David's eyes opened wide as he reached the same conclusion.

The room fell silent; all action came to a halt. Julia and Blythe stopped soothing Megan, their hands frozen in midair. Megan's sobs ceased and Graham stopped pacing.

"Claire!" I yelled, as David stumbled backward away from Elsie, lost his balance, and fell into an ungainly heap.

Claire ran in from the terrace, her cell phone in her hand. Her eyes went from Elsie's outstretched arm and cane, to David sprawled on the rug. The color drained from Claire's face. "Mother! You didn't!"

"No, I didn't," replied Elsie, with more than a little regret in her voice. "But that doesn't mean I won't. Now get this jackass out of my sight, or I swear to God there'll be another body going over to the county morgue today!"

"Go upstairs, David," she hissed. "Now."

For once David didn't resist Claire's advice. Pulling himself to his feet, David shot Elsie a look of malice and turned and left. When the sound of his footsteps echoing to us down the long hallway faded, Claire turned to Elsie. "I will not allow you to threaten my husband," she said. "I don't know what he said to that detective about Harry, nor do you. Until we do, you leave him alone. Do you understand?"

Elsie did not speak. Slowly, she lowered the cane and nodded. "Fine, Claire. I'll leave him alone—for now. But if I find out that he was responsible for getting Harry arrested, I'll—"

"You won't do anything," said Claire, turning to go. As she left the room, headed after David, I heard her mutter, "I will."

SEVENTEEN

No good deed goes unpunished.
—Clare Boothe Luce

MINUTES LATER, Claire and David left. They were having lunch downtown. If there was to be any kind of calm, it was obvious that David would have to be kept away from Elsie. And vise versa.

My hope that David's departure would result in a chance for sensible ruminations was ridiculously short-lived. No sooner had the front door slammed than Bridget yanked Colin, Peter, and me into the foyer. Anna skittered after us, her tail wagging in anticipation of a walk.

Bridget lost no time. Laying her palms on the hall table, she leaned toward us, her gaze stern. I'd seen that look before, and it did not bode well: Bridget had gone into battle mode. "Colin," she said, her voice brisk, "I want you and Peter to keep everyone downstairs. Elizabeth and I are going to search everyone's room, starting with David's."

"Are you crazy?" I yelped. Next to me, Anna sensed my agitation and barked excitedly.

"Hush, they'll hear you," Bridget admonished. It was unclear if she was talking to me or the dog. "Look, this may be our only chance. We don't know how long Claire and David will be gone. If we want to help Harry, we need to work quickly."

Words failed me. I turned in mute appeal to Colin, but he had been struck dumb as well. Only Peter retained the power of speech.

"You want us to what?" he stammered. It wasn't a brilliant oration, I'll admit, but inasmuch as it was five words more than I was capable of stringing together, my heart swelled with pride.

"Come on, guys," Bridget pleaded. "Harry is at the station right now; they're probably getting ready to arrest him. He's my cousin, for Christ's sake! I have to help him. I don't know what else to do!"

"But what do you think you'll find?" asked Colin.

"I don't know, really," Bridget admitted. "I realize it's a long shot, but then again you never know—we might actually find something that helps Harry. Someone killed Roni. It wasn't Harry. We need to find out who it was!" she finished, slapping her hand on the table. The lacquered blue-and-white vase shuddered in response, sending yellow rose petals plummeting to the table.

Bridget stared at me, her eyes pleading. The idea of rummaging through the Matthewses' personal belongings made my stomach twist in protest, but she was right—there *was* a murderer on the loose. I knew Harry didn't do it, and despite Bridget's conviction that David was the killer, I wasn't convinced. Which meant that the killer was probably in the house this very minute. The hairs on the back of my neck rose at this thought. The last thing I wanted to do was get caught searching the room of the person who'd brutally stabbed Roni. However, from the steely expression in Bridget's eyes, I realized that she was going to search with or without me. I couldn't let her do that alone.

I glanced at Colin and Peter. From the expressions on

their faces, I think they felt as positive as I did about our endeavor. My left temple throbbed. Then my right. Then both eyeballs. After that, I gave up tracking the pain.

"I need aspirin," I mumbled.

"There's some in my dopp kit," said Peter. "Grab yourself a few while you're in there searching."

"Very funny. Have you any idea—" I began but was interrupted by Bridget.

"Come on! Enough chitchat. Let's move!" Grabbing my hand, she yanked me down the hallway and up the stairs. Anna padded happily along. With a cautious glance in both directions, we crossed the hallway to the door of David and Claire's room. I felt like we were teenagers again, sneaking back into the house after curfew. Except this time, the repercussions if we got caught were far worse than being grounded.

With a quick twist of the knob, Bridget swung the door open and marched into the room. After glancing uneasily over my shoulder to make sure we hadn't been noticed, I threw myself in after her and shut the door behind me.

David and Claire's large room held a mahogany queen-size four-poster bed and two massive dressers. The walls were a soft white, and the linens and upholstery were various shades of green and blue. On either side of the bed, a long window overlooked the side terrace. To the left of the bed was a blue- and green-striped club chair and matching ottoman. A crumpled blanket and sheet thrown across the chair indicated that it had also served as a bed.

Bridget crossed to one of the dressers. Yanking open the top drawer, she stuck her hands in and felt around. After a second, she gave a triumphant cry.

"What is it? Did you find something?" I asked, pushing my frame off the door.

"You could say that," Bridget said. In one hand she held a pair of men's black dress socks. In the other was an empty vodka bottle. "I'd say it's a safe bet that this is David's dresser," she said, proudly thrusting the bottle toward me.

"I would have thought the black socks would have told you that."

"Whatever. I'll search this one. You get Claire's."

"Claire's?" I repeated stupidly.

"Yes, Claire's. I don't suspect her, of course, but David might have hidden something in her things."

"Hidden what?" I asked.

"That's what we're looking for!"

Reluctantly, I thrust my hand into the drawer and prayed that "something" wasn't in there.

WE WERE IN THE ROOM for only about ten minutes, but it felt like two hours. My palms were sweaty and my nerves were shot. Every noise, every creak sent a fresh wave of adrenaline pumping through my veins. I half expected someone to burst into the room and attack us. Pathetically, our efforts yielded two empty vodka bottles and a pack of rubbers. Finding the latter among David's things had escalated my headache to that of a migraine. It also explained the nausea.

Unfortunately, our dismal results did nothing to dampen Bridget's enthusiasm. If anything, she grew more determined.

"Okay, so we didn't find anything," she said, as we cautiously slid out into the hallway. "We'll just have to keep searching."

My right temple throbbed again and I remembered

that Peter had aspirin in his room. "I'm going to Peter's room," I said, turning in that direction.

Bridget followed. So did Anna. "Hey," she said, "I don't think we need to search there, do you? Unless… do you think that David might have planted something in Harry's things?"

"What I think is that you're crazy," I replied. "I just need some aspirin."

She didn't seem to hear me. "I wonder if that's what he did," she muttered to herself. "I wouldn't put it past him. He steals the necklace, then panics and hides it in your room. Maybe he thought he was putting it in Harry's room. He goes around half drunk, I could see him making a mistake like that. It might explain why he was so intent on pointing the finger at Harry this morning."

I ignored her and entered Peter and Harry's room, aka the green room. The room was actually painted cherry red. Its name came from Elsie's father. He had been color-blind, a limitation he steadfastly refused to acknowledge, and to him, the red looked green. He always referred to it as the green room, and eventually the name stuck. Even if David was three sheets to the wind, I doubted that he couldn't notice he wasn't in a bright red room.

I opened the leather dopp kit on the dresser and dug through it. I pulled out bottles containing vitamin A, B, C, herbal supplements, and No-Doz, but no aspirin. I was wondering when Peter had become such a health nut when I realized that I was digging through Harry's kit. I quickly repacked it and found Peter's kit and the aspirin two drawers down. Shaking two tablets from the bottle, I glanced up at Bridget. Seeing that she was intently searching the closet, I dumped two more into my palm for good measure.

As soon as Bridget declared that the room was "clean," we returned to the hallway. Thirty minutes later, we had finished all the rooms—David's, Harry's, Millie's, Elsie's, and even Roni's. All we had learned was that David preferred light vodka, Harry was a health nut, Millie was painfully neat, and Elsie had a stash of miniature Snickers bars in her nightstand. Roni's room, which we'd hoped would shed some light on her murder, was the worst. Her flowery perfume still lingered in the room—a faint, sickly reminder of her presence. We were forced to nix a search of Avery's room as it was downstairs and we doubted we could get in and out unseen.

We returned to my room. I collapsed on my bed, the four aspirin starting to take effect. Bridget restlessly paced the floor.

"Nothing," she moaned. "We found nothing. If only we had more time…"

I was only half listening. Events and facts swirled in my head. I was missing something—something important—something about the *time* of the murder. If I could just remember what it was. Suddenly, the increasingly murky surface of my brain cleared and the solution to the puzzle swam to the surface.

"Wait!" I cried, pushing myself off the bed so suddenly that Bridget started backward. "I think I have it!"

EIGHTEEN

Santa Claus has the right idea; visit people once a year.

—Victor Borge

WITHIN MINUTES, I was once again seated opposite Detective Grant in the study. Only this time, I was in a good mood. Although Peter would need to speak with Detective Grant himself, I hadn't pulled him into the room with me yet. First, I wanted to confirm that my suspicions were correct.

"You said that the murder was committed between one and three a.m.?" I said.

"Yes," said Detective Grant slowly.

"Then Harry couldn't have done it!" I cried triumphantly.

"I see. And how do you figure that?" he asked, leaning back into the desk and folding his arms across his wide chest.

"Wait and I'll tell you!" In two quick strides, I was across the room. Swinging open the heavy door with a flourish, I looked out into the living room for Peter. Once again, Chloe stood close to his side. I swallowed the words I wanted to shout and instead merely bit out, "Peter! Can you come here?"

Within seconds he was in the doorway. I ushered him in and shut the door. With a wary glance at Detective Grant, he asked. "Are you all right? What's happened?"

As there weren't enough hours left in the day to co-herently catalog all the things that were currently wrong with me, I opted to ignore his first question and focus on the second. "According to the coroner, Roni was killed between one and three a.m.," I said. "If that's true, then Harry couldn't have done it! You and I were with Harry right after his fight with Roni." Peter nodded. I contin-ued. "Immediately after which, Harry took a shower while we waited for him in the hallway. And then…he went to bed. And…"

Realization dawned in Peter's eyes. "And I was with him the rest of the night!" he cried.

"Exactly!"

Detective Grant did not share our enthusiasm. His bulky frame remained reclined against the desk. "Yes, but that doesn't mean that he didn't leave the room once you fell asleep" was his calm reply.

"But he didn't—he couldn't have!" said Peter.

Detective Grant's brows snapped together. "Why not?"

"Because I couldn't get to sleep last night. I stayed up reading until around three! After that, I tried to sleep but Harry snored like a jackhammer. Trust me, if he had stopped, I would have noticed."

I looked expectantly at Detective Grant. He said nothing, but he did blink several times. After an eter-nal pause, he asked, "Would you testify to this if nec-essary?"

"Of course," Peter replied.

"Well, then I guess I need to make a few phone calls about Harry," said Detective Grant with a sigh. He reached for his phone.

Peter turned to me, a wide grin on his face. I mo-mentarily forgot my anger with him and returned it. Detective Grant spoke rapidly into the mouthpiece before shutting the phone with a loud click.

"Well?" I asked.

"I've asked one of my deputies to drive him home. He should be here later this afternoon."

"That's great!" I said.

Detective Grant nodded slowly. "It's great news for *Harry*. But I wouldn't say it's great news for certain people," he said with a meaningful look at me.

Without thinking, I said, "People? I ain't people." However, quoting from *Singin' in the Rain* didn't seem to change Detective Grant's low opinion of me, judging by the scowl on his face.

Shit. My brilliant deduction had just opened up the spot of main suspect for someone else in the Matthews family or for me.

This kind of crap never happens to Nancy Drew.

THREE HOURS LATER, everyone was gathered in the living room anxiously awaiting Harry's return. No one spoke, preferring the soothingly monotonous ticking of the grandfather clock's swinging pendulum to conversation. At the first sound of tires crunching over Barton Landing's driveway, everyone scrambled outside to the front steps. Well, almost everyone. David was absent from our group, opting instead to stay in his room and keep a previous engagement with a fresh bottle of vodka.

Gingerly pulling his long, bedraggled frame out of the squad car, Harry quietly surveyed us with a shadow of his old smirk. "I have an announcement to make," he said. "Contrary to popular belief, jail is *not* good for you."

Although his tone was light, I could see that he wasn't kidding. His pale complexion and bloodshot eyes were evidence of his obvious miserable state. Granted, he was hungover, but I doubted that was the sole cause of his haggard appearance. Any of his friends had seen him hungover a dozen times, but I'd never seen him like this.

With a muffled sob, Megan pushed past the rest of us and flung herself into Harry's arms. "Oh, I'm so glad you're home," she said, her voice thick with tears.

"Well, that makes two of us," he joked. Hearing Megan's soft sobs, he wrapped his arms protectively around her. "Don't cry, Meg," he said, his voice soothing. "It's all over. How are *you*?"

Megan lifted her face to his. "Better now," she said with a watery smile. "I was just so worried."

Elsie let out an impatient grunt. "Move over, Megan," she said. Using her cane to put those words into action, she gently but firmly moved Megan to one side, saying simply, "I want to see Harry."

After staring searchingly into Harry's wan face, Elsie said, "Did they treat you all right? Were they abusive?"

Harry managed a smile. "Abusive? Far from it. I was quite the hit. In fact, I believe one of the other inmates proposed."

Avery cleared his throat. "Harry?"

At the sound of his father's voice, Harry turned. "How are you, Dad?" he said softly.

Avery nodded. "I'm glad you're home."

Harry moved to hug Avery, while Elsie shooed the rest of us back into the house, saying, "Let's give them a minute, shall we?"

As we dutifully filed into the living room, there was almost a new lightheartedness in the air, an easiness that had been missing ever since…well, ever since Avery married Roni. I stood back a bit, watching as everyone settled into their seats, smiling at each other with obvious relief. Roni was gone and Harry was home. I was half surprised that Elsie didn't crack open a bottle of champagne. Like them, I was happy that Harry had returned, but I couldn't totally share in their celebration. I wondered if one of them had really tried to divert attention from Harry by throwing me into the glare of Detective Grant's bright spotlight. The fire blazed in the hearth, but I was overcome with a chill that no amount of external heat could chase away.

My eyes stung and I knew I was seconds away from bursting into tears or screaming in rage. Someone had planted Roni's necklace in *my* room—among *my* things! Someone had tried to frame *me*! My mind reeled. The Matthews family was an extension of my own, yet one of them had tried to pin Roni's murder on me. I was both furious and sick to my stomach.

I made my way to the study. I needed to be alone. I needed to regain my composure. I stepped inside and reached to shut the door, when Peter pushed it back open. Poking his head around the wooden frame, he said, "Elizabeth? What's going on? What's wrong?"

Looking up at his concerned face, my self-control broke. "What's wrong?" I repeated. I let loose a small laugh that didn't sound normal even to my overwrought ears. "Where would you like me to start? With finding Roni's body? With finding her necklace planted in my room? With knowing Detective Grant thinks I may have had something to do with all of this?" I felt hysteria rising. "Or should we skip all that and just focus on the fact that *you* seem to have gone completely gaga over some…some anorexic, Prada-wearing catering Nazi?"

Peter's face flushed. "Elizabeth, I can explain about Chloe. I've wanted to tell you, but I just didn't know how. You see…"

His words buzzed in my head. *I can explain about Chloe.* Had he really just said that? Explain what? I couldn't do this now, I simply couldn't. Hearing Peter confess anything about Chloe would push me over the edge—from where I now teetered on one toe. I shoved him away from me—hard. "Get out," I hissed. "Get out now. I'd like to have my nervous breakdown *without* an audience, if you don't mind."

Peter's lips parted in protest, but I gave him a final shove that caught him off guard and he stumbled backward. Taking advantage of his inadvertent retreat, I shut the door in his face, locking it for good mea sure. He knocked several times and jiggled the handle, but I ignored him. After a few minutes, he gave up and went away and I got angry with him all over again.

I sank into the leather chair behind the desk, happy for once not to be on the other side of it and facing Detective Grant. His unsmiling face as he all but accused me of covering up aspects of Roni's murder swam up before me. I buried my head in my hands to try and block out the memory, but to no avail. I had to get a grip on myself. I wasn't thinking clearly. I needed to talk to someone. Unfortunately, the two people I usually turned to when in crisis were in the next room. I couldn't very well tell Bridget that I thought her family had used me to clear Harry, and I wasn't speaking to Peter at the moment.

Thinking of my mother, I reached for the receiver of the old-fashioned black phone on the desk. I glanced at my wristwatch and saw that it was six o'clock. My mother was in Dublin attending a symposium on James Joyce; it was after midnight there. Dropping my hand from the receiver, I idly played with the coiled black cord while I considered my options. I knew my older sister, Kit, would be at home, but I doubted talking to her would be the best thing for my psyche. Kit is married to a nice man named Tom and is the mother of my nephew, Tommy. In Kit's adept hands, these normal facts have become "achievements," and achievements that only certain special individuals, like herself, can attain. As such, one of Katherine's favorite topics is What Is Wrong With Elizabeth and How If She Only Listened to Me, She Would Be Okay. I think she may even be attempting to get her doctorate using me as her thesis. Over the years, I've learned not to willingly hand her additional material for her research. Telling her that I'd once again stumbled upon a dead body would be bad enough, but admitting that I was on the verge of losing yet another boyfriend would no doubt be the equivalent of handing her the degree.

I stared dumbly at the phone for another minute until the obvious solution hit me. Aunt Winnie! I needed to talk to Aunt Winnie.

Aunt Winnie is technically my great-aunt. She is seventy-three years old and like no other woman I know. As a young woman, she inherited a substantial amount of money from her parents, and after years of wise investments she tripled that inheritance until she was an extremely wealthy woman. She has never married, always repeating the old line that marriage is an institution and she doesn't want to be in an institution. Besides, she says she prefers the freedom of affairs. Two years ago, while on a visit to Cape Cod, she impulsively bought a house and turned it into a bed-and-breakfast, despite the fact that she had no experience running such a venture. She promptly named the place the Inn at Longbourn, a testament to her admiration (read: obsession) with all things Jane Austen. That obsession is just one of the many reasons we get along so well.

I quickly dialed her number, offering a prayer that she would be at home. For the first time this weekend, the Fates smiled on me, and her familiar voice answered the phone.

"Elizabeth!" she cried, when she heard my voice. "Thank God! I've been worried sick about you! What the hell is going on down there?"

I pressed the receiver close to my ear at her words and shut my eyes. I hadn't realized just how much I missed her until now. I wished I could squeeze myself through the phone and into her house. "Oh, you know—betrayal, murder," I said, keeping my tone light to prevent myself from crying. "Just your typical Greek tragedy, really."

She saw through me, of course. She's been doing that since I was six years old. "Betrayal?" she said. "Peter told me about the murder, but he didn't say anything about a betrayal." She paused. "Or is the reason he didn't say anything because he's the one who did the betraying?"

"You know, you can be downright spooky sometimes," I mumbled, choking back tears.

"Elizabeth, for goodness' sake! Stop trying *not* to cry. I can't understand a word you say when you do that. Let it out and tell me what's going on!"

As she no doubt expected, as soon as she told me to cry, my body did the exact opposite. Sitting straighter in my chair, I took a deep breath and launched into my tale, bringing her up to date on the goings-on of the last seventy-two hours. It wasn't the most coherent recital of my life, but I managed to get the more salient points across.

"What an unholy mess," Aunt Winnie said when I finally finished.

"I know."

"Do you want me to come down? I could be there by tomorrow morning."

I was seriously tempted by her offer. Knowing I had someone on-site firmly in my corner would be nice, but it didn't seem fair to drag her hundreds of miles just to boost my self-esteem.

"No, I'll be okay," I said. "I'm sure this will all be straightened out soon enough. And then I'll be up…" My voice quavered. I was going to visit Aunt Winnie. The question was, was Peter still going to come with me?

"Elizabeth," Aunt Winnie said firmly, "you are wrong about Peter. He cares for you. I know he does. I don't know who this Chloe person is, but Peter is not the sort of man to be swayed by a pretty face." My spirits buoyed somewhat at this, until I wondered what that comment meant about *my* face. Before I could ask, Aunt Winnie went on. "You've always been insecure, Elizabeth. I don't know why, but you have. And I think you're letting your insecurities cloud your judgment on this. Why don't you simply *ask* Peter what's going on rather than make yourself sick imagining the worst?"

"You make it sound so simple."

"Well, that's because it is simple, dear! This is Peter we're talking about—not one of your scummy ex-boyfriends." With a slight laugh, she added, "Besides, what did you expect me to say? That he is not the only man worth having? That with your pretty face, you will never want admirers?"

That wrung a smile out of me. She was right, of course. She usually is. "Okay, Aunt Winnie, I'll talk to Peter." With a hollow laugh, I added, "Right after I clear my name of murder."

"No, talk to Peter first."

"Why?"

"Because I suspect it will be the harder of the two tasks."

"Gee, thanks."

"Seriously, Elizabeth. Do you want me to come down? I could catch an early flight."

"No, thanks, Aunt Winnie. I'll be okay."

"Would it help if I called Detective Stewart and had him get in touch with the police down there? Maybe it would help if he vouched for your character."

Detective Stewart had led the investigation of the murder at Aunt Winnie's inn last New Year's. In the end, I'd helped him solve the case. In the beginning, however, we did nothing but butt heads and I think he was well on his way to developing a facial tic at the sound of my name—similar to how Inspector Dreyfus reacts at the mention of Clouseau. I dreaded to think how he would react if he learned that I'd not only landed in the middle of yet another murder investigation, but was also suspected of tampering with the evidence.

"No," I said again, this time more firmly. "I don't think you need to call him. I'll be fine. I'll straighten this out and be up by the end of the week. I promise."

"Okay," said Aunt Winnie, "if you're sure. But if you change your mind, let me know."

"I will."

"And Elizabeth?"

"Yes?"

"Go talk to Peter. Now."

I sighed. "Okay," I said, wondering why hearing Peter say that he preferred Chloe over me scared me more than the thought of Detective Grant arresting me for interfering with a murder investigation.

After replacing the receiver, I remained slumped in the leather chair for several minutes. This was silly, I told myself. I couldn't sit in the study and hide forever. It was time to face all the messiness that lay on the other side of the door. However, I resolved to face it calmly and without my usual show of hysterical emotion. I would not cry or fall apart. I would be calm.

I opened the door. Everyone had left the living room—except for Peter. He sat in one of the fireside chairs, his long legs stretched out in front of him. Seeing me, he jumped to his feet and rushed across the room.

"Can I talk to you now?" he asked.

I nodded and walked to the chair opposite the one he'd vacated. The fire's blue-and-yellow flames leaped and swayed to an unknown beat. With a sigh, I sat down on the plush seat cushion and stared at my lap. Peter settled across from me. Leaning forward in his chair, he took my hands in his.

"Elizabeth? I know I should have told you this before, but I just didn't know how. Chloe and I know each other." He glanced uneasily at me to gauge my reaction. I gazed calmly back at him. "You...you don't seem surprised."

"That's because I'm not. Chloe already told me."

He swallowed. Hard. "Chloe told you?"

"Yes. Chloe. Funny how *she* managed to find the time."

"When did she tell you?"

"During the reception, but then I saw you two for myself. It was pretty obvious you two hadn't just met."

Peter flushed. "I didn't know you'd seen us talking. You seemed to be spending a lot of time dancing with Harry."

I shifted in my seat. "I believe you were telling me about *Chloe*."

Peter sighed and nodded. "Sorry. Our parents are close friends and so we were thrown together a lot as kids. There was this general assumption that Chloe and I would eventually date, and, well, we did." He paused, his eyes shifting briefly to the floor. "We were pretty serious, actually. Anyway, we talked about the possibility of taking it to the next step, but there were some things that we just didn't agree on—kids, for instance. I wanted them and she wasn't sure."

Chloe's absurdly indulgent behavior toward Ashley suddenly made sense—she was trying to show Peter how over-the-moon about kids she'd become. God, I *really* hated her.

Peter continued. "Anyway, we agreed it would be a good idea to see other people before we made any major commitments. I had no idea that she was going to be here."

My heart plummeted and I nodded dumbly, staring at my hands entwined in his. This was harder than I thought it would be. There is a difference, I thought wryly, between the expectation of an unpleasant event, however certain the mind may be told to consider it, and certainty itself. At least now I understood why Peter had never discussed marriage with me. The only reason he was dating *me* was to discover if he wanted to marry Chloe. My resolve failed. I wished the conversation was already over.

Yanking my hands out of his warm grasp, I said with a steadiness that belied my true feelings, "So, have you been in touch with her the entire time we've been dating?"

"Not really. She called once or twice, but that's all."

"Did you tell her about me?"

Peter hesitated and I knew his answer before he gave it. "No, I didn't. I don't know why. I guess I just assumed that she'd moved on. But after seeing her this weekend, I realize that she hasn't." I stared at him in silence, waiting for him to elaborate. "Chloe can be pretty...direct sometimes," he finally added.

"I'll give her direct," I muttered.

"Elizabeth, I'm sorry about all of this. I should have told you."

"Yes, you should have. But the fact remains you didn't." A numbing sensation seeped through my veins, as if my brain dosed my body with a kind of emotional novocaine. I sat very still and was grateful for the feeling—or lack thereof. For once, I just might be spared from making a colossal ass of myself. "Peter," I said with a steadiness that surprised me, "we've been dating for more than eight months. During that time you never told me about Chloe, and more important, you never bothered to tell Chloe about me. I think that says it all."

"What do you mean?"

I raised my eyes to his. "It means that you still have feelings for Chloe. If you didn't, you would have called her and told her about me. You would have ended it completely with her."

He looked like he was going to interrupt. I didn't want to hear any more. I *couldn't* hear any more. I just wanted to get out of this room before the novocaine wore off. I wanted to be alone when I finally burst into tears. "I can't do this again, Peter. I *won't* do this again."

"Won't do what?" he asked, confusion registering across his face.

Get dumped for the other woman. "Peter, a relationship where someone is always wondering about what might have been is no good. There's no point in being with someone when you're confused."

"Elizabeth, I...I don't know what to say. I don't want to end things. Frankly, it sounds like *you're* the one who wants to...see what could have been."

I had no idea what that meant. I could only hear the blood pounding in my ears as the novocaine wore off and the realization that Peter and I were breaking up caused my heart to shudder and thud unevenly.

I stood up. "Peter, I really like you, but I think it's best if we just go back to being friends."

"But we never really were friends," he said with a small attempt at a smile.

I couldn't return it. "Yeah, well maybe that was part of the problem."

Before he could say another word, I turned and left the room, tears already blurring my vision. I went upstairs and headed for the bathroom. I splashed cold water on my face until I finally stopped crying. Then I grabbed my purse and car keys. I needed to go for a long drive. When I got back downstairs, Peter was gone.

I walked out to the side terrace in the hopes of finding Bridget so I could tell her what had happened and where I was going. She wasn't there. However, Harry was. He was walking toward me, a bunch of roses in one hand, a clipper in the other. My face must have registered my misery, because he looked at me with evident surprise.

"Elizabeth! What's going on?"

Rather than launch into what had happened with

Peter, I focused instead on the flowers. "Those are pretty," I said mechanically. "Who are they for?"

Harry glanced down at the roses. "Oh. These. They're for Megan." He looked uncomfortable admitting this, and I wondered if he thought I'd be upset to hear they weren't for me. "I thought they might cheer her up a little," he continued. "But I guess that's asking a lot from a bunch of roses."

"I think it's very sweet."

"Well, I'm glad you think so. Just don't tell Elsie. I cut them from the trellis. She'd tan my hide if she knew." He peered closely at my face. "What's wrong? You look like you need your own bouquet of flowers."

I shoved my hands deep into my pockets and willed myself not to cry. I focused on staring at the intricate stone design of the patio to distract myself. That lasted a whole ten seconds. Before I knew it, Harry had gently pushed me into one of the chairs and had pulled another up alongside it. Putting down Megan's roses, he took my hands in his. "Okay, kiddo, give. What's wrong? Is it Peter?"

I could only nod. I didn't quite trust my voice to come out in a decibel appropriate to human ears. I suspected that I was capable of producing only sounds discernible to chipmunks.

"Would you like me to do something about him?" he asked teasingly. "I could make it look like an accident."

I laughed hollowly and shook my head. "No, thanks. I think one violent act for the weekend is enough."

Harry's face clouded over at my words, and I cursed my insensitivity. Harry may not have liked Roni, but she had been married to his father.

"I'm sorry, Harry," I mumbled.

"Don't be," he said after a moment's pause. "Now, tell me what's going on with Peter."

I numbly launched into what was becoming a repetitious story in my life. I meet someone, like him, only to get dumped a short while later for someone better. But this time I hadn't just liked someone. I'd fallen in love with someone.

My story told, I stared at my lap. I didn't want to see the pity in Harry's eyes. After a few moments of silence, I ventured a glance in his direction. He was looking at me with bemused frustration.

"You're a silly ass, you know that, right?"

"How so?"

"Peter is not in love with Chloe. He dated her, but so what?"

"So what? Have you seen her? She's perfect. There's no comparison."

"I agree there's no comparison, but not in the way you obviously think. Yes, Chloe's beautiful, has a great figure, is smart—"

"This is really helpful, by the way. I'm feeling loads better. Thanks."

Harry ignored me and continued. "She is all those things, but she's not *you.* You still see yourself the way you were when you were twelve. Cute but not, perhaps, having reached your potential. I wish you could see yourself the way others see you."

"If I'm so wonderful, why has every guy I've dated broken up with me—usually for someone else?"

"Because you've dated idiots. Peter is different."

I shook my head. "I don't think I can take another rejection, especially from him."

Harry rolled his eyes. "Wow, you've got it bad." He pulled me to my feet. "Come on, let me take you out to dinner. I'll flirt wildly with you and make you forget all about Peter." I glanced uncertainly at him. "Don't worry," he added quickly, "I know I can't compete with Peter, so I won't even try, tempting as it is. But I insist on dinner."

I smiled up at him and nodded. "Okay, dinner it is."

"Great, just let me give these to Megan. I'll be back in a flash."

As promised, he was back in no time. He walked me to his car, making a huge production of opening the door and getting me settled inside. Then we were off.

IT WAS AFTER TEN by the time we got back. The house was dark. As I stepped out of Harry's car, a movement out of the corner of my eye caught my attention. I peered into the darkness. It was Peter.

He was leaning against the driver's-side door of his Jeep, his arms tightly crossed against his chest.

"Peter?" I said, my heart jumping. I crossed over to him, hoping against hope that he would pull me into his arms and tell me this whole mess was a giant misunderstanding. "What are you doing out here?"

"I was waiting for you. I didn't know where you were." His eyes flashed as they touched upon Harry before settling back on me.

"I think I'm going to turn in," Harry said quickly, glancing between the two of us. "See you guys in the morning."

"Good night. Thanks for dinner," I called after him. Peter said nothing; his eyes remained trained on my face.

"Have a nice time?" he asked, after Harry shut the front door.

"Harry took me to dinner," I said.

"So I gathered," he said, his voice hard. "I just wanted to let you know that I've checked into a hotel downtown."

My heart sank. So this was it. I wondered if Chloe was waiting for him somewhere.

"You didn't have to do that," I said weakly.

"I know."

Peter said nothing: he was probably trying to figure out a way to leave without being obvious. "Well, I think I'm going to hit the sack," I finally said.

"Right." He didn't move.

"Good night," I said, turning.

"Elizabeth?"

I turned back. I couldn't see his face in the darkness, just his shape. "What?"

He paused. "Nothing." He abruptly pushed himself off of the door. In one quick move, he yanked the door open and swung his frame inside. "Good night," he called out before slamming the door. Within seconds the engine burst to life and the car pulled out of the driveway.

"Good night," I whispered as the taillights turned onto the main road. I stood for a moment before exhaustion overtook me. I desperately needed to collapse into my bed. I let myself into the house and quietly made my way up the stairs and opened the door to my room. Peering into the inky darkness, I wondered if Megan was already in bed. Out of habit, I moved to flip on the light switch before I remembered that it didn't work.

Blindly making my way to my bed, I switched on the night-stand lamp. I saw with relief that Megan was asleep. I wasn't up to small talk to night. My brain felt as if it were stuffed to the brim with odd bits of information needing to be sorted and filed. Harry's flowers were in a vase on her nightstand. I hoped they helped her a little.

No sooner did my head hit the pillow than one of these bits of information burst forth from my subconscious. Claire had said that she had seen Avery asleep in his bed the night of the murder. But she couldn't have. None of the light switches next to the doors worked. If Claire had opened the door to Avery's room, she would have seen exactly what I had when I opened my door just now. Nothing.

Claire had lied. But had she lied about seeing Avery, or about going to his room?

NINETEEN

Sleep is when all the unsorted stuff comes flying
out as from a dustbin upset in a high wind.
—William Golding

THAT NIGHT I DREAMED I had been dumped into the muddy confines of a cold, desolate marsh. As I struggled to free myself from the rushes' suffocating embrace, my leg caught on something and I was dragged even deeper into the water's inky depths. Frantic, I looked down and saw Roni's necklace wrapped tightly around my calf, its brilliant diamonds gleaming eerily in the dark waters. At the other end, a hand pulled the sparkling cord with slow determination, steadily dragging me lower and lower. I clawed desperately at the necklace, trying to free my leg from its deadly grasp, all the while straining to catch a glimpse of the face beyond the hand. With a horrific crack, the necklace snapped in two and both the glittering cord and the disembodied hand faded from sight. With a pitiful muffled sob, I broke through the water's surface and flung myself to safety.

I lay disoriented for several seconds, the sheet, damp from my sweat, twisted around my leg. With a shiver, I pulled the heavy comforter off the floor, wrapping it tightly around my body to ward off both the night's cold air and the lingering terror of my nightmare. As the images of the dream faded and my mind cleared, I became aware of two things. One, the pitiful sob in my dream had not come from me. It had come from Claire, whose low cries I could hear emanating from the room next to mine. And two, unless I was very much mistaken, the terrible cracking sound of the necklace was made by David's hand as he struck his wife.

The wall between our rooms muffled their voices but not their emotions. David's anger was as palpable as Claire's misery. I was able to catch a few of David's words, but they told me only that he was adept at spewing run-of-the-mill obscenities.

I pushed the covers back and swung my legs out of bed. David scared the hell out of me when he was drunk and mad, but that didn't mean I was going to cower under my covers while he smacked Claire around. Megan was still asleep. Thinking she'd been through more than enough over the last two days, I opted not to wake her. I looked around the room for something to use as a weapon in case David decided to smack me, too. Unfortunately, the only thing I could find was my hair dryer. I grabbed it anyway, preferring to have *something* in my hand when I faced him.

With my heart pounding in my ears, I eased my bedroom door open. Just as I did, David stormed out of his room and disappeared down the hall, his unsteady gait confirming his drunkenness. I sank back against the wall in relief, the hair dryer hanging from my limp arm. I shook my head—what the hell did I think a hair dryer was going to do? Although, I suppose to a man as hair-obsessed as David, threatening to dry out his follicles might slow him down a bit.

Cautiously tiptoeing down the hall, I gently rapped my knuckles on Claire's door. There was a brief pause, during which I could hear her blow her nose, before the door cracked open an inch. One red eye peered cautiously out at me.

"Oh! Elizabeth, it's you," Claire said in a remarkably normal voice. Hearing it, my heart twisted in sadness. Claire was obviously no novice at having to hide the pain David caused. "Is everything all right?" she asked.

"Actually, that's what I was going to ask you. I... uh...I heard what happened, Claire. Can I get you anything?"

The eye blinked several times before filling with fresh tears. Letting out a sigh, she stepped back, easing the door open a few more inches. Her eyes were red and puffy from crying. Her left cheek was red as well, although I knew crying wasn't the source of that irritation. Giving me a weak smile, she shook her head, saying, "Oh, that. I'm fine. Really. It was just a silly misunderstanding. I'm sorry if we woke you." She moved as if she was about to close the door, so I stuck my foot out and pushed my way into the room, shutting the door quietly behind me.

Surprised, she fell back a step. "Elizabeth! What are you doing? I said I was fine."

"Claire, I'm sorry, but you are anything but fine. I heard David hit you."

Her face crumpled at my words and she sank down onto the ottoman, the one that Bridget and I had noticed was being used as part of a makeshift bed. For some reason, that made me all the angrier. Not only was David a bullying drunk, but he'd co-opted the bed as well.

"Claire, do you want me to call the police? I'd be happy to tell them what I heard. We would get him away from you—at least for a day or so. It would give you enough time to decide what you want to do."

"No!" she cried, a note of real panic in her voice.

"Not the police! Whatever you do, please don't call the police."

The violence of her reaction startled me—until I remembered her lie. I sat down on the edge of the bed and faced her. "Claire," I said as gently as I could, "I know that you lied to the police about seeing Avery that night. Is David threatening you with that fact? Just because you lied doesn't mean that he gets a free ticket to use you as a punching bag."

With a half sob, Claire buried her face in her hands. I let her cry for a minute, before moving off the bed and onto the chair beside her. Putting my arm around her, I said, "Please let me help you, Claire. You can't let this go on!"

"Can't let it go on?" she repeated with a bitter laugh. "It's been going on for years. He's not going to stop now."

"Then you make him stop. Call the police. Leave him. Bash him in the head with something heavy. Do *something*."

She lowered her eyes. "If I do, he'll tell the police about Avery."

My hand involuntarily tightened around the hair dryer's handle and I half wished David was still in the room. Very few things would give me as much pleasure as bashing in his adulterous, abusive head. Taking a deep breath, I said, "Claire, do you really think that Avery would want you to endure this for his sake?"

She rubbed her hands over her face. "Of course not. But that doesn't change anything. I won't go to the police."

"Tell me about that night. What happened? Why did you lie?"

Beneath my arm, I felt her body stiffen. Raising her

head, she looked at me, her brown eyes wary. "How do you know about this, anyway? I'm not sure I should even be talking to you."

I nodded at the light switch on the wall. "You told Detective Grant that you went down to talk to Avery but changed your mind because you saw that he was sleeping. As none of the wall switches are working, you couldn't have seen anything by just opening the door. You would have had to go into his room and turn on a lamp. But you said you just stuck your head in, saw he was sleeping, and left."

Claire's face paled. "Oh, God. How stupid of me."

Through the door, I thought I heard the sound of a creaking floorboard. Was someone in the hall listening? Had David returned? I eyed the door anxiously, wondering when he would come back. I wanted to find out why Claire lied, but I knew that once David reappeared, she'd clam up. "Claire, maybe we should go somewhere else," I began.

She raised confused eyes to mine before my meaning sunk in. "Oh, don't worry about David. He won't be back. He's downstairs drinking himself into a stupor. I usually have to go down in the morning before everyone else wakes up and drag him back to our room."

"Oh," I said, relaxing my grip on the hair dryer. "Maybe you should tell me about that night."

Claire said nothing for a long moment. "I guess you're right," she finally said. Taking a deep breath, she looked at me, the beginnings of a steely resolve flickering in her eyes. "I suppose I should start with the fact that Roni was screwing my husband."

I tried to react with genuine surprise at this, but Claire saw through me. "Christ. Are you kidding me? You knew? Does everyone know?"

"No," I said hurriedly. "I happened to overhear something between them and, well, wondered. That's all." I couldn't tell her that it had actually been Bridget's deduction that David and Roni were having an affair. To do so would only add salt to the wound.

Claire eyed me skeptically but continued. "I figured it out about a month ago. David came home late one night, drunk as a lord and reeking of that god-awful perfume of hers. He claimed he was at a client dinner. Obviously, I didn't believe him, so I checked his secretary's appointment book. There was no mention of it, and she writes down *everything*. Well, that was the proverbial straw for me. It made me sick. For the love of God, she's his sister-in-law! It's practically incest! I mean, I knew that David had…well," she broke off, embarrassed.

"Did Avery know?" I asked, hoping to save her from another embarrassing confession about her marriage.

"I don't think so. But seeing the way Roni went after Harry—hearing her threaten him—I couldn't take it anymore. I wasn't going to sit idly by while she destroyed another person in this family. After I brought David upstairs that night, I went back down to tell Avery everything. But…but when I got to his room, he wasn't there. His light was on, but the room was empty. I didn't think anything of it at the time, but later, after we found out that Roni had been killed, Avery told that detective that he'd been in his room all night. I didn't know what to do!" She grabbed my hand hard and looked at me, her eyes beseeching. "I didn't want to tell the police the real reason I went to talk to Avery—it would give Avery a motive for her murder! And on top of that, he'd lied about being in his room!" She dropped my hand and looked away. "Besides, if he did kill Roni, well, who am I to blame him? There were times when I could have cheerfully murdered her myself. That's when I decided that I would back up Avery's lie. I would protect him."

"How did David find out?" I asked.

"He was awake when I came back up. I was still angry and I stupidly told him that I'd gone to tell Avery but he wasn't in his room. I told David that I still planned on telling Avery. I'd had it. But then later, David realized that Avery had lied about being in his room all night and what that meant. David is many things, but he's first and foremost an opportunist. He threatened that if I told anyone about the affair, he'd tell the police about Avery's lie."

In my mind's eye, I saw David lean in toward Claire during Detective Grant's questioning of her. At the time I thought there was something menacing in the movement; it appeared I had been right.

"So once you saw that Avery's room was empty, what did you do?"

"That's when I heard the thump. It sounded like it came from upstairs. I thought that David had fallen. He's done that before. He's always too drunk to hurt himself, of course, but I didn't want him waking everyone else."

"So you ran back upstairs and then what?"

"And then nothing. David was in bed. If he had fallen, he'd already pulled himself back into bed. Anyway, I decided to wait until morning to talk to Avery. I went to sleep soon after."

I sat quietly, thinking about what she had said. "Did you see anything or anyone when you were downstairs?" I asked.

"No. Well, other than seeing Chloe in the kitchen when I went downstairs. But she wasn't in the kitchen when I came back up."

I stared at the floor trying to puzzle out what all this meant. Could Avery have found out about Roni and David and snapped? And if he had, was it physically possible for him to stab her in the chest while sitting in his wheelchair? I rubbed my hand across my face, suddenly very tired and very confused.

"None of this makes sense," I said. "Especially when you add the fact that Roni's necklace ended up in my bureau."

"I don't know how that happened. I swear."

"That makes two of us," I said with a sigh. "But Detective Grant sure as hell thinks I do."

Claire suddenly stood up. Clutching the edges of her green terry cloth bathrobe tightly together at the neck, she looked down at me, her expression inscrutable. "I wish I could help you, Elizabeth, I really do," she said. "But I don't see how telling Detective Grant that Avery wasn't in his room will do you any good. It's not as if Avery could manage the stairs, anyway."

The memory of Avery struggling to push himself out of the chair to face David's and Millie's horrified reactions floated before me. Was Claire's assertion true? Was Avery really bound to the chair? Caught up in that memory, I did not immediately respond.

She continued, a note of urgency in her voice. "I appreciate your concern, Elizabeth, I do. But I'm okay now." Giving me a rueful smile, she added, "Unfortunately, I've been through this before. The drama is over for the night."

Pushing aside the possibility that Avery might actually be able to walk, I focused on the more important matter of Claire's safety. "Are you sure you don't want to sleep in my room tonight? Claire, I don't like leaving you like this."

"I'll be fine, Elizabeth. Really. If anything, it'll be worse if he comes back and finds you here." She opened the door. There was nothing left to say. Reluctantly, I pulled myself to my feet. "Well, if you're sure," I said.

"I'm sure."

I cautiously peeked out into the dark hallway. I paused in the doorway and turned around to say good night. Claire looked at me, a defiant tilt to her chin. "Elizabeth?" she said, her voice barely above a whisper.

"Yes?" My voice dropped to match hers.

Claire paused. "I think you should know that if you tell anyone about what happened tonight, I'll deny it."

"Claire, you can't pretend that David isn't abusive!"

"I'm not talking about David," she said. "I'm talking about Avery. I'll modify my story about the lights if I have to. But if Avery did have something to do with Roni's death, I will do whatever it takes to protect him. He's my brother," she said simply.

"Claire…"

"No, Elizabeth. Roni was a terrible person. She hurt everyone in this family. Avery is a good man. I'm sure he had his reasons for…well, for telling the police that he was in his room all night. He's been through enough. I will not add to his misery by contradicting what he said."

Looking at her now, I realized that Claire had inherited some of her mother's toughness after all. Her eyes held that same steely firmness that I'd seen displayed in Elsie's hundreds of times. "I wish I could help you," she continued, "but I just can't." She abruptly stepped toward me. Instinctively, I stepped back, out into the hallway. With a decisive movement, she shut the door in my face. Standing in the empty hallway, still clutching my hair dryer, I heard the soft click as she turned the lock.

I was halfway back to my room when something Claire said hit me. She had said that she usually got up early and went downstairs to drag David back to their room.

Had she done that the morning after the wedding?

TWENTY

Getting out of bed in the morning is an act of false confidence.

—Jules Feiffer

I SLEPT LATE the next morning. Megan was already gone. I was glad to not have to talk to her right then, and I couldn't help wondering if her absence had something to do with the discovery of Roni's necklace. Whether that "something" was a suspicion I had actually taken it or personal knowledge that I hadn't wasn't a detail I felt up to dwelling on at the moment.

I glanced out the window over my bed; the weather matched my mood. Rain spit at the glass, and the sky was an endless blanket of gray. I couldn't blame the weather for my bad temper, though. Who needed a mass of storm clouds to make you feel lousy when you had murder, betrayal, spousal abuse, and lies to do it for you? Pulling myself into a sitting position, I rested my head against the bed's wooden headboard and tried to mentally organize questions I had about the night of the murder.

First, why had Avery lied about being in his room all night? Where had he been? Had he been lying about the state of his recovery? Could he, in fact, walk? And if he could walk, did Millie know? Was she a willing participant to this lie?

Second, Claire claimed to have immediately come

back upstairs after realizing Avery wasn't in his room, but had she?

Third, David had definitely been having an affair with Roni, just as Bridget suspected. Had he gone downstairs the night of the murder to drink more as he had last night? If so, what did that mean? Could David have killed Roni in a drunken rage? If so, why did he have a room key from the Jefferson Hotel?

Fourth, what was the source of the thump heard by Claire and Chloe? Could they be lying? Why would they both lie? Was Chloe's reason for being here more than just professional?

I don't know how long I sat lost in thought, letting the questions swirl about unanswered in my head, but eventually they were interrupted by loud banging on my door. Pulling on my bathrobe, I eased the door open an inch and peeked out. It was Bridget, her face incredulous.

"You broke up with Peter?" she hissed at me as soon as she saw me. "You're such a shit. Are you okay?"

I sighed and opened the door, and she swept in, highly agitated. I shut the door behind her. Seeing my face, she pulled me into a tight hug. She continued to berate me as she held me.

"I can't believe you! Peter is the greatest guy you have ever dated and you break up with him? Why?" she demanded.

"Because he was about to marry Chloe a few years back," I said, pulling away from her. "The only reason they haven't tied the knot is they decided to take a break and date other people. They wanted to make sure they were 'meant to be,'" I said, illustrating the thought with air quotes. "I'm nothing more than litmus paper for their relationship. He never even *told* her about me."

Bridget's mouth fell open at this and she sank down onto the bed. "Peter used to date Chloe? Peter was going to *marry* Chloe? Impossible! I can't believe it. When did you find this out?"

"The day of your wedding. Chloe made a point of telling me."

Bridget gaped at me. "You've known since then and you didn't tell me! Why?"

"It was your *wedding day*! I wasn't going to bother you with my dramas! Then afterward, well, it seemed unimportant in comparison with Roni and helping Harry."

"So you've been worrying all this time about Peter and Chloe? God, no wonder you're not thinking straight. When left with only your own imagination, you always invent the worst possible scenario."

"I didn't invent this! Peter finally admitted to me last night that they used to date!"

"Exactly, Peter told you that they *used* to date. So what? He's not dating her now—he's dating *you* now. Or at least he was, until you stupidly broke up with him!"

"I broke up with him because it's clear to me that I'm nothing more than a test for his relationship with Chloe! He never bothered to call her and tell her that he'd moved on—permanently."

Bridget rolled her eyes and stood up. "So what are you saying? That they had some melodramatic plan to stay apart for a year, dating other people, and at the end of that year, they'd meet up again. Say, for instance, on the top of the Empire State Building?"

"Don't mock me. I have no idea what their exact plan was, I only know that there was one. Besides, aren't you the one who's always rattling on about people having only one true love in life, that anything else is just a pale copy? I don't want to be the pale copy. I want the real thing. And the real thing doesn't neglect to break it off with the old girlfriend!"

"Listen to yourself! You're the one who's always telling me not to be guided by my emotions! Yet here you are, letting your fear of losing Peter paralyze you."

"What do you mean, paralyze? *I* broke up with *him*!"

"You took the safe, coward's way out because you're afraid of getting hurt. But if you want Peter, you're going to have to take a risk. Fight for him!"

I folded my arms across my chest and shook my head. "No. I will not run around acting like an idiot over this. I have some dignity. Not a lot, granted, but some."

Bridget shook her head in disgust. "I don't understand you at all. You're just going to give up?"

"It's not giving up. I know when it's pointless to fight."

"How can you be so blasé about losing Peter? You love him! None of this makes any sense to me. You can't mean any of this. And if you think you're going to get me to agree that breaking up with Peter was a good idea, you're crazy!" Pausing, she added, "You know, Elizabeth, that this is a kind of talking which I cannot bear. If you only hope to have your assertion contradicted, as I must suppose to be the case, you ought to recollect that I am the last person in the world to do it. I cannot descend to be tricked out of assurances, that are not really wanted."

I tried to smile but couldn't. "Not now, Bridget."

"Wow. You are in bad shape if a little Jane can't bring you around."

"I don't want to talk about this anymore," I said, heading off another lecture. "Besides, there's something more important we need to discuss," I added, remembering the events of last night. I paused, unsure how to begin. Bridget was not going to like what I had to say.

She looked at me expectantly. "Well?"

"I'm not sure how to tell you this and I want to make sure I say it the right way."

"Oh, for God's sake, don't give me that namby-pamby crap. Just spit it out!"

"I'm going to, but I want you to understand that what I have to tell you won't be easy to hear—"

She stamped her foot in annoyance. "It can't be any harder than listening to you *not* say anything. Now give!"

"Fine!" I said, now equally vexed. "Last night I heard David hit Claire and found out that Claire lied about seeing Avery in his room the night of the murder. She went to Avery's room, but he wasn't there. After Avery told the police he'd been in his room all night, Claire decided to back up his lie with one of her own. And you were right about David and Roni. According to Claire, they were having an affair."

Bridget's eyes widened in surprise and she sank slowly back onto the bed.

I continued, trying to get the worst part out in a rush. "Detective Grant doesn't believe that an outsider killed Roni, especially not after our discovery of the necklace. He thinks the room key and the note were planted to make us think that."

"Holy shit," Bridget said after a stunned moment. "Jesus, you'd make a lousy diplomat, you know? I can't believe you just dumped all that on me like that."

I rolled my eyes in exasperation. "Well, you didn't exactly give me another option. Besides, I have a pound-ing headache, I haven't eaten breakfast, and I'm work-

ing on roughly four hours of sleep. Peter…" My voiced
cracked. I closed my eyes.

"Elizabeth?"

"I'm fine. I'm fine."

Bridget rubbed her hands across her face and mercifully did not press me. Knowing that I was shutting
down, she changed the subject. "So David hits Claire,
does he? Is Claire all right?"

I nodded. "That rotten bastard," she continued. "I
mean, I guess I'm not surprised—we've all known for
years that he's an SOB, but to actually have evidence
is different." She looked up at me. "Does Elsie know?"

I shook my head. "No, nobody knows but you."

Bridget shook her head in silence. "Well, I'll tell you
this much, I want to be there when she does find out. I
want a front-row seat for what she does to David."

I hadn't thought about that. Bridget was right. Elsie
would go after David with the vengeance of a lioness
protecting her cub. Maybe I'd better make sure that Detective Grant was on hand when I told Elsie. As much
as I despised David, I couldn't in good conscience leave
his punishment in her hands. It would be signing his
death warrant.

"Before we tell Elsie, we need to find out where
Avery was and what he was doing when Claire went
to his room."

"None of this makes any sense," Bridget said. "Why
would Avery lie?"

I paused, unsure how to put it into words. I didn't
need to bother. Bridget's head snapped up, anticipating
my next words. "No!" she cried. Springing to her feet,
she stepped back from me. "Is that what you think?"
She eyed me incredulously. "You can't really believe

that *Avery* killed Roni? It's absurd! This is Avery we're talking about!"

I took a step toward her. "I'm not saying *anything,* Bridget. All I know is that Claire told me Avery wasn't in his room when he said he was. And I think we should find out why."

Bridget ran her hand through her spiky red hair. "What could he have been doing that he felt he needed to lie about it?"

I hated this. I had hated having to tell Bridget that Avery had lied and now I hated having to make assumptions as to why. The throbbing of my temples increased and my face began to ache. "I was wondering, well, I was wondering, if maybe Avery might be able to…"

"To what?" she snapped.

I took a deep breath. "To walk."

My words were greeted with stunned silence. Bridget burst out, "Are you crazy? Why the hell would Avery lie about being able to walk?"

"I don't know!" I said, raising my hands in frustration. "I don't know why he lied at all!"

"Well, to suggest it's because he can *walk* is one of the stupidest ideas I've heard from you in a long time!"

"It's not stupid! Did you see him yesterday when he went after David? He almost pushed himself out of his chair. I think if Millie hadn't shoved him back, he would have gotten out of it!"

"Your imagination is getting the better of you."

"That may be true," I conceded. "But I don't think we can just ignore the possibility. Who knows, maybe it's the reason he lied."

"I don't understand."

"Well, if he *can* walk, maybe he was up that night and saw something. Maybe he saw the murderer."

"But if he saw the murderer, then why wouldn't he say so?"

"Given what we've just learned about Roni and David, maybe he was afraid that no one would believe him. Maybe he couldn't see her attacker. Maybe he was afraid the police might suspect *him*. If he can walk, he has means and motive."

Bridget slowly nodded. "I see what you mean, but I'm still not convinced. I want Colin to hear this. Let me get him—and my parents." She paused. "Oh, shit. They went out to run some errands. I think they're going to be gone for a while. Oh, well, never mind. Meet me and Colin in the boat house in ten minutes. We can figure out what to do there."

I threw on jeans, a sweater, and my jacket. I glanced at my reflection in the mirror and sighed. I had never been one of those girls who spring from bed dewy fresh and lovely. However, this morning I had managed to surpass my usual unkempt look. There is a simple equation in my life: with the rain comes humidity and with humidity comes frizzy hair. True to form, my hair was obeying this equation in spectacular fashion. I was now a good three inches taller and my head was several inches wider. I shrugged. It wasn't as if Peter was going to be around to see me.

I made it down the stairs and to the terrace without being seen. It was still raining. I pulled the hood of my jacket over my head in a purely reflexive gesture—the rain certainly wasn't going to make my hair look any worse—and sprinted across the wet grass to the boat house, where Colin and Bridget were waiting for me.

I shook some of the rain off my jacket and glanced questioningly at Bridget.

"I've brought Colin up to date," she said briskly.

"How is Claire?" Colin asked. "I can't believe that bastard hit her."

I shrugged. "She's fine. I think she's dealt with it so often that she's almost becoming numb to it."

Colin shook his head in disgust.

"I explained your theory about Avery, too," said Bridget. It was clear it was a theory that she was still reluctant to believe. "I guess that *if* he could walk and did see something that night, he *might* lie about it out of worry that he might become a suspect, especially if he didn't have a good description." She bent her head and stared at the worn wooden floor as she processed this scenario. As she did, Colin glanced at me with worried eyes. I knew what he was thinking. It was the same thing troubling me. There was another reason Avery might have lied about seeing Roni's attacker: because he *could* describe her attacker.

"Bridget?" said Colin. "The three of us can stand around and guess all day and it won't help anything. Why don't we just ask Avery why he lied?"

I looked at Bridget. She stared back at me, her expression sober. "Okay," she said softly, "let's go find Avery."

WHEN WE GOT BACK to the house, Avery was in the living room. Against the backdrop of a cheery fire, he, Julia, and Megan were bent over the low coffee table, playing Scrabble. Julia and Avery teased Megan over a word choice while Megan good-naturedly deflected their barbs. Millie sat in one of the nearby fireside chairs, reading a book. It looked like a family scene out of the pages of *Southern Living*. In fact, so natural and effortless was their banter, it was hard to believe that instead of an average family enjoying a rainy day inside, they were suspects in a murder case.

My step faltered and I glanced uncertainly at Bridget. Coming up with the plan to confront Avery about his lie had been the easy part; enacting it, I suspected, would be another matter. At our entrance, they all looked up. Avery greeted us with a relaxed smile, and I thought with sadness that it had been a long time since I'd seen him so at peace.

"You three look like drowned rats," Julia said affably. "What in heaven's name were you doing out in this weather? It's dreadful out there."

Suddenly tongue-tied, none of us replied. We stared dumbly first at each other and then back again at Avery. Being an intelligent man, he sensed our tension. His eyebrows pulled together and he asked tersely, "What's happened?"

Out of the corner of my eye, I saw Millie lay her book down on her ample lap. Bridget threw me a pleading look and I realized with a sinking feeling that if we were going to learn anything, it would be up to me. "Nothing's happened, exactly," I said slowly, as I sat down in one of the empty chairs. "It's just…it's just that I talked to Claire last night."

Avery started to shake his head as if he didn't understand, then the meaning of my words hit him. With an apprehensive glance at Julia, he said, "Oh, I see."

Both Julia and Megan tensed at the tremor of nervousness in his tone. Megan turned to me, her face pale. "What's going on?" she asked.

Avery looked at her with pained eyes. "Nothing's going on," he said, forcing his voice back to normal. "But I think I need to talk with Elizabeth alone for a minute."

Julia said firmly, "I don't think that's a good idea."

Giving her a desperate look, Avery nodded almost

imperceptibly toward Megan. Megan's eyes were focused on Julia, so she missed it. However, Millie, with her uncanny sensitivity to her patient's wants, did not. "Megan," she said in a brisk tone that left no room for argument, "please come with me. I need you to help me make tea."

Realizing that she was being got out of the way, Megan threw a curious glance at us before pulling herself to her feet and trailing on reluctant feet after Millie to the kitchen.

"What is this about?" asked Julia, her tone uneasy.

I looked at Avery.

He sighed. "I…I lied to the police about where I was the night Roni…" His words caught in his throat. He tried again. "I lied about where I was the night Roni… died." He did not look at Julia as he spoke. "Claire knew and lied to protect me."

Julia shifted uncomfortably in her chair. Avery's eyes fell to his lap and stayed there.

"What really happened?" I asked.

Avery's anguished eyes briefly landed on Julia before turning my way. His next words came out haltingly. "I wasn't in my room all night as I told the police. Around one thirty, I went to the study to make a phone call. My cell phone was dead and there isn't a phone in my room."

"And you called…?" I asked.

Avery did not respond. He fixed his eyes on his lap again. I repeated the question. "Avery, who did you call?"

"He called me," Julia said suddenly. "He called me," she repeated quietly.

"Julia…" Avery began.

"Avery, it's okay," she said, but Avery interrupted her. "No, it's not. Let me tell them."

His eyes swept over Bridget and Colin still stand-ing stiffly in the doorway, before focusing on me. In a tentative voice, he said, "As you probably know, Julia and I were…were very close before…before I married Roni." He shrugged quickly as if to ward off hurtful memories. "When I first met Roni, I thought…well, I guess I thought she was wonderful."

Julia's face bunched in pain. Seeing it, a different kind of agony crept into Avery's expression. With a cheerless shake of his head, he continued. "After we were married, I still thought she was wonderful, even when faced with evidence to the contrary. The mind can play funny tricks on you, I guess." He stared blankly at the leaping flames in the fireplace. Dragging his eyes back to mine, he went on. "Anyway, I managed to blind myself to all the ugliness, but when I saw Julia again at the reception, it was as if someone suddenly ripped the blinders away. In that one moment, I saw everything clearly: Roni's shallowness, her greediness, and her pro-pensity for cruelty—especially with Megan. I realized what a horrible mistake I'd made and how much I'd lost when I…when I ended my friendship with Julia."

I remembered the change in Avery's demeanor after he talked to Julia at the wedding. He had seemed to sud-denly withdraw into himself. His mood certainly caught Roni's attention, but like her, I had believed his explana-tion that he was merely tired. Now I saw his odd silence and desire to be alone for what it was—a man under-standing what a giant mistake he had made with his life.

Julia reached over and grabbed Avery's hand. The gesture was Avery's undoing and tears welled in his eyes. Seeing that Avery was incapable of speech, Julia picked up the narrative. "What Avery is trying to say," she said with a melancholy smile, "is that he called me that night. I wasn't home yet, so he left a message. He was very upset. He told me…well, you don't need the exact transcript, but the gist of it was what he's just told you." Still holding tightly to Avery's hand, Julia turned her eyes on me. "When I got in from the wedding, I went straight to bed. I didn't get his message until the next morning. But when I did hear it, it scared me. Avery sounded like a man at the edge of a deep, dark hole. I was afraid that he was in danger of doing something rash."

My expression must have registered alarm, because Julia quickly clarified her words. "Not to anyone else, of course! I merely meant I was afraid he was in danger of hurting himself," she said firmly. "That's why I dashed over here as soon as I heard his message. And then…when I saw the police cars…I was terrified that my suspicions had been right and I was too late."

My mind jumped back to that chaotic morning and Julia's clearly distressed state when she arrived at Barton Landing. She'd been desperate to see Avery, but there was something else. She'd also taken a special interest in Megan.

"You were very kind to Megan," I said.

Apparently, Bridget was right when she told me that my diplomatic skills are worthless. Julia arched her eyebrow and studied me. Choosing her words with care, she said, "I was very concerned about Megan, but not in the way you seem to think. As a counselor, I've seen the terrible damage an overbearingly critical parent can do to a child, especially a sensitive child like Megan." With a swift glance at Avery, she continued. "Megan was in danger of losing herself under Roni's abuse. Even the little I saw of them together at the wedding told me that. I could see that unless something happened to change

Roni's behavior, Megan's wounds would only deepen. I...I wanted to help her." Softening her tone, she added, "Anyone would have wanted to, really."

"Megan is very special," I said, tipping my head in agreement. "But I still don't understand. Why the need to lie about the phone call?"

Disquiet radiated from both of them; they did not look at each other. Taking a deep breath, Julia finally answered. "I think Avery had some old-fashioned notion about protecting me." She seemed faintly amused by the idea. "He didn't want me involved. It was very sweet of him," she said, flashing a brief smile in his direction, "but completely unnecessary. I can take care of myself."

Avery returned her smile, but I could see that he was unconvinced by her declaration and troubled about the revelation.

That's when it hit me: each one had initially suspected the other of Roni's murder. Avery wondered why Julia hadn't been home when he called, and Julia wondered if Avery's despair had transcended into a murderous rage.

Watching them now, as they sat with their hands entwined but not making eye contact, I realized that on a certain level, each still harbored that uneasy suspicion.

TWENTY-ONE

*Any fool can tell the truth, but it requires a man
of some sense to know how to lie well.*
                                        —Samuel Butler

MEGAN ENTERED THE ROOM carrying a wooden tray laden
with lime green teacups and matching saucers. Colin
rushed over to her, taking the tray and placing it on the
coffee table. "Thanks," Megan said with her shy smile.
"That was heavier than I expected. I'll be just a second;
I'm going to help Millie with the rest."

Realizing there was no polite way to question Avery
about his ability to walk, I decided my only hope was
to tackle Millie on the subject. Given her obvious devotion to Avery, I hoped that she wouldn't tackle me—
in actuality—for what would no doubt be considered
highly inappropriate questions. "Oh, let me get the rest,"
I said, and rapidly set off for the kitchen before Megan
could argue.

Elsie's kitchen was exactly how I would design one—
if I had a couple of hundred thousand dollars to spend.
She had renovated it a few years ago, modernizing the
appliances without destroying its old-fashioned charm.
Exposed wooden beams still lined the ceiling, and the
original wide wooden planks ran the length of the floor.
The walls gleamed white except for blue Spode tiles that
served as the backsplash. In front of the room's small
stone fireplace was a long wooden kitchen table. Millie

stood at it, her broad back to me, pouring steaming hot water into a large teapot. Hearing me, she said, "Oh, Megan, can you pour the cream into the pitcher? And I think there are some cookies in the cupboard."

"Actually, it's just me, but I'm happy to help."

At the sound of my voice, Millie whirled around, clearly startled. I couldn't fathom why. "Oh," she said, her voice now brisk and professional. "Yes, thank you. I just need some cream."

I opened the refrigerator's chrome door and pulled out the container of cream. Pouring a generous amount into the green-and-white pitcher, I watched Millie from the corner of my eye as she busied herself with the teapot.

"So, how is Avery doing?" I asked, trying to keep my voice neutral.

Millie's movements slowed as she considered my question. "I think he'll be okay," she said, dunking several tea bags into the pot. "Of course, terrible shocks like these can be a real setback to a recovery."

"I'm sure they can," I agreed, placing the pitcher of cream on the counter, "but his recovery was going well before…before all of this, right?"

Millie turned to face me, her eyes unreadable. "He was doing quite well. Why do you ask?"

I shrugged. "No reason, really. I just wondered. He's always been so active. I imagine living in a wheelchair is very hard for him." I took a gamble and continued. "Now that he's able to walk on his own again, it must be a huge relief for him."

Millie set down the heavy teapot with a loud thump and stared at me in disbelief. "What are you talking about?" she asked, shocked. "Where did you ever get the idea that Avery—I mean Mr. Matthews—can walk?"

"I…I don't know, really," I stuttered. "I guess maybe when he almost went after David the other day. It…it seemed like he was trying to stand up."

Millie let out a sharp bark of laughter. "Trying to stand up?" she repeated, eyeing me in amazement. "Are you serious? That man could no sooner stand than I could…well, than I could land on the cover of the *Sports Illustrated* swimsuit issue." She shook her head in disbelief at me. "Did you really think he was trying to stand up? And do what? Fight David?"

I felt my face flush under her bemused scrutiny. Millie shook her head again. "Trust me, Mr. Matthews needs that chair. At least for now he does." She shrugged and added, "But, truth be told, I wouldn't have blamed him *had* he tried to go after David. He's almost as bad as *she* was."

I didn't need to ask Millie whom she meant by "she." I opened a box of shortbread cookies and spread some out on a small blue plate. My empty stomach growled at the sight of them. I grabbed one and took a large bite. "David is a pain in the ass," I agreed, once I'd finished chewing. "And I know it isn't nice to speak ill of the dead, but Roni wasn't very nice, either." I shoved the rest of the cookie in my mouth and took another.

"She was pure poison," Millie agreed with force. "Mr. Matthews is well rid of that woman, but if you ask *me,* he never really loved her. How *could* he love someone like *her*?" Pausing, she added, almost to herself, "Now that she's gone, I think he'll realize that."

"Well, I just hope that he finds some peace soon," I said, once I'd finished the second cookie. Still hungry, I dug into the box and grabbed two more. "He's such a nice man."

"He's a *lovely* man," she said softly.

Something in her tone distracted me from the short-bread cookies—no small feat there. Pausing with the cookie halfway to my mouth, I considered her. Could her devotion to Avery go beyond that of a dedicated nurse? "I wonder if he'll remarry," I mused, with what I hoped was a casual tone.

"Oh, I think he will," Millie said with brisk assurance. "He's the type that needs a woman in his life. The right kind of woman, mind you, especially now that it's just him and Megan. Now *that's* a girl who needs a steady woman's influence in her life."

"Maybe he'll marry Julia," I suggested innocently. "After all, I believe they used to date."

Millie's head jerked up and her thin, red lips pulled down. "Julia?" she repeated doubtfully, her eyes inadvertently straying to the doorway to the living room. "No, I don't think that's likely." She shook her head as if to confirm the absurdity of the idea. "No. If he really cared for her then he'd have never left her in the first place. Besides…"

Whatever Millie was going to say was lost in the arrival of Bridget. She burst into the kitchen and Millie's professional mask slipped back into place. Placing the teapot, pitcher of cream, and plate of cookies on the tray, Millie quickly excused herself and returned to the living room.

"Did you learn anything?" Bridget whispered.

"Well, Millie was pretty adamant that Avery can't walk," I admitted.

Bridget rolled her eyes. "I told you I was right about that! I don't know how you ever came up with that idea in the first place!"

I still wasn't convinced, but I held my tongue. "There's something else. I think Millie might have feelings for Avery, feelings that go beyond that of professional interest."

"You're kidding!"

"No. You should have heard the way she was talking about him just now. And when I intentionally mentioned that he and Julia might get back together, she got upset. I wonder if Avery has any idea."

Bridget stared thoughtfully at the door through which Millie had exited. "I wonder, too" was all she said.

"I guess this means we're back to square one," I said, popping the last cookie into my mouth.

"I wouldn't go that far," Bridget said. Anna scurried into the kitchen, followed by Elsie. Catching the smell of the cookies, Anna immediately flung herself at me, plopping down at my feet, her furry expression hopeful. Elsie poured herself a glass of water and surveyed us with a bemused expression.

"What's the matter with you two?" she asked.

"We're trying to solve this whole thing with Roni," Bridget answered.

"But Harry's home," Elsie replied with a grateful smile. "You've already done your job."

"Not completely," said Bridget. "We still need to find her killer so we can be done with Detective Grant and all his crazy suspicions."

Elsie shook her head. "No. I want you to stop. I wanted Harry cleared of this crime and that's the reason I asked you to get involved. Now I want the police to focus on someone outside this family. The idea that one of us could have committed such a heinous crime is ludicrous. But someone did, and the murderer is still out there! I don't want you two risking your necks trying to find him or her. This person is deranged and dangerous! I will not let you expose yourselves to more danger. Harry is home. We can now leave it to the police to solve."

"But Elsie," Bridget argued, "you're forgetting that someone planted Roni's necklace in Elizabeth's room! We still have to clear her name! And the only way we are going to do that is by finding the killer." Bridget drummed her fingers on the granite countertop. "What we need to do is find out who wrote that note to Roni. Whoever put that note in her purse is the killer."

My mind jumped back to the night of the wedding as I sat across from Roni and watched her pull out her pink purse. Her pink purse. What had I seen...? And then the memory of Elsie covertly stuffing something into a pink purse flooded over. My eyes flew to Elsie's. She was looking at me over the rim of her water glass, her expression bland. Beneath my feet, the floor seemed to tip and tilt. The cookies in my stomach threatened to pop back up and my lungs felt as if they'd shrunk three sizes. Bridget chattered on with her plan to find Roni's killer, oblivious to my churning emotions. "We need to go to the Jefferson. After all, the note was written on their stationery. Maybe the staff might be able to help us," she said.

"Are you all right, Elizabeth?" Elsie suddenly asked, setting her glass on the counter. "You look pale."

I forced myself to meet her eyes. Her expression was normal. I suspected mine was anything but. Taking a step toward me, she said, "Honey, what's wrong? Do you need to sit down?"

"No!" I said, backing away. "No. I'm okay. I feel a bit queasy. I probably need some fresh air, that's all." Stumbling backward, I fled the kitchen. Bridget watched my retreat with a perplexed expression. Elsie's expression, I noticed, was less mystified.

I hurried to the foyer, telling myself that lack of sleep was turning me into a melodramatic paranoid. Bridget trailed after me.

"Elizabeth? Really, are you okay?"

"I'm fine," I said in as normal a voice as I could muster. "I like your idea of going to the Jefferson. In fact, I think we should go now." I tried to keep the desperation out of my voice.

Bridget misinterpreted my rush to leave. Her face brightened. "Really?" I nodded dumbly. "So do I. I have a good feeling about this," she said. "I bet we're going to find the killer's identity today."

The hairs on my neck bristled at her words and I had a sudden fervent wish that we wouldn't.

The rest of the day was a blur. Colin, Bridget, and I arrived at the Jefferson, where we followed Bridget around as she alternately interviewed, badgered, and threatened the hotel's bewildered staff. They had no more information than what Detective Grant had already learned—that the electronic keys are useless after checkout. The picture of David that Bridget brought with her also failed to strike a chord of recognition with the staff. The only information we gained that was of lasting use is that desk clerks find it highly annoying when their little bell is rung incessantly.

I didn't speak much on our outing; I was too busy trying to prevent myself from thinking. It's hard to make conversation when you're focusing on keeping your mind a peaceful blank. Thankfully, Bridget talked enough for three people, so my silence wasn't noticed.

It was late by the time we returned to Barton Landing, the three of us having decided to eat dinner in the city. Bridget and Colin tried their best to convince me to join them on the patio for a drink with Blythe and Graham, but I refused. I was exhausted and I didn't want to talk anymore about finding Roni's killer.

I said good night to them and dragged myself upstairs, eager to crawl into bed. I pushed open the door to my room and saw that Megan was lying on her bed reading.

Seeing her, my mind finally unthawed and the thoughts and realizations I'd kept buried all day burst forth. The truth had to come out. It was time.

At my entrance, Megan smiled and put her book on the nightstand. "Hey there," she began, then peered closely at my face. "What's wrong? You look terrible."

I sat down heavily on my bed. "Megan, I don't know how to tell you this, so I'm just going to say it."

When I entered the room, Megan tensed and sat up straighter in her bed. "What's going on?"

I wearily rubbed my hands across my face. "If you saw someone on the terrace that night, Megan, then you need to tell Detective Grant."

Her face blanched and she pulled her comforter around her. "What are you talking about?" she said, her voice cracking nervously.

"Don't play games, Megan!" I snapped, my voice raised. "This is murder we're talking about! The murder of your mother! If you know something, then you have to tell the truth! How would you feel if the wrong person was arrested? Could you really live with that?"

She stared horrified at me a moment before bowing her head in silent acknowledgment. "You're right," she said. "I'll talk to Detective Grant in the morning."

"I'm sorry, Megan, I really am," I said softly. For a moment I debated asking her just who it was she saw, but I couldn't bring myself to. Call me a coward, but I wanted just one more night of happy oblivion. I gathered my pajamas. On my way to the bathroom, I heard a floorboard in the hallway creak. I peeked out, but the hallway was empty.

After changing into my pajamas and brushing my teeth, I returned to the room. Megan was gone.

TWENTY-TWO

There are bad times just around the corner.
                                                    —Noël Coward

I LAY DOWN ON my bed and waited for her to return.
I must have dozed off because the next thing I knew
there was a pair of very large brown eyes staring into
mine. The eyes were Anna's; she was sitting on my bed,
her furry black face positioned not three inches away.
I smiled sleepily at her and reached out to scratch her
behind her ear when one of the basic facts concerning
Anna penetrated my tired brain: Anna's presence always
heralded Elsie's. My hand froze midair and I turned my
head. Before me, calmly perched on Megan's empty
bed, was Elsie.

I sat up swiftly and upset Anna, who fell backward
and slid off the bed. Giving me as dirty a look as a dog
is capable of, she crossed to Elsie and flopped down
at her feet.

Pulling the comforter tightly around me, I glanced
uneasily around the room. With a sinking feeling, I saw
that the door was shut. I wondered how quickly I could
get across the room and out the door.

"Elizabeth, goddamn it, calm down," Elsie said.
"You're flailing about like some poor trapped animal."

I eyed her suspiciously and tried to regain my shattered composure. "No, I'm not. You...you just startled

me, that's all. What's up?" I asked, hoping my voice sounded casual rather than terrified.

She sighed heavily. "This is ridiculous. I had a feeling earlier when we were in the kitchen, but still…" She broke off, shaking her head, her silver upsweep tilting precariously from side to side. In one fluid movement, she rose from Megan's bed and crossed to mine. Sitting down on my bed, she roughly grabbed one of my hands. I winced at the sudden pressure but fought to keep my composure. Leaning in so close to my face that I could clearly make out the indigo swirls of pigment in her eyes, she said, "I understand that you are tired and under a tremendous amount of stress, but I want you to listen very carefully to what I am about to tell you." She paused as if to make sure she had my full attention. "I did not kill Roni."

She continued to hold my hand and stare at me. "Why would you think—" I began, but she cut me off.

"Goddamn it, Elizabeth! You still don't believe me! I had a feeling you had jumped to some terrible conclusion when I saw you in the kitchen today. But to think that you would actually think I…" She turned away from me, releasing my hand with a disgusted grunt.

I pulled my legs up to my chest and wrapped my arms around them. "Elsie—" I began.

She interrupted me again, which was a relief, actually, as I had no idea what I was going to say. "I overheard Roni on her cell phone talking to some man," she said, her lips curling in revulsion at the memory. "She was obviously having an affair with him and was planning on tricking Avery into selling the Garden." A look of pure hatred flashed across Elsie's face; I gave an involuntary shiver. If she was trying to convince me of her innocence, she was doing a lousy job. She continued. "I knew that Avery would never believe me unless I had proof." Straightening her spine, she looked down at me. "I took her cell phone when she wasn't looking. I'm not proud of myself, but I had to find out who Roni was dealing with. It was the only way that I would ever be able to convince Avery that Roni was two-timing him." Grabbing my hands again, she said, "What you saw during the reception was me putting Roni's cell phone back into her purse, nothing else!"

"Her cell phone?" I repeated stupidly.

"Her cell phone," Elsie echoed with an emphatic nod.

I realized it did make sense. I had already guessed that it was Elsie's footsteps I had heard hurrying away after listening in on Roni's phone call. For her to take Roni's cell phone to track the call was entirely consistent with the special brand of morality that Elsie employed when her children were concerned.

Giving my hands a shake, she peered at my face closely. "You do believe me, don't you?"

I looked into her eyes and, with a wave of relief that made me grateful I was already sitting down, I knew that I did. Seeing my expression, she pulled me into a fierce hug. "Oh, thank God. You've no idea how terrible I felt thinking that you thought I…"

"I'm sorry, Elsie. I don't know what got into me. It's been such a horrible couple of days; I guess I wasn't thinking straight." I gave a rueful laugh. "As you have no doubt already realized, I'm not the great detective that Bridget makes me out to be."

Elsie placed her hands on my shoulders and eased me back. Staring into my face with a sober expression, she said, "I wouldn't say that, my dear. You've learned quite a lot. And don't forget, you saved Harry. For that, I will be forever grateful. You are a very special young lady.

I knew that the very first time I met you." She added, a glint in her eyes, "And remember, I have the 'sight.' I know these things."

I scoffed. "Elsie, you told me that I was destined to marry a rocker and live a life of international travel."

Elsie shook her head. "No, dear. I said that you were destined to marry a 'rock,' not a rocker."

"I'm meant to marry a rock?"

"When you get a minute, look up the meaning of the name *Peter*," Elsie said kindly.

I blushed at her words. Changing the subject, I said, "Well, I hope this investigation gets cleared up soon. I have a feeling that until it does, Detective Grant is going to want to keep a very close eye on me. I don't think he believes me about finding the necklace."

Elsie nodded. "I think you may be right. But I know that it'll get straightened out. In the meantime, get some sleep. You look like you could use it."

She left, Anna padding happily along behind her. I stared blankly at Megan's bed, wondering where she could be. I don't know how long it took me to notice that the bedpost where she hung her purse was bare. Shit. Where had she gone? I looked at the clock; it was a little after ten. Where would a seventeen-year-old go at that hour? I knew the answer almost immediately: she was at the boat house smoking pot. Enough is enough, I thought. If I was going to catch her in the act, I'd have to hurry. I slipped on my robe and slippers, reasoning that the sight of my ensemble might be enough to scare her straight. As I grabbed a hair tie off my nightstand to pull my hair back, I saw Megan's flowers. Some of the roses were already dying, their pink heads bent low, their stems limp. I continued to stare at them as another memory swirled. The impact of that memory made my knees buckle. Thankfully, the bed caught me as I sank backward. I'd been looking at the whole thing upside down!

It all made sense now—the calls to Roni's cell phone, the source of the thump, the letter from the hotel.

I sat there in shock, struggling to find a flaw in my reasoning, but for once there was none. Only Megan would be able to tell me if I was wrong. I made my way downstairs and slipped outside into the darkness, intent on finding her.

The moon hung behind thick clouds, transforming the wide lawn into a maze of shadows. Carefully making my way to the boat house, I could hear Bridget and Colin's murmured conversation from the patio. Soon their voices faded, seemingly swallowed up by the night. Ahead of me a branch snapped. A second later, the sound was repeated. An uneasy premonition slid down my spine. Hurrying, I had just rounded the curve leading to the boat house when I heard a sickening thump. My heart thudding in my chest, I picked up the ends of my robe and ran toward the sound.

I had gone only a few steps when I saw the dark crumpled heap. With terrible certainty, I knew it was Megan.

TWENTY-THREE

Don't overestimate the decency of the human race.
—H. L. Mencken

Running over to her recumbent body, I was dimly
aware that I was screaming. I hoped Colin and Bridget
could hear me, but my voice sounded like it was origi-
nating from the end of a long tunnel. I came to a skidding halt over Megan's body and knelt beside her. Blood
streamed down her face and onto the grass. There was
a large gash from her forehead almost to her crown. A
heavy black flashlight lay on the ground next to her.
Numb with terror, I frantically felt for a pulse and went
weak with relief when I felt a faint and thready one. Just
then, I saw a flash of movement out of the corner of my
eye. A dark figure darted furtively across the back lawn
in jeans and a black shirt. I couldn't make out many
details, but I saw the black ski mask over the face.

Before I knew what I was doing, I was bounding
across the lawn in full pursuit. The grass was slick from
rain and I discovered quickly that bunny slippers do
not provide much, if any, traction, but I wasn't going to
let the bastard who attacked Megan get away without
a fight. Luckily, her attacker appeared even more unsteady than I was, and soon I was within arm's reach.
With a burst of speed, I hurled myself at the runner's
waist and the two of us fell to the ground. I had the
upper hand for a moment, the element of surprise being

on my side. But with an embarrassingly easy shove, I was flung off. I had a brief sensation of weightlessness as I soared through the air before I crashed back down to the ground in an ignominious heap. The jolt of the landing knocked the wind out of me and I desperately sucked at the air. Flopping on the ground like a fish out of water, I was helpless as my attacker jumped up and took flight. But after only three or four steps a quick-moving blur to my right tackled the form. To my surprise, I realized that the blur was Peter. This time the figure wasn't able to toss aside its attacker, especially after Colin joined the fray.

Writhing in pain, the dark figure let loose a stream of obscenities that left me with no doubt as to its identity. Even before Peter ripped off the black ski mask, I already knew it would be David's face underneath.

Colin and Peter managed to drag David back to the house, although it wasn't an easy task. David is not only a big man, but he was also drunk, and the alcohol surging through his blood gave him added vigor. I ran back to where Megan lay; Bridget joined me a second later. Together, we gently carried her to the house. The fact I kept tripping on my slippers' bunny ears didn't help matters.

We lay Megan on the living room couch. She was terribly pale but, thankfully, conscious. The house was suddenly alive with activity. Julia, who had been visiting Avery, let out a small scream when she saw Megan. Hovering over her with anxious desperation, she knelt beside the couch, her face ashen, and gently cradled Megan's battered head in the palms of her hands. Time seemed to slow for me and I realized that my earlier deduction had been right, after all. Megan was the key to all of this. It had been about her all along. It explained everything—the source of the mysterious thump, the key, and the note. The realization and its implications almost made me throw up.

In the distance, I heard sirens screaming toward the house, and for the first time since I'd arrived I hoped that they brought Detective Grant with them.

Peter and Colin shoved the struggling David into a chair and stood over him with the fireplace poker while Elsie ran to the kitchen for something to secure David with. Claire stared aghast at her husband, uttering only one anguished word: "Why?"

"Goddamn you, Claire, you stupid idiot, get me out of here. Tell these morons to let me go," he screamed at her.

"Shut up, David," Bridget said, her voice furious. "You can't bully her anymore. We've got you. You're done." Elsie returned to the room and tossed a roll of duct tape to Colin.

"Sorry," she said with an apologetic shrug, "it's all I could find."

"It'll do," Colin replied, and immediately knelt behind David and secured him roughly to his chair.

David struggled against the tightening bonds, all the while staring at us with wild eyes. "What are you talking about?" he sputtered.

Bridget looked at him with disgust. "What are we talking about?" she repeated sarcastically. "How about murder? You killed Roni. And now you tried to kill Megan! Why?"

David's eyes widened in panic. "You think I killed Roni? I didn't kill Roni!" Seeing our disbelieving expressions, he continued. "Okay, I…I took her necklace, yes, I admit it, but that's all!" He shut his eyes, trying to pull a coherent narrative out of his alcohol-soaked brain. "She was already dead, don't you see? She was dead and she owed me money. She promised me that money!" He looked wildly about for a sign that we either understood or believed him. He found none. "I went downstairs to make myself a drink. That's when I found her dead and…I…took the necklace. I figured she owed me. But then Megan said she saw someone on the terrace. She said that I could make it right. I figured she meant the necklace! She wanted the necklace!"

I struggled to understand David's rambling story. Looking over at Megan, I saw that she had revived enough to respond. With Julia pressing a large towel to her bleeding head, Megan whispered, "You're crazy! I don't know what you're talking about!"

"But you have to," David pleaded. "You said that if I could figure out how to help you, you'd listen to me."

"You're crazy!"

I pressed my fingers against my eyes. Some of what David was saying did have a familiar ring to it. I tried to remember why. Then it came to me. After trying to pin Roni's murder on Harry, David had told Megan that he was sorry for her mother's death and asked her if there was anything he could do. Megan's response echoed in my head. *"Anything you can do? Just what do you think you can do, David? From what I've seen, you've done quite enough!"*

I struggled to remember the rest of the conversation. David had pressed her, obviously trying to win her over. What had he said? *"I know you're upset. But I'd like to help."*

And then Megan had responded. *"Help. Here's an idea, David—how about you do the right thing? For once, why don't you just do the right thing?"*

On a certain level, it made sense, especially to someone as drunk as David. He had taken the necklace and then panicked when he thought that Megan had seen him on the terrace. His exchange with Megan had left him with the impression that she would keep her mouth shut about what she'd seen if he only gave her the necklace.

"*You* put the necklace in my bureau," I said suddenly.

David glanced at me and nodded. "I thought it was Megan's bureau. It was what she wanted me to do!"

"I didn't want you to do anything! I don't understand what you're talking about!" Megan protested faintly, then fell back against the cushion as the effort caused a fresh spasm of pain. Julia gently stroked her cheek and tried to calm her.

"But you do!" countered David with a pathetic whine. "You have to!"

More of the puzzle fell into place. "You were in the hallway earlier, weren't you, David?" I asked. "You heard me tell Megan that she had to go to the police. You were afraid that she was going to tell Detective Grant that it was you she saw that night on the terrace."

David's glance slid away from mine. "I didn't kill Roni," he said, his lips pulled into a petulant pout.

I heard the front door slam open and the sound of rapid footsteps. Detective Grant burst into the room and took in the scene before him, from Megan on the couch to David taped to a chair. Two paramedics rushed in behind him and immediately made their way to Megan. Within minutes, they had removed her from the room and were on their way to the hospital. Julia and Avery followed, anguish etched on both faces.

Detective Grant eyed David with abhorrence. "Enjoy attacking young girls, do you, Mr. Cook?"

"It's not my fault," David retorted. Turning a loathing eye on me, he said, "If you hadn't found the necklace, none of this would have happened. She would have kept quiet if she'd had the necklace!"

Looking into his bleary, unfocused eyes, I realized that he was so drunk that basic logic was beyond his grasp. With a sob, Claire buried her head in her hands. "I can't believe you did this, David. You tried to kill Megan! What kind of a monster are you?"

"Oh, shut up," came his illogical reply. "She's fine, isn't she?"

A fresh burst of tears came from Claire and she looked away.

Detective Grant stepped forward. "David Cook, I'm arresting you for the murder of Roni Matthews and the attack on Megan Matthews."

David thrashed wildly upon hearing these words. "I didn't kill her!" he screamed. "I didn't!" With a sudden burst of strength, he broke free of the tape. Grabbing the chair, he flung it at us. It caught Detective Grant square in the chest and he fell back with a crash. In a flash, David sprang out of the room, onto the terrace, and disappeared from sight.

Pulling himself to his feet, Detective Grant darted after him. The rest of us followed. As we reached the terrace, we saw Detective Grant round the corner of the house and head for the front lawn. I sprinted after them and had just reached the front steps when I saw David's car charge down the driveway. Detective Grant ran for his car, yanking open the driver's-side door. His ignition had roared to life when another, louder sound took its place—the sound of crunching metal. Running down the driveway, I saw the source. Wrapped around the base of one of the ancient magnolia trees that lined the stately drive was the shattered remains of David's car.

Detective Grant got there first. He reached into the

driver's side of the wreck, and after a minute, pulled back. Seeing our expectant faces, he slowly shook his head.

Beside me, Claire moaned and covered her face. Detective Grant walked back to us.

"Is he dead?" Elsie asked in a strained whisper.

"I'm afraid so," Detective Grant said.

Her face a mask of sadness, Elsie wrapped her arms around Claire. "I'm so sorry, Claire," she murmured. Claire nodded mutely.

I looked at Detective Grant. I had to ask him the question, but at the same time I dreaded it. "What about Roni's murder?" I said.

Detective Grant studied me thoughtfully. "Well…"

Claire raised her tear-stained face from Elsie's shoulder. "It was David, of course," she said, after an uncertain glance in my direction. Turning to Detective Grant, she said, "They were having an affair, you know. David and Roni. But then Roni tried to double-cross him." Her voice grew stronger as she continued her story. "She wanted Avery to sell the business so she could run off with yet another man. When David found out, he was furious. David has"—she squeezed her eyes shut—"*had* a terrible temper."

"Claire—" I began, but she interrupted me.

"No, Elizabeth," she said with a firm shake of her head. "David killed Roni. He tried to kill Megan, too. We all saw that. He's a killer!"

Detective Grant's cell phone rang and we all fell silent. "Yes, sir," he said. "Well, sir, we may have made some progress, actually." He glanced at Claire and she nodded. "I think we have our murderer," he said.

Claire looked at me, her red-rimmed eyes pleading. "Please," she said in a low whisper. "It's all over now."

I'M NOT SURE how long after that Detective Grant left. Time seemed to take on a different quality for me. At times, it flew by in lighting-fast spurts; at others it dragged with maddening slowness. Like now.

It was well past midnight. Peter sat next to me on the terrace—the back, not the side. Idly, I wondered if I'd ever be able to sit in that area of the terrace again. Neither of us had spoken for what seemed a long while, but maybe that's just because my perspective was so screwed up.

"So," Peter finally said.

"So," I agreed.

After a beat, I asked, "How did you happen to be here, anyway?"

"Colin and Bridget called and invited me over for a drink." Suddenly, I understood their interest in getting me to join them as well.

"What are you going to do now?" Peter asked.

"I'll stay for the funerals, and then I'm going to the Cape. I've got some vacation time I can use. This whole weekend has thrown me, I guess. A lot of things that I thought were solid, were unalterable facts, just got thrown out the window. I think I need some time to sort through everything."

After a long silence, Peter said, "Well, I'm leaving next week for London. I'll be gone for at least three months. When I come back, maybe we can get together or something..." He trailed off.

Just don't be engaged, I prayed. I wanted to tell him that I still wanted him to come to the Cape with me, but somehow the words wouldn't come out. The fact of Chloe—the fact that he hadn't told me about her—raised every red flag in my head. The awkward, fat girl inside me still had too strong a pull. I heard her familiar taunt of "Yeah, right, like he's going to stick with *you* when he could have Chloe," and stayed silent.

After another minute, Peter stood up to go.

LATER IN THE DAY, Megan came home from the hospital. She'd suffered a slight concussion and needed a tremendous amount of stitches, but she was going to be all right. Julia and Avery sat with her; every once in a while one or the other would reach over to touch her as if to reassure themselves that she was really there. Harry stayed near them, an expression of calm on his drawn face as he watched Avery and Julia together. He'd had a rough couple of days, I thought. I hoped now that he would be able to find some peace.

Bridget and Colin had booked another flight to Bermuda. They were scheduled to leave immediately after the funerals and were obviously excited to finally start their honeymoon. Blythe and Graham both offered them last-minute advice, advice I could tell Bridget had every intention of ignoring.

Claire and Elsie sat in the two hearthside chairs. Between them a fire danced happily inside the grate. I noticed that while they spoke very little, there seemed to be a quiet understanding between them that I couldn't ever remember having seen before.

I leaned back in my chair. So was this it, then? Roni is killed and David is posthumously judged to be the murderer and the Matthewses experience some peace. I looked around wondering how long it would be before Elsie returned to dictating everyone's lives and they were all grumbling in frustrated protest. For now, though, they were a family unit once again—and for me, that would have to be enough.

RONI'S FUNERAL WAS held the next day. It was a subdued affair, just as Avery wanted. David was buried the day after. By Claire's request, it was also a quiet remembrance. Detective Grant attended both funerals. At each, he nodded gravely at me but said nothing.

The next day, I packed to leave for the Cape. Bridget and Colin had left early that morning. All that was left was for me to say good-bye to the rest of the family. Standing in the driveway, Blythe and Graham said good-bye, making me promise to come and visit them again very soon. Elsie's good-bye was more meaningful. Giving me a long hug, she said, "Thanks again for everything, kiddo. You were amazing." After searching my face carefully, she said, "You gave us back our family. And for that I can never thank you enough."

I nodded, unsure what to say. Claire stepped forward next. She wasn't wearing a headband and her bangs were pushed over to one side. It was a tiny change, but I hoped it was the first of many. Pulling me into a tight embrace, she said, "Thanks, Elizabeth. Thanks for everything. We'll be fine now."

Megan, Julia, and Avery were next. I was relieved to see that Megan seemed to be handling the traumatic events of the last few days quite well. I suspected that Julia's calming influence and professional expertise had much to do with that.

Harry was last to say good-bye. Grabbing my hand with a flourish, he said, "Ah, Elizabeth, parting is such sweet sorrow."

Giving him a level look, I said, "And a rose by any other word would smell as sweet."

Confusion crossed his face. "Don't you mean, 'A rose by any other *name*'?"

"No."

Something in his expression changed. "You always were smarter than me."

Before I could answer, he pulled me close. Wrapping his arms around me, he whispered into my ear, "Thank you, Elizabeth. Thank you...well, for everything. I've always known you were special, but I don't think I knew exactly how special until this weekend. I missed my chance with you. Don't make the same mistake and miss your chance with Peter."

"Good-bye, Harry," I said, turning away before I started to cry.

He leaned forward and placed a chaste kiss on my forehead. There was nothing else to be said. I got into my car and headed for the Cape.

TWENTY-FOUR

The truth is rarely pure and never simple.
                                        —Oscar Wilde

Three months later

I sat in Aunt Winnie's reading room at her Cape Cod B and B, the Inn at Longbourn. As I had last year, I was spending New Year's Eve with her. Unlike last year, there would be no murder dinner theater—no point in tempting fate again. A large fire danced and crackled in the hearth, helping to ward off winter's chill. Lady Catherine, Aunt Winnie's large white Persian cat, lay curled up in her basket on the hearth. If this suggests a cozy arrangement, it was anything but. Lady Catherine has no manners to speak of and dislikes me almost as much as I dislike her.

In my hand was a letter I'd just received. I think I always knew it was coming, but I didn't realize how hard it would be to read it. I saw with some sadness that the handwriting was faint and weak.

Dear Elizabeth,
By the time you read this, I will, as they say, have moved on. I'm not sure how I feel about that, to tell you the truth, but it will be a relief to not have to fight this illness anymore. The leukemia was just too strong for me this time.

Unlike others who don't know when their death is coming, I'm trying to stay positive and look at this as an opportunity to reflect on my life. I think you should know that I've decided to categorize you as my Greatest Regret. Leave it to me to have the perfect girl right under my nose and not realize it until it's too late. Don't make the same mistake I made, Elizabeth. I know you love Peter. Don't be an ass and ruin it just because you're afraid of getting hurt. If you don't fight for what you want, you run the risk of missing too much.

I shifted uncomfortably. I hadn't talked to Peter since he'd left for London. I'd hoped he would call me, but he hadn't. I had begun to resign myself to the fact that he never would. I focused on the letter again rather than deal with my own emotions.

I also want you to know how much it meant to me to have this short time with my family. You have no idea how much peace I feel seeing my dad happy again and knowing that Megan is going to be okay. When Dad told me that he was going to marry Julia, I knew they'd be all right. And really, what more can I ask for?

And now for the real reason for this letter: I know that you deciphered the truth about that terrible night—nice with the "rose by any other word" bit, by the way. Roni was truly evil, Elizabeth. She was using my dad for his money and she was destroying him. Megan was well on her way to becoming a wreck because of Roni. I caught Megan smoking pot a couple of times—it was like watching Becky self-destruct all over again. When

I found out that my leukemia had returned, I had a feeling that this time it would win. Like Elsie, I'm a firm believer in premonitions. Laugh all you want, but I do believe that certain members of our family have a kind of "second sight" (except for Bridget, of course, so don't ever listen to her predictions). Anyway, knowing that my time was limited was torture because I knew I wouldn't be around to help anyone. I had to stop her. It was my last chance.

I tried to set it up so that the police would think someone outside the family killed Roni. I swiped one of those electronic keys from the Jefferson Hotel and wrote her a blackmail letter on their stationery. Then I called her cell phone a few times from their lobby. I figured the trail would eventually grow cold and her case would never be solved. I stumbled in that night pretending to be drunk and intentionally picked a fight with her, knowing that afterward she'd go outside for a cigarette. She always ran outside for a cigarette when she got upset.

I suspect you know the rest. We scrambled around that roof too many times as kids for you not to guess what happened. I turned the shower on and crawled out the window and onto the roof, climbing down the trellis to where Roni was. I had hidden the knife in one of the cushions earlier. It took only a second. I stuffed the blackmail note in her purse, covered her with the blanket on the chaise, dropped the key on the terrace, and then I was back on the roof and in the bathroom. This time I took a real shower. The whole thing lasted less than ten minutes.

I stared at the fire, remembering the trellis. On the day of Bridget's wedding, the roses were healthy and vibrant, yet the next morning, after I'd discovered Roni's body, some were already dead and dying. I didn't register that fact until later. When I'd run into Harry on the terrace, he told me he was getting some roses for Megan, but in reality, he was clipping off the damaged ones, the ones he'd crushed while climbing the trellis. It wasn't until I saw the roses on Megan's nightstand, wilted and limp, that I realized the truth. I concentrated on the letter again.

I had hoped that the police would think it was an outsider who committed the crime, but David ruined that by stealing Roni's necklace. For a while, it looked like I was going to end up in jail anyway, but then you stepped in. I guess you know now that I arranged that, too. I slipped a few No-Doz into Peter's drink so he could vouch for my being in the room. While I never would have let someone else take the blame and was quite prepared to step up and go to jail should the need arise, I also wanted to take every precaution that the need wouldn't arise. I wasn't kidding when I said that jail didn't agree with me. After they let me go, I really thought that Roni's murder would get tossed into the unsolved file and that would be that. But then David attacked Megan. After he died, the police decided they had their man. Everyone seemed to accept it, even Claire. Everyone seemed to find a kind of peace in that solution. At least that's what I convinced myself of, anyway.

That's my little story. Now that I'm gone, I'm giving it to you. You can decide what you want to

do with it. I am literally leaving it in your hands.
Take care of yourself, Elizabeth, and keep an eye
on the family.
Love, Harry

I dropped the note onto my lap as tears streamed down my face. Soon after the wedding, Harry had started radiation, but this time it didn't work. His funeral had been both beautiful and heartbreaking. I clutched the letter a little harder; it was my last contact with Harry.

My mind reviewed the horrible events of that weekend. I don't know when I first suspected Harry; it was nothing concrete, just a lot of little things that didn't add up. The thump from upstairs (which was the sound of Harry on the roof), the No-Doz in Harry's dopp kit along with all his vitamins, and Megan's reluctance to tell who she saw that night on the terrace. It was Harry she had seen, of course. She hadn't ever seen David. Once she realized what had happened and what it meant, she had lied about not being able to see the figure. Harry was the only person Megan would lie for, but I didn't register that fact right away. David certainly didn't; he thought she had seen him and was lying about it so she could get the necklace from him.

All his short life, Harry had tried and failed to save the people he loved. First his mother, who died despite his fervent prayers, and then Julia's daughter, Becky, died because Harry hadn't known to get her to a hospital. I think that's when I knew for sure my suspicions were right—when I saw Julia with Megan after David had attacked her. Julia worried over Megan like a mother. Julia also saw that Megan was on the same path of self-destruction that Becky had taken. Harry obviously realized this, too, and looked upon Megan as his last chance to "get it right." In his mind, Harry began to believe that for Megan to live, Roni had to die. The only thing I didn't pick up on that weekend was that Harry was sick again. I should have. We all commented on how tired he looked and both Julia and Bridget noticed that he'd lost weight. I'd even found all those vitamins in his dopp kit. I guess none of us ever wanted to think he'd get sick again, so we attributed it to the strain of dealing with Roni.

I stared at the heavy cream paper for a long moment. Then I slowly got up and knelt before the fireplace. Lady Catherine eyed me with distaste for invading her space and angrily twitched her tail. I ignored her. With once last glance at the letter, I threw it into the fire. The flames licked at the paper faster and faster until it lifted and curled, its edges blazing red before fading to a dull white. Within seconds, it was gone.

The doorbell chimed, startling me out of my reverie. From the other room, Aunt Winnie called out, "Could you get that, Elizabeth? I'm in the middle of something."

"Sure thing," I called out, pulling myself into an upright position. I crossed to the foyer and swung open the door.

It was Peter.

"What are you doing here?" I blurted out in surprise.

"I got a letter," he said simply. He stood stiffly on the door-step, his hands jammed into the pockets of his jeans.

"A letter?" I repeated stupidly, staring up into his face. He moved slightly and the familiar scent of his aftershave floated over me. I briefly closed my eyes to savor the smell.

"From Harry," he clarified.

"Harry!" My eyes flew open. "What did he say?" Had he confessed to Peter as well?

"Well, to paraphrase, he said you could be a silly ass at times, but that you were worth it."

I paused a moment to take that in. "He really said that?"

"Yep."

"You needed Harry to tell you that?"

Peter looked down, a small smile on his lips. "No, that much I knew. It was the part about you two just being friends that I didn't know."

"I don't understand."

Peter sighed and said in a rush, "I thought the reason you were breaking up with me was because of Harry. I thought you were using the whole mess with Chloe as an excuse."

"Why on earth would you think that?"

"It was pretty obvious that Harry liked you—hell, he announced at the rehearsal dinner that he wanted to run off with you. Then at the wedding you danced with him an awful lot."

"Only because you were off with Chloe!"

"Well, I didn't know that at the time. And then after breaking up with me, you disappeared with Harry for a couple of hours. It wasn't too much of a leap to wonder if you weren't interested in him, especially given how calm you were about everything. You really didn't seem to care."

I let that sink in a minute, somewhat dumbfounded by the sad fact that the one time I managed to control my emotions, it completely backfired on me.

"But then I got Harry's letter," Peter continued. "And, well, it made me think that maybe I should try again."

Same old Harry, I thought with a smile, still trying

to fix things—even from beyond the grave. Suddenly, I noticed that Aunt Winnie hadn't appeared to see who'd rung the doorbell. I might be an ass, I thought as I reached out and happily pulled Peter to me, but I wasn't so big an ass to fight the machinations of both the living *and* the dead.

* * * * *

REQUEST YOUR FREE BOOKS!

2 FREE NOVELS
PLUS 2 FREE GIFTS!

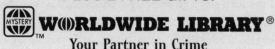

MYSTERY

W(O)RLDWIDE LIBRARY®
Your Partner in Crime

YES! Please send me 2 FREE novels from the Worldwide Library® series and my 2 FREE gifts (gifts are worth about $10). After receiving them, if I don't wish to receive any more books, I can return the shipping statement marked "cancel." If I don't cancel, I will receive 4 brand-new novels every month and be billed just $5.24 per book in the U.S. or $6.24 per book in Canada. That's a saving of at least 34% off the cover price. It's quite a bargain! Shipping and handling is just 50¢ per book in the U.S. and 75¢ per book in Canada.* I understand that accepting the 2 free books and gifts places me under no obligation to buy anything. I can always return a shipment and cancel at any time. Even if I never buy another book, the two free books and gifts are mine to keep forever.

414/424 WDN FEJ3

Name	(PLEASE PRINT)
Address	Apt. #
City	State/Prov.	Zip/Postal Code

Signature (if under 18, a parent or guardian must sign)

Mail to the **Reader Service:**
IN U.S.A.: P.O. Box 1867, Buffalo, NY 14240-1867
IN CANADA: P.O. Box 609, Fort Erie, Ontario L2A 5X3

Not valid for current subscribers to the Worldwide Library series.

Want to try two free books from another line?
Call 1-800-873-8635 or visit www.ReaderService.com.

* Terms and prices subject to change without notice. Prices do not include applicable taxes. Sales tax applicable in N.Y. Canadian residents will be charged applicable taxes. Offer not valid in Quebec. This offer is limited to one order per household. All orders subject to credit approval. Credit or debit balances in a customer's account(s) may be offset by any other outstanding balance owed by or to the customer. Please allow 4 to 6 weeks for delivery. Offer available while quantities last.

Your Privacy—The Reader Service is committed to protecting your privacy. Our Privacy Policy is available online at www.ReaderService.com or upon request from the Reader Service.

We make a portion of our mailing list available to reputable third parties that offer products we believe may interest you. If you prefer that we not exchange your name with third parties, or if you wish to clarify or modify your communication preferences, please visit us at www.ReaderService.com/consumerschoice or write to us at Reader Service Preference Service, P.O. Box 9062, Buffalo, NY 14269. Include your complete name and address.

WWLI1B

FAMOUS FAMILIES

YES! Please send me the *Famous Families* collection featuring the Fortunes, the Bravos, the McCabes and the Cavanaughs. This collection will begin with 3 FREE BOOKS and 2 FREE GIFTS in my very first shipment— and more valuable free gifts will follow! My books will arrive in 8 monthly shipments until I have the entire 51-book *Famous Families* collection. I will receive 2-3 free books in each shipment and I will pay just $4.49 U.S./$5.39 CDN for each of the other 4 books in each shipment, plus $2.99 for shipping and handling.* If I decide to keep the entire collection, I'll only have paid for 32 books because 19 books are free. I understand that accepting the 3 free books and gifts places me under no obligation to buy anything. I can always return a shipment and cancel at any time. My free books and gifts are mine to keep no matter what I decide.

268 HCN 0387   468 HCN 0387

Name _____ (PLEASE PRINT) _____

Address _____ Apt. # _____

City _____ State/Prov. _____ Zip/Postal Code _____

Signature (if under 18, a parent or guardian must sign)

Mail to the **Reader Service**:
IN U.S.A.: P.O. Box 1867, Buffalo, NY 14240-1867
IN CANADA: P.O. Box 609, Fort Erie, Ontario L2A 5X3

ReaderService.com

Manage your account online!
- Review your order history
- Manage your payments
- Update your address

**We've designed
the Reader Service website
just for you.**

Enjoy all the features!
- Reader excerpts from any series
- Respond to mailings and special monthly offers
- Discover new series available to you
- Browse the Bonus Bucks catalogue
- Share your feedback

Visit us at:
ReaderService.com

RS12